Rise of the Alliance II
The Blood Mage Texts

SARTORIAS-DELES BOOKS

HISTORICAL ARC
"Lily and Crown"
Inda
The Fox
King's Shield
Treason's Shore
Time of Daughters (two volumes)
Banner of the Damned

MODERN ERA
The CJ Journals
Senrid
Spy Princess
Sartor
Fleeing Peace
A Stranger to Command
Crown Duel
The Trouble with Kings
Sasharia En Garde

AND
THE RISE OF THE ALLIANCE ARC
A Sword Named Truth
The Blood Mage Texts
The Hunters and the Hunted (late Jan 2022)
Nightside of the Sun (late Feb 2022)

RISE OF THE ALLIANCE II
THE BLOOD MAGE TEXTS

SHERWOOD SMITH

Book View Cafe

Published by Book View Café
304 S. Jones Blvd., Suite #2906
Las Vegas, NV 89107
www.bookviewcafe.com

ISBN: 978-1-61138-983-8

A Brief Summary of Book One,
A SWORD NAMED TRUTH

Agents of Norsunder, a bastion of power, have reappeared in the world, amassing resources and sowing instability. The most recent, previous to the start of the book, was a world-wide enchantment by a young Norsundrian mage named Siamis. It was unsuccessful, but with numerous nations led by young rulers brought too early to their thrones, the world is hardly safe from another attempt.

Atan is still uncomfortable with her new queenship, gained after her country was freed from a Norsundrian enchantment that left it frozen outside time for a century.

Senrid has been striving to establish rule of law, after deposing his brutal uncle. Still only a teenager, Senrid has to exert control over rebellious jarls and a distrustful military academy.

Jilo never expected the responsibility of leading his nation, but when its evil king vanished after a Norsundrian attack, Jilo stepped into the power void, taking the reins of a country so riddled with dark magic that its citizenry labors for mere survival.

Clair and CJ led a band of misfits against magical threats that overshadowed their tiny country, including a direct incursion from the Norsundrians.

Tsauderei, a powerful and much-respected maverick of a mage way past the age of retirement, tries to oversee as much as he can, but as mages are forbidden to meddle with governments, there is little he can do outside of offer advice. Especially with young rulers from such a wide range of nations.

Those in power are not the only individuals working to subvert the plans of Norsunder. Liere, a young shopkeeper's daughter, battled her own debilitating insecurities to live up to her reputation as a former savior of the realm—helped by Senrid, her first friend.

Hibern, a mage's apprentice, tries as a liaison between national leaders, negotiating politics still foreign to her, as a way to overcome the devastation of being shunned by her own family.

Rel, a traveling warrior, brought friends and allies to action, encouraging common folk to take up arms.

This disparate group soon realized that any significant victory against Norsunder would require an alliance. Yet good intentions began to fracture in the face of personal grudges, secrets, and inexperience.

As the Norsundrian attacks turned into outright war in Sarendan and then in Everon, and Siamis began to spread his enchantment once again, the tenuous alliance ended up on the sister world Geth, where they distracted the enemy long enough for local mages to avert catastrophe.

A list of characters and a glossary can be found beginning on page 241.

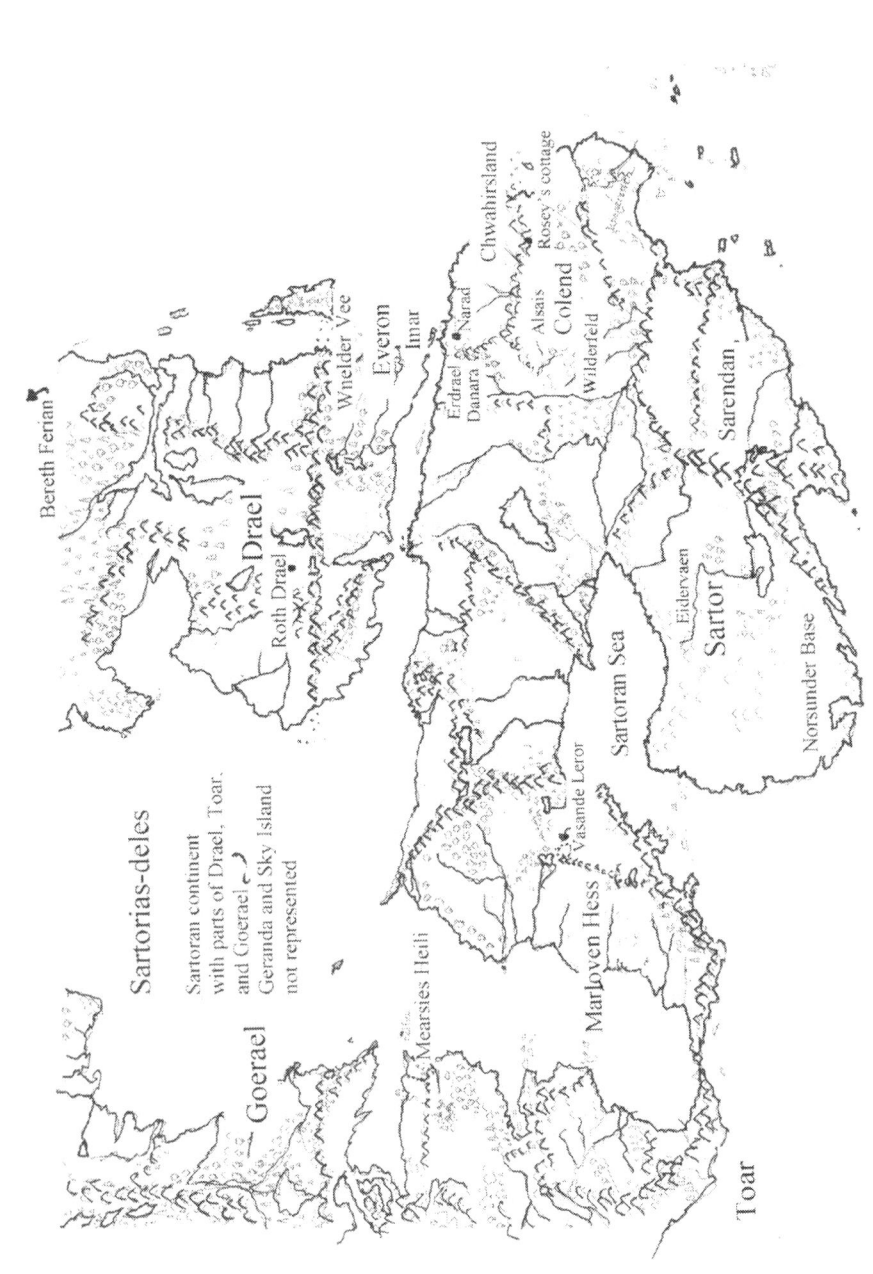

Sartorias-deles

Sartoran continent
with parts of Drael, Toar,
and Goerael
Geranda and Sky Island
not represented

Goerael

Bereth Ferian

Drael

Roth Drael

Wnelder Vee

Everon

Imar

Mearsies Heili

Chwahirsland

Rosey's cottage

Erdrael
Danara   Narad

Alsais
Colend

Wilderfeld

Marloven Hess

Vasande Leror

Sartoran Sea

Eidervaen

Sartor

Sarendan

Norsunder Base

Toar

THE BLOOD MAGE TEXTS

As I write this second segment of the history of the Young Allies, I'm convinced that the primary requirement for anyone hoping to understand the tangle of relationships and changing loyalties is a healthy sense of irony.

I must begin at Norsunder Base, the fortress located south of Sartor in otherwise barren land.

Though generalizing about any group of persons is risky, it's safe to say that everybody at Norsunder Base relished a fight. Some liked the spectacle, others the exertion, but all pretty much agreed that the pinnacle of entertainment was a clash between commanders. You had to be nimble to make certain you weren't part of the spillover, but risk was part of the thrill.

Word of Norsunder's recent setback on the sister-world Geth-deles had begun spreading through the fortress when Dejain, head mage and occasional commander at the Norsunder Base, returned.

The moment she had recovered from the excruciating wrench of transfer-magic, she summoned the mages for a more detailed report. "The chief reason for the defeat is that Siamis tried to turn on dear Uncle Detlev. And lost," she finished with the savor of hatred. "The Geth-deles mages have united to destroy the between-worlds transfer tunnel. I expect it's going to be a long time before we see the return of Uncle — "

The word *Detlev* coincided with a skull-ringing *VOOM*.

The fortress's ancient granite blocks ground together as air expelled from the collapsed cross-world transfer blasted through, hurling warriors to the painted stone floor in the Destination chamber. They slowly got to their feet, checking themselves for broken bones, as all over the fortress grit sifted down from ceilings.

Word flashed along the halls and byways, faster than fire: *Detlev is back.*

The mages with Dejain recovered, several turning caustic gazes her way.

She made an effort to shrug, hiding the throb in her bones. "If Siamis survived that transfer, he might wish he hadn't."

And she strolled out, brushing grit off her dainty lace-trimmed rose gown and running her fingers through her golden curls. As soon as she was sure she was away from watching eyes, she closed her eyes, concentrating on erecting the mental brick wall of her mind-shield, then hurried downstairs to the command center's back entrance.

In the Destination chamber, Detlev's elite picked their weapons off the cracked stones and clattered off to the barracks, some giving sideways glances at Detlev, who had managed to stay on his feet.

Detlev left in the direction of the command center. Those who dared watched from shadowy alcoves, anticipating bloodshed as Detlev paused at certain doorways, as if seeking someone who was not there. For a man of such sinister reputation, Detlev was ordinary enough in appearance, above medium height, brown of hair, hazel of eye. He rarely wore weapons, an idiosyncrasy only a fool took as invitation.

Dejain had reached the commander center first, and observed from the back as Detlev entered the main door with a quick glance around. Looking for . . .? *Siamis*, she thought, laughing inside. If Siamis was still alive, and smart, he should be halfway around the world by now. And still running.

Detlev ignored desk jockeys as he walked to the trays where reports and messages were relayed in by magic transfer, and flicked through papers in a methodical manner.

The silence was so profound that all heard the approach of leisurely footfalls.

Eyes turned to the door as Siamis walked in. Dejain glared as he smiled gently, his sword — four thousand years old while he was still maddeningly young — held casually by the sheath, as though he had been wielding it too recently to slide it back into its baldric. She hated him for his youth, his fair hair, and for his offensive insouciance over still being alive.

Alone of all in that fortress, Siamis and Detlev had been born thousands of years ago, in the lost days of Ancient Sartor. Until recently had rarely emerged from Norsunder. Siamis's outrageous impatience with his uncle's constraints was obvious to everyone.

Detlev looked up at his errant (*arrogant*, Dejain thought, and she was not alone in that opinion) nephew.

Siamis spread his hands, his smile rueful as he said something in Ancient Sartoran.

"What's he saying?" a mage hovering at Dejain's shoulder asked in a whisper.

"Says something about how he had to try. Bored. Wants, um, responsibility," Dejain whispered back. She hated having to admit that her understanding of Ancient Sartoran, with its millennia-old idiom and layered figurative language, was rudimentary at best. But she knew it better than anyone else in that place, save those two who'd been born when it was spoken.

Detlev glanced at the papers on the desk, as the watchers held their breath. Then he said — in everyday speech, so that all the listeners could understand — "Prove it. I believe the time has come to secure the Arrow."

"Arrow," the mage whispered. "Impossible. Tsydes died trying to *find* it."

He died trying to cross me, Dejain thought, but kept a prudent silence. The mage was not altogether wrong; everyone there knew the reference. The magical construct known as The Arrow was the name for the enchantment that'd bound the magic of the Venn for eight centuries. If any of their mages tried the smallest spell outside their borders, it would mirror back and kill them.

Even those who knew very little about magic understood that complicated spells—or enchantments—had to be bound to something specific, or the magic dissipated like vapor. Some objects held magic better than others, and even more rarely, amplified it in a way no one understood, which meant that the layers of complex spells would not have to be renewed.

The Arrow was one of these, hidden so well that no one had been able to find it, though enterprising mages in both light and dark magic had searched all through the northern reaches.

That included Norsunder mages, who knew that anyone who possessed it would effectively control the Venn—the empire once the most powerful force in the world.

"But it took two centuries for the Venn to be bound," Siamis said. "Three, if you include Erkric's death and its aftermath."

Detlev's tone remained equable. "Then you had better get started, hadn't you?" He added something quickly in Ancient Sartoran, and turned back to the dispatch desk.

Siamis laughed. "Well, if it was easy, it wouldn't be fun," he remarked and sauntered out, as if he had not just been dismissed before the eyes of all watchers.

The mages watched him without a word. Most were disappointed that Detlev hadn't reduced his obnoxious nephew to a bloody smear, but the more discerning knew the dismissal for what it was: Siamis had effectively been demoted from Commander of Norsunder Base to errand boy. Then given an impossible errand.

The moment Siamis entered the hallway, there was Bostian, one of the military-side commanders who had tried three times to challenge Siamis for control of Norsunder Base. A huge man a little older than Siamis, bristling with weapons, he took a preparatory step, an anticipatory grin on his face as his hand closed on the hilt of the knife he called the Carver.

Without slowing, Siamis snapped a palm-heel strike to Bostian's chin and an elbow into his breastbone, his sheathed sword still held in the other hand. He was halfway down the hall before Bostian, gasping, crashed to the ground.

Those inside the command center heard the crunch, the thud, and Bostian's harsh breathing. No one moved. No one spoke. The only sounds were the rustle of papers as Detlev continued to read, and the diminishing tread of Siamis's footsteps. Then silence.

No one wanted to be the first to move, lest they catch Detlev's eye. Time passed with the speed of snow melt, drip by drip, then Detlev laid down the last page and vanished, leaving a room full of people who resumed breathing.

As soon as he was gone, Dejain unlocked her knees. Everyone knew Detlev and Siamis were the best mind-readers outside of Norsunder's Garden of the Twelve, wherein dwelt the sinister figures who had built that place beyond time and space. She had seen him strike with only his mind. But mind-reading had limitations, she had discovered after painstaking research, and you could shield your mind against them. Though it took concentration. She let her mental grip on her mind-shield relax — her head throbbed faintly — as the mage whispered, "Did you understand that at the end?"

"No," she lied, pushed past, and trod upstairs again. She'd only heard part of Detlev and Siamis's exchange, specifically the words, *Blood magic.*

The most powerful and deadly type of magic, and the rarest, it was blood magic that the Venn mage Erkric had been seeking nine hundred years ago. That single-minded, destructive quest had resulted in an entire kingdom's mages being bound inside their border.

Dejain had to find out who had what, where, and get to it first.

PART ONE

One

End of Winter 4743 AF
Tser Mearsies

IT WAS A QUIET day in a part of the world so quiet it seldom appears in histories, except in lists. I will begin here on an early spring day as a horseback rider emerged on the common path.

The lone rider passed from shadow into light and then into shadow again between the tall, barren elms growing alongside a road in the northern part of Tser Mearsies.

"Rel's back!"

A party of workers pulling up a stump paused as the rider and his big horse passed into the sun again: very tall, broad through the chest, a quantity of badly cut waving dark hair falling to his threadbare collar in back. At first the strength obvious in the contours of those arms, and the deep-set eyes in a craggy face, appeared to be those of a man, but the weak late-winter sun falling on the smooth downy cheek made it clear that this rider had not quite crossed that threshold, big as he was.

"It *is* Rel! Ho, I've got to tell the Khavnans!"

Rel still wore shabby traveler's clothes, but there was the gold-chased hilt of a beautiful sword jutting from the saddle sheath, and a knife hilt gleaming at the top of a tall riding boot, hints that maybe some of the wild stories about his adventures were true.

The man sprinted across the Holder Raneseh's Khavnan's southernmost fallow field, flushing from the thawing ground the birds who'd been rooting for seeds.

Rel recognized two of the workers at the stump. "Need some help?"

The eldest called back, "We've got it, young Rel. The Holder will be wanting to see you."

Rel lifted his hand in greeting, and rode on.

As soon as she heard of Rel's arrival, Pralineh made her way to the kitchen to give orders for her foster-brother's favorite dinner to be prepared. She found Cook and all her assistants buzzing around, a startling sight in the customary calm, well-ordered routine. When she saw that they'd forestalled her, Pralineh smiled and backed out.

A short time later Rel himself stepped through the kitchen door, head stooping under the lintel. Everyone paused to stare. Had he grown even taller? Pralineh thought he'd grown better in-to his bones, making him even more handsome—a catch for someone who didn't mind that he would never settle down. Grateful for her own betrothed Tasmon, she exclaimed, "Welcome home!"

Though Rel recognized how his little foster-sister had blossomed into a pretty young woman, it was an observation, not a reaction. His heart had room for one image: tall, long-faced, brown-haired, on the verge of womanhood, whose rank set her at an unreachable distance.

"Thanks, Pralineh," Rel said with a sudden, rueful smile. "It's good to be back."

Raneseh entered then, bald, bearded, mild of eye. He and Rel greeted each other with heartfelt pleasure, and Rel asked after everyone in the neighborhood.

As Raneseh began a catalogue, Pralineh glanced around the familiar room, trying to imagine what it must look like to a world traveler who knew the legendary Sartora, the girl who'd once ridden a horse made of lightning from south to north and east to west to free the world from Siamis's evil enchantment. Rumor had it that Rel had aided in the freeing of Sartor from Norsunder's century-old spell, and most recently he'd fought (at the express invitation of King Berthold) with the Knights of Dei when Norsunder invaded Everon on the other side of the strait.

Didn't they give rewards, these powerful people? She eyed the threadbare, elbow-patched shirt molding his shoulders, and over that, a dusty, travel-worn vest whose weaving Pralineh instantly recognized as some of their own. Those dark brown riding trousers were an unfamiliar cut and cloth, and the fine blackweave boots were new, at least.

Ah, but this was *Rel.* He might have been offered rewards, but she suspected he wouldn't take anything he couldn't fit into his knapsack.

"And you, Pralineh?" Rel turned her way. "How are you?"

"As you see," she replied. "My life is quiet. I like it that way. You?"

He smiled. "Different every day. I like it that way."

Pralineh laughed.

"Different seems an understatement," Raneseh observed. "You must know the entire valley will have heard by now that you're back again. They'll want to see you, and hear about your exploits firsthand."

Rel thought back to the horrible losses in Everon, a war that only ended because Norsunder withdrew for some reason of their own. He thought of the death of Derek Diamagan, the high-hearted young leader, trusted friend of the King of Sarendan, and shook his head. The quiet local society wanted stories; it was a regrettable part of human nature to find entertainment in faraway tragedy.

He couldn't speak the words. "I can only stay tonight," he said. "I'll be gone come morning. I want to get north before the weather changes."

Raneseh and Pralineh were disappointed, but not surprised.

"It's nearly sunset now." Raneseh indicated the merging shadows in the garden beyond his prized etched-glass doors. "You must be hungry."

Rel enjoyed this gentle reminder that in quiet Tser Mearsies, farm people considered it civilized to eat when the sun vanished. "I never turn down a meal."

"Then get yourself ready, and we shall talk over dinner."

Pralineh watched him go, feeling a little wistful. "He seems restless," she'd said to her father after the last of Rel's departures — two years ago? Three? "Do you think he will ever settle down?" she asked.

"Oh, it might come to pass," Raneseh said, after a long gaze toward the eastern horizon. "But do not expect him to settle among us. I don't think he's ever found his home here, though we've done our best to give him one."

Pralineh thought about that conversation over dinner, as Rel sat there in the new tunic she'd embroidered between his last visit and this one. It was his favorite forest green, with leaves of the same color worked around the cuffs and the high collar, and it made him look as handsome as any noble — and she knew from the self-conscious way he moved in it, careful not to get his sleeves in the food, or spill his redcurrant wine on it that he would carefully fold it away, and on his leaving, put on the old patched shirt and vest.

They had drunk their egg soup, and eaten their rice balls cooked with the first spring vegetables of the season, before Raneseh said, "Come, Rel, we've talked over the stables, the crops, the quality of this year's wool, and all the neighbors' doings, but you have yet to mention what you've seen out in the great world."

"Ah, I've been here and there. Colend, most recently. I have new friends there, Thad Keperi, and his sister Karhin. They're scribe prentices. So they're always in the middle of news crossing the continent."

What Rel didn't mention was that the Keperis were the communication center of the alliance of under-age rulers and student-mages that had recently formed.

He continued, "I thought I might go north to Bereth Ferian, see the sky lights, and study a little."

"What would you study?" Pralineh asked, amazed to have gotten that much. Rel's answers were usually a lot more terse.

"A friend nicknamed Arthur offered to tutor me, to better my knowledge of Ancient Sartoran," Rel said, to the others' surprise.

What a boring subject, thought Pralineh.

And Raneseh thought, Ah-h-h-h. So this is the time.

When the servant brought in the baked compote with the last of the winter apples, Pralineh saw in the subtle lift of Rel's strong cleft chin, and the way Raneseh stroked his beard, that they were going to go off and talk alone.

Rel and Raneseh walked in silence back to the study, where Raneseh shut the door. "Ancient Sartoran?" he asked.

"I can read a little of it now," Rel said. "That is, I know the alphabet. The principal verbs. Not a lot else."

"That's good enough." Raneseh moved to one of his bookshelves.

The books were propped up by a variety of fine art objects: a statue of a famous centaur, a vase, a cherry-wood carved box. This latter he took down and opened. Inside was another box, this one very old, its carving blurred with centuries of age. Raneseh touched the lid. A spark of protective magic flashed blue, then he opened the box and removed a little scroll made of heavy, cream-colored rag paper, tied by a rumpled, thread-loose black hair-ribbon of the sort worn in the previous generation.

Raneseh looked down at the letter, then lifted it out with both hands. "As promised, here it is."

Rel took the letter with both hands, signaling he understood this was an important moment. Then he regarded the man who had raised him. "Do you know what it says?"

"I do not," Raneseh replied. "I only know what I told you when you were a boy: that I had something for you if and when you learned enough Ancient Sartoran to read a letter."

"Do you know who wrote it?" Rel asked.

"Yes," Raneseh said. "And again, I apologize for the secrecy. It . . . was deemed necessary at the time."

Rel stared down at the letter, then slid the ribbon off, and opened the heavy, cracking paper. In Ancient Sartoran, it said:

> *Rel, I am alive. For you this ought to be enough. If*
> *it isn't, regard me as dead. But I expect my son is*
> *equal to the chase.*

Rel had waited most of his life to read that; he read it through again, then laid it on the desk. "I understand that you can't tell me who wrote this note. Nor can you tell me where. Perhaps you can tell me why."

"That, I may." Raneseh sat back in his chair. "Your father and I were good friends when we were young. But there was much about his past that I did not know, and he would never tell me. We shared a number of adventures —"

"In Everon."

"You've figured that much out." Raneseh smiled.

Rel said, "It might explain why Roderic Dei broke the strict rule about only recruiting Everoneth for the Knights of Dei when he invited me to join. While it was flattering to think it was owing to my beginner's skills, I never believed that to be true. I also have vague memories of the place. Can you tell me if I was born there?"

Raneseh glanced up at the map on the wall of his study. "You were not." He hesitated as he looked from the map to Rel and back again. "I do not know Roderic Dei's reasons for wanting you in his Knights, though I suspect he saw your potential. What happened to place you here with me is going to sound arbitrary — no, more like a whim. To the world, until very recently, it was necessary. Shall I go on?"

Rel said, "Please."

Raneseh opened his hands. "I know very little beyond your father's present situation. This I can tell you. You were not born in Everon, but you spent some time there as an infant after your mother was murdered."

"Murdered!"

"Yes. Again, I was not there, and at the time, we were unable to discover who, or why. Shortly thereafter, you came here to live with me, which protected you and freed your father to investigate."

Rel said, "I've always appreciated your generosity. Now I value it the more."

Raneseh smiled. "Mind, I would've been happy if you and my daughter had grown up fond enough to marry. I would love to see you share the responsibilities of this Holding with her, and become my son through marriage. But I could see by the time you were ten years old that it was unlikely to happen. And she's found a good match in young Tasmon."

"I remember him, the stonemason's boy, right?"

"Yes." Raneseh tapped his desk lightly with his fingertips, and glanced at the letter lying between them on his handsome desk. "This is more difficult than I had envisioned, though I've practiced this conversation in my mind over and over, your entire life. I think . . . I think perhaps I'd better leave that subject. What I can tell you is this. In addition to your father's private cares, we fought desperately hard in Everon, but found ourselves defeated by Norsunder. In recent years we've seen that Detlev and his evil allies can be as dangerous to one another as they are to us. "

Rel's right hand flexed. A small movement, but Raneseh saw in that tiny betrayal evidence of experience with the sinister and terrible Detlev.

He continued. "At the time our high-minded beliefs in our own powers were dashed. I retired from the hero trade to take up my life here, but your father had his own cause. And so, to protect you, as far as the world knew, you had no father, and he no son. Whereas I gained a ward from some unnamed intermediary who had given you up on a whim."

Rel said, "Have I ever seen him?"

"No. He was very careful about that. But, I assure you, he has watched from afar. Now, he accepts that you might want to get on with your life, and forget the past that cannot after all be retrieved. He accepts that you might be angry. He accepts that you might only want to find him in order to lay blame. All these things, he says, are reasonable. But I say, do not seek him if you have anger in your heart. For then I would know that I have failed you."

Rel said, "I'm surprised, I'm confused. I'm intrigued. But I'm not angry."

"Thank you, Rel," said Raneseh, bowing over his hands in the old formal mode.

Rel also bowed over his hands, more deeply. "Thank you, Raneseh, foster-father. He may have given me life, but you saw to it that my life was a good one."

Two

Early Spring, 4743 AF
Chwahirsland to Marloven Hess

NOT FAR TO THE northeast of Tser Mearsies lie the formidable mountains dividing Chwahirsland from the rest of the eastern end of the Sartoran continent. Chwahirsland had been isolated from the rest of the world for centuries.

That was going to change.

But no one in Chwahirsland knew it, certainly not teenaged Jilo, who held an empty throne that no one dared to fill. Not with the threat of Wan-Edhe's return, the mage-king who had ruled the vast kingdom with a remorseless grip for nearly a century.

Jilo had scarcely arrived in the partially ruined castle where the remnants of his family lived when one of his magical tracers gave him the inward poke of a warning. It meant someone had dared venture into Wan-Edhe's private chambers back in the royal fortress halfway across the country.

Many would have run. Jilo held himself still, the old fear rushing back. He reflected that even if he ran, Wan-Edhe would spare no effort to hunt him down, so he may as well go back.

He turned to his cousin Aran, a girl his own age, and said, "Please tell Uncle Shiam I have to return to Narad."

Aran's eyes widened, but long-enforced custom kept Chwahir girls from ever protesting, or even responding — at least directly. She ducked her head, her black hair so much like his swinging forward to hide her face, and he braced himself for the wrench of another transfer.

When he'd recovered, he slunk down the empty hall in the upper reaches of the fortress, hands out. Fingers spread.

Something had broken one of the tracer wards he'd set over the former king's magic chambers. Wan-Edhe never used his name: he had required the Chwahir, and the world, to use his title: *wan edhe* meant *the* king, as if there had never been a king before, and would never be again.

Whoever had breached the magic chambers was not Wan-Edhe.

Jilo had stepped into an empty throne when Wan-Edhe was forced into Norsunder by Prince Kessler, but no one, from the smallest Chwahir girl scraping up wax droppings from the torches after a military march, up to the army commanders, believed that Wan-Edhe, terror of the Chwahir for eighty years, was really gone forever.

And there were a very few in high places who not-so-secretly wanted him back.

Jilo didn't call himself a king. He didn't think of himself as a king. He did what he believed must be done, but he was aware that most Chwahir assumed Wan-Edhe would return from Norsunder, angrier and more powerful than ever, if Prince Kessler (rumored to be still alive, unlike the rest of the royal family) didn't ride over the border with an army from Norsunder to take the throne himself.

Jilo licked absently at chapped lips, and breathed slowly, fingers out as he tested the air.

The person he feared second to Wan-Edhe was Prince Kessler. No one else would dare this terrible place, still full of hidden magic traps, in spite of Jilo's protracted efforts to undo decades — centuries — of accumulated evil intent.

Jilo had replaced some of the killing wards with tracers, and had altered the rest to target Wan-Edhe, and no one else. If and when Wan-Edhe did return, Jilo hoped for enough warning to get out of reach, because despite his work, he knew he had merely dismantled the surface of what Wan-Edhe had wrought for decades.

So he returned to his room and fetched from a painstakingly hidden crack between two stones the book where he kept record of the spells he had discovered, and carried it back to the hall that led to the magic chamber. Somewhere along there a person had transferred in and the alert spell had caught them.

He braced himself against a wall and murmured the long spell that Wan-Edhe had prepared to reveal any trespassers.

He hated using the spell, first for the physical effects, but the more ever since he had learned from Senrid Montredaun-An of the Marlovens how the dark magic gained its power: from the life forces of the fortress denizens. At least this spell would be brief, compared to the drain that he still labored to eradicate altogether.

He completed the spell, and held his breath as his heart labored in his chest. He tried not to move, loathing the sticky, heavy drag that even the slightest movement sustained, leaving his muscles trembling.

His eyelids stung. His nose watered from the burned metal stench of intense dark magic. The time smear revealed a flash of light out of which a man emerged: slender, tense shoulders. Black curly hair cut short, pale skin, pale blue eyes. Plain white shirt, black trousers over riding boots.

This had to be Prince Kessler. He carried two slim books in his hand as he walked slowly toward the magic chamber.

Jilo gritted his teeth and pushed his way into the thick air to follow. It was like trying to run in honey. He saw slow ripples in Kessler's shirt, the fabric molding over the hard contours of the young man's arm as he lifted the books.

Two steps, three, and Kessler gestured with his left hand in magic signs that Jilo recognized. A low burbling hiss: speech.

The books winked out in a tiny flash of light, followed by a brief wink high up on one of the shelves where the worst magical protections had clustered. Then another transfer—a blink of shadow opening up, affording a glimpse of a far Destination—and Kessler was gone.

Jilo opened his mouth, striving to suck in air as he released the spell, then stumbled forward, panting.

After he recovered, he stared up at the bookcase, uncertain what to do. Prince Kessler hiding something *here*, of all places? He had to assume that Jilo did not know about the protections. Fear kept Jilo immobile until he forced himself to investigate. It was better to find out.

He dismantled the protections with painstaking care, then stared down at a pair of thin books he had never seen before. These had not been part of Wan-Edhe's collection, at least since Jilo had begun cataloging what lay on the shelves. He cautiously extended his hand over one of them. Though Kessler had handled them, Jilo knew better than to assume that he could. By now well practiced in seeking Wan-Edhe's many magical traps, he sensed broken wards, nasty ones whose magical residue felt like greasy, metallic smoke and old, dried blood.

He extended a cautious finger. He'd learned that when it came to layers of evil intent, *no one* outthought Wan-Edhe. Kessler might be the same.

Touch.

Nothing happened.

Jilo slid his finger along the edge of what felt like very, very old binding material, lifted the cover, glanced down . . . and recoiled, breathing hard.

He retreated down the hall to the room he'd temporarily adopted as a bedchamber. Nothing was in it but a bed and a cleaning frame. The latter was new, made by Jilo himself. Until Wan-Edhe's disappearance he had owned little, and Wan-Edhe would have destroyed that, too, if it did not serve his purposes. Jilo still kept his occasional attempts at drawings hidden a continent away.

This bedroom was as safe as he could make it, surrounded by spells to alert him to anyone's proximity. Wan-Edhe had warded his personal space against his own subjects, but Jilo cast his spells as protection against Wan-Edhe.

He sat on the bed, running his knuckles over the thick wool of the blanket. He knew he needed help, but he had to figure out whom to trust.

The obvious answer was the alliance. Jilo still had trouble believing he was a part of this. . . net of lighters no older than he was. Why would they call him to their aid? They wouldn't. And he didn't believe that any of them, excepting maybe Senrid Montredaun-An, the boy king of Marloven Hess, might come to his.

So far, Senrid had been closest to what Jilo assumed a friend might be like, though he still wasn't sure what that word really entailed. But Senrid had been helpful when Jilo needed help, and he'd asked Jilo's aid when they were all up in the mountains after the villain Siamis made another try at the world with his enchantment.

So Jilo pulled his new notecase out of his pocket, fetched pen and paper, and wrote a note.

Then he sat and waited.

At the other end of the continent, in the largest interview chamber at the Marloven royal castle, an angry, irritated, greedy, speculative gathering of city merchants stared at their king as he stared back at them.

Then Senrid felt the internal tap of the notecase he had trained himself to carry, and eased it out of his pocket as a huge blacksmith tried to shout down the rest of the crowd.

"But there wasn't an attack," the blacksmith said, sending a glance Senrid's way under furrowed blond brows before he turned back to the company. "That means there was no war, which means the guilds don't disperse a copper to shoe your horses. And I'm not doing the work for free."

This was the tenth reiteration of a similar statement, from ten different people, and Senrid knew what they really meant: The boy king got scared and sent the entire army into hiding for nothing.

Senrid shoved the notecase back into his pocket, but kept his fingers on it as he said, "There was an attack. Two attacks. Just not here. Norsunder went to war in Everon and Sarendan. They were turned back before they made it this far." He hated repeating himself. To his ears, he sounded defensive, as if he made excuses. But it was the truth.

Everyone had to comment on that to their neighbor; using the hubbub as cover, Senrid slipped the note out. His heart sank. Jilo? Anything with him was never easy.

A break in the noise occurred when a guild representative stood up, a tough old woman with a bitter sneer. "It wasn't a war *here*. When there is no war, then the guild war chest isn't opened. You all agreed to that when you joined your guilds."

"But we sent our horses to the plains all the same — "

" . . . entire academy emptied, no business all summer . . ."

"Tradition is quite clear, the war chests are only broached after an actual war."

Several faces turned Senrid's way, and he wondered, did they really expect him to pay for the whole fiasco from crown funds?

He could. It would make a grand gesture—it would feel generous.

His hand stirred. He flexed his fingers, knowing there was something wrong with that easy solution. He remembered Commander Keriam telling him when he was small that the crown traditionally paid for war games. Senrid's uncle, the regent, had never ordered a defensive war game because he lived in fear of conspiracy.

Last summer's kingdom-wide retreat, a defensive plan Senrid had worked on for over a year, had been no war game. Senrid had truly believed they were about to be invaded.

But Norsunder had not come in force—to Marloven Hess.

" . . . my cousin said East Army spent the entire . . ."

I was wrong. Is that what you want to hear? He could say it, and what would be the consequences of that? He was a coward, he was too young to rule, he had never been to the academy . . .

He looked down at the Jilo's note, longing to get away, but he had to settle this problem himself, and without Commander Keriam, his trusted tutor. Because if they saw grizzled Keriam whispering advice, then Keriam might as well call himself king.

As the argument spiraled out from horse shoes to horse training, and a thousand what-ifs, Senrid considered fast. Maybe Jilo's problem was something the alliance ought to know about.

When a blacksmith stood up to air his views for the third time, Senrid pulled a tiny square of paper from the top part of his notecase, dipped his pen, and wrote:

> *Hibern: Jilo needs help. Isn't this what the alliance is for? Meet at Roth Drael?*

He tucked that into the notecase, sent it, and when he raised his head, he caught several speculative and worried looks. So it was intimidating to see him writing?

Excellent.

With a sharp look his way, a woman from the harness makers got to her feet and reiterated her argument even more forcefully.

Hibern's answer came back:

*Not here. I suggest the Keperis. Call it neutral
ground.*

That surprised Senrid. Hibern was studying light magic under
a mage, but she'd been born a Marloven. She was also the one who
had brought Senrid into the alliance. Something else was going on.
He'd have to talk to her.

He glanced up. The speeches were definitely repeating.

He leaned over, picked up a pen, dipped it in ink, and while
the latest ranter showed no signs of running out of words, he
wrote three fast notes: to Jilo, Hibern, and then to Karhin Keperi,
the scribe student in Colend whose letter writing seemed to be
putting her at the center of the alliance's lines of communication.
He suggested a meet tomorrow. Maybe by then he wouldn't be
one step from losing his throne.

At the other end of the continent, Jilo had meant to get something
to eat, but sank into reverie.

When his notecase signaled a response, he jumped, alert and
wary. He took out the slip of paper, and recognized Senrid's neat
hand, the words in Sartoran:

*If you think this is related to Norsunder in any
way, the rest of the alliance ought to be in on it. If
you agree, transfer to the Keperis. Tomorrow,
midday your time — here is the transfer
Destination pattern. . .*

Jilo's first instinct was to say no. But last year, when the
alliance faced the Norsunder attack, Senrid had explained the
Marloven concept of inside lines of communication. It was alien
thinking to the hierarchical Chwahir, but Jilo had been reading
about the Marloven plains warriors, whose successes far
outstripped those of the Chwahir. He had seen first-hand the
damage possible when one set of allies kept crucial information
from another, and Senrid had also pointed out that young rulers
may as well band together even loosely, as alone, they had enough
problems hanging onto their thrones even when Norsunder was
not a threat.

Finally, Jilo was intensely curious about Colend, oldest enemy
of the Chwahir.

Relieved to have a decision taken care of, he cast a warning spell tied to Colend's time and lay back to shut his eyes . .

Three

Colend

"WHOSE ROOM IS BETTER?"

In the scribe house central to the village of Wilderfeld, Thad and Karhin Keperi faced each other, each seeing a mix of excitement and consternation in their sibling. Karhin was the first to look about her, surveying their familiar house as she wondered how it was they had ended up this way, hosting a meeting between two kings! And one of those a Chwahir, the ancient enemy. Granted, these kings were teenaged, and neither would be traveling with an entourage, but still. Kings. In provincial Wilderfeld, where nothing of import ever happened.

"I think we ought to use your room," Karhin said finally.

"Mine?" Thad, younger, his hair a brighter red, put his hands to his chest. "Our rooms are the same. Both our windows look out over the village square. There is no difference."

"It being farther from the stairs, we might be better assured of privacy," she said, and they both knew she meant their younger sister, who if she saw Karhin's door open, or heard visitors, would insist on being included.

"Ah-ye," Thad responded, fingertips touching. "But Adam is painting in there."

"And?" Karhin held out her hands. "It was Rel himself who brought him. Is he not therefore part of the alliance, even though he's new?"

So — aided by the ever-obliging Adam — they set about cleaning, dusting, and squaring an already clean room in the rambling house. The village lay alongside a river-canal, as did most trade towns and villages in Colend, especially at the country's western end.

Because Thad, Karhin, and their house became crucially important to the Young Allies, here's a little about each.

The house sported a sign over its awning:

Wilderfeld Scribes and Messengers

The Heralds' Guild had bestowed on the Keperi family the Seal of Law, commonly known as the magic-imbued *sved*, which guaranteed constant business: at least two scribes had to witness every contract they drew up for people, enter it into the civil law ledger, then send a copy to the Heralds' Guild in the capital, where official records were kept.

Thad and Karhin's mothers, who served as chief scribes, were well respected in guild and town, but neither parent had any idea that their two eldest were part of a secret alliance. Thad and Karhin worked hard to keep it that way, aided by the fact that the house saw a constant stream of custom not only from the area, but scribe-couriers on the road.

Karhin, older than her brother, had at ten set out to become the scribe student with the most correspondents, a benign sort of competition popular among scribe students. By the time she boasted 110 pen-friends, she had begun to tire of using the prescribed phrases whose many gradations scribe students began memorizing at an early age, as they practiced their handwriting. At first it had charmed her to see that they worked, eliciting the correct responses.

But around the time that many of those correspondence-collecting friends also began to tire of predictable exchanges, they practiced their polite closings on one another, and Karhin began looking for pen-friends outside Colend's borders. At the same time, Thad, who was a scribe student only because it was the family business, liked making friends with couriers and travelers who came through the small town. Though he was a diligent student, he preferred talk to text.

It was Thad who had befriended the oddly named Mearsiean vagabond Puddlenose, which led to more friendships with other teenaged wanderers. These turned up once word spread about Wilderfeld's new coffee house, now that Sartor, after nearly a century of enchantment, once again was trading their excellent coffee and leaf.

Due to a felicitous marriage, Wilderfeld's coffee house got one of the best cooks in the entire western province, which guaranteed the trade village becoming a regular stop for caravans, messengers, couriers, and wanderers.

Among the wanderers Puddlenose brought was Rel the Traveler, who in turn brought Adam the painter. Karhin, through Rel's and Puddlenose's encouragement, had found herself writing regularly to three young monarchs—the queen of Sartor, Puddlenose's cousin, the young queen of Mearsies Heili, and the princess in Everon—which had gradually widened out to more young royals.

And today, Senrid had proposed another first: a meeting, at their house, between him, Hibern the mage student, and the new Chwahir king!

Think of it . . . a Chwahir in the alliance—and in their very house!

The magical alert woke Jilo abruptly. He discovered he'd fallen asleep so deeply he'd drooled down the side of his face.

He got up, joints creaking as always because of the magical toxins left by Wan-Edhe. He put himself through his new cleaning frame, and carefully did the transfer spell that Senrid had written for him. Then he stumbled dizzy and nauseated out of the painted Destination square in an attic room. He was met by a skinny girl about his age, with bright red hair, blue eyes, and freckles, wearing layers of cream and pale pink, with green edging. She put her hands together, then opened them in the most formal version of the gesture known as the peace.

Jilo stared in complete incomprehension.

What Karhin—dressed in her best, and making a formal welcome—saw was a gangling slouch of a boy, thinner than a fence slat, wearing badly dyed black clothing. His pale, sallow face under matte-black hair was obviously Chwahir. A Chwahir, in Colend!

"You must be Jilo," she said uncertainly, reminding herself that Senrid had spoken for him as an ally. She held her fingertip to her lips in a gesture Jilo didn't understand. "Please, come this way quietly."

Jilo thought he understood. She didn't want anyone knowing that a Chwahir was polluting her house. The impulse to transfer back to Chwahirsland was strong, but if this was the only way to talk to Senrid, he'd put up with Colendi arrogance.

So he forced himself to follow as she flitted on soundless feet along a hallway with flowers and stylized figures painted high under the wood-patterned ceiling. Jilo breathed in the scent of flowers and baking corn bread. His stomach wrung, and it occurred to him that he hadn't eaten since . . . as usual, he couldn't remember.

Senrid Montredaun-An hated to be late, but even at sunup in Marloven Hess, his day had already become complicated.

When at last he was able to get away and transfer to the Keperis in Colend, he didn't wait for Karhin. He remembered the way to Thad's room, and paused in the doorway.

Five young faces took in Senrid: short for mid-teens, curly blond hair square-cut in back above his white linen shirt collar. None of the others had ever seen him wear anything but those black riding trousers with the tan stripe down the side, a white shirt, and riding boots. Knowing what the rest of the world thought of Marlovens, he seldom wore his black-and-tan tunic outside his own borders.

He returned the scan: besides the redheaded Karhin and Thad, there was black-eyed Hibern, who lived with her magic tutor, and proudly wore her mage student's blue robe. Her nearly black hair and brown skin were a contrast to pasty-faced Jilo with his lank, unkempt blue-black hair and moon-pale skin.

Senrid noticed the tightness in Hibern's long, unremarkable face. Whatever had happened to Hibern since they'd all returned from Geth-deles seemed to have turned her into a semblance of stone, except stone didn't work all the time.

Hibern, seeing his surprised expression, said, "I came straight from up north."

"Up north" meant Bereth Ferian and its magic school, where Liere, Senrid's first real friend, currently lived.

Senrid squashed the impulse to ask about Liere in front of the fifth person he saw there, a stranger. Dressed in paint-stained travel clothes, the boy was thin, and so slight in build he could be any age between twelve and sixteen. Above mild wide-set brown eyes mushroomed sun-streaked light brown hair so wild it often looked as if a goat had chewed it. Not helping that impression, his hair also streaked with blotches of green and yellow and a splatter of blue on one side. Paint grimed his fingernails, too.

"Who's this?" Senrid asked.

"Meet Adam," Karhin said.

As Senrid perched on the edge of Thad's desk, Karhin went on, "Rel brought Adam. Found him being attacked on Sartor's border."

Thad added, "Adam's been here almost a month, and he fit in so well we told him about the alliance. He offered to help."

Senrid opened a hand, his version of a welcoming gesture. They had all agreed they needed to expand the alliance if it was to work, recruitment to be handled one youth at a time.

But he still felt they ought to be careful; some in the alliance had been invited either because the adults they should have had as guides couldn't be trusted, or were dead. They didn't know anything about this Adam, so until they did . . .

Adam squinted at the newcomer, then at the rest of the company, seeing them in ever-shifting hues: Karhin's sky-deep blue shading toward the silver of question and wariness, Thad's gold also silvering; Hibern's a subtle complexity of greens shading to very deep; Senrid's colors were the most muted, hidden behind a shield of reflective steel.

Jilo's were the most interesting, the entire spectrum shimmering with light-on-water intensity, but underneath the slow boil of thick, rust-tasting mud of never-ending worry, and below that a luminous thread, diamond-bright. Odd, so much color from a slouching boy who didn't seem to be able to meet anyone's eyes.

Adam noted the others' attention on Jilo, who studied his hands as if his future lay there.

Adam thrust his colored chalk behind his ear, adding another blotch of color to his hair, and said, "My art master told me you don't get good unless you draw from life. Best way to draw from life is to see it." His smile twisted. "Some brigands trampled everything I'd done into the mud. So I had to start over." He tipped his head toward a travel-stained tube made of lacquered canvas sitting next to his knapsack. "I'm going to sketch the trumpet flowers against the walls. Midday, I noticed, the light is perfect in that corner."

No one stopped him from leaving, so his guess was right: they wanted to be private.

As soon as Adam was out the door, Thad closed the window, and Karhin peered out the door in both directions, then pulled it shut, too.

Jilo got to his feet. "If it's my presence you object to, I'll take myself off."

Karhin and Thad listened in horror, then Thad whirled around so quickly that he fell against his own desk and tumbled to the floor in a flurry of papers. "I crave your pardon—we never meant—oh." He saw in Jilo's tight face and averted gaze what he had assumed. He mumbled an apology, his face as red as his hair, then dashed out of the room.

Karhin stood with her hands to her cheeks. "Oh, please!" she said—even in extremity, it was difficult for a Colendi in polite mode to use the word *no*. "The objection—that is, we do not, we never would *object*—it's just . . . It's my sister."

Her hands clapped together in the peace, then flew wide in a gesture of appeal. "Our stepsister Lisbet is a dear, but she cannot keep anything to herself. When a duchas's daughter was here for the window-box festival last month, we overheard Lisbet bragging that we'd had three princes visiting us. She didn't quite get to talking about the alliance, but I'm afraid it's only because the duchas's girl snubbed her. We daren't let Lisbet overhear anything that she might chatter about to anyone who will listen. Please, *please* know you are welcome—"

At that moment the carillon pealed noon. It was so beautiful a sound, so utterly unexpected, that Jilo was distracted.

Before the last chords died away Thad returned with the family's finest tray, polished wood with chestnut blossoms carved around the edge. It bore their finest porcelain, containing lemon-ice pastry shaped like roses, a pot of Sartoran steep, and a tiny painted dish with Colendi rice wine, a petal floating in it.

Wilderfeld being a village, all they had were three bells, but they were perfectly tuned. Adam smiled in appreciation as he descended the rest of the stair, stepping into the sunlight as the last echoes died away.

He entered the square at the same time that Thad and Karhin's step-siblings, skinny, brown-haired Lisbet and fair-haired Aural (known as Little Bee for the way he had hummed constantly when very small), were crossing back for the midday break, after Little Bee's morning at the village school.

Little Bee's chin lifted, and he turned his face from side to side. "Adam is over there. I heard his step."

Lisbet cast an impatient glance around the square, her mood brightening when she saw the artist boy sitting down on one of the stone carved benches.

Adam saw them coming, and obligingly held out a hand to meet Little Bee's groping fingers, then guided Little Bee to the bench next to him.

"May I stay with you?" Little Bee asked.

"Sure."

Lisbet put her hands on her skinny hips and tossed a brown braid over her shoulder. "Are they talking secrets again?"

"Secrets?" Adam asked.

"You know, that stupid thing, where they blab about watching out for Norsunder. As if Norsunder would let *them* know if they ever really planned an attack against Colend. Which has never happened yet." Lisbet tossed her other braid back with an air of *so there!* "I *can* keep secrets, *if* people just tell me why. *I* think they just like pretending to be important." She ran off to join a couple of friends who had appeared on the other side of the square.

Little Bee sighed. "She's not supposed to talk about that."

"Do they tell you secrets?" Adam asked, laughing.

"They tell me none," Little Bee said. He kept to himself the truth: that if he really wanted to hear them, he could. "Tell me more colors, please?"

This had begun when Adam first arrived, and he'd found Little Bee curled up in the dormer window. Little Bee had said, "I hate it when they talk about colors. It doesn't make any sense."

"How?"

"They say gold is so beautiful, but when I touched a Sartoran six-sider, it was hard and cold. It tastes like metal."

"I'll tell you what gold is," Adam had said. "It's the first real day of spring, when you go outside, and lift your face to the sun, and it's so warm on your skin after all the days of cold. That is gold."

Little Bee's whole demeanor had transformed. "Yes! And how does it taste?"

Adam wasn't used to anyone listening to him talk about the feel, sound, or taste of colors without scoffing. He'd ventured cautiously, "Gold is warm pudding, the kind made with lots of eggs and butter and vanilla-bean."

"I thought that was green."

"It might be green, too, but it's my idea of gold. How about lemon juice beaten into egg-white?"

"That's close to orange, flavors akin."

"I think of gold as something that tastes warm and perhaps slightly sweet, like that sun on the first spring day."

"Oh, yes!"

Little Bee was eight, and he worked hard at the village school, as he was determined to follow in the family trade and become a scribe. Since he was blind, he would work entirely with memory, so he spent a lot of time trying to get ahead by playing memory games with anyone he could get to listen.

But whenever he and Adam were alone, they talked about colors. "Bees," Little Bee said as he lifted his chin and turned his ears from side to side. "There are bees around the honeysuckle. Did I tell you they called me Little Bee because I learned to hum from bees? I can tell where I am in the house when I hum. Every room sounds different, but bees sound different in the same place. What color is their honeysuckle hum?"

Adam tipped his head. "Green."

"What color is the sound of angry bees?"

"Red."

Little Bee sighed. "Karhin's voice is fire right now. Mixed with thunderstorm purple."

"Do you hear the words, or just the tone?" Adam asked. "The . . . thunderstorms and fire and things?"

"That. Sometimes the words, if I listen close. I don't know how it is, because sometimes I can hear them when I am walking down by the stream, but only when . . ." Little Bee halted, looking unhappy. "Some people don't believe I hear like that. Everyone says I shouldn't."

He waited for Adam to add his disapproval, but Adam only

said, "Why don't we sit on this bench and count how many insects we hear? No one would mind that. We'll have a contest."

Little Bee settled himself happily on the bench, face uplifted, and silence fell between them.

Directly above them in Thad's room, Jilo did not recognize the beautiful tray and dishes, the delicate pastry and the best rice wine as a peace offering anymore then he'd recognized Karhin's formal welcome. All he was aware of was that amazing, delicious first bite of the pastry, followed by the exhilaration of the rice wine. Never in his life had he tasted such subtle flavors. The alcohol in the wine warmed him to the core, making his nerves sing.

Senrid looked impatient. Hibern caught his gaze and turned her hand flat in a gesture to wait as Karhin poured out steep for everyone, her gestures careful and precise. The single cup of rice wine had been for Jilo, a silent apology that completely passed him by.

Jilo devoured his third pastry and thought about the sour, flat clangs of Chwahir bells. Was that another requirement of Wan-Edhe? Except most bells were old. Why didn't his people make bells that sounded good? Bell-casting could not be a secret art.

When Karhin sat down again, at last, Senrid said, "Jilo, what did you find?"

Jilo shifted uncomfortably. "These books. I'm almost certain that it was Kessler Sonscarna who left them."

Senrid turned his empty cup around and around, a restless movement. He'd been in some foul places, but the fortress in the center of Chwahirsland's capital was right up there with Norsunder Base's prison for sinister and terrifying.

Hibern gave the texts the squint-eye. "Did he talk to you?" And on Jilo jerking his head in negation, "Did you discover he'd been there in that enemy book of yours?"

Jilo tightened in reflex at the mention of that book. "No." He reddened, remembering how he'd fallen asleep instead of checking. "That is, not exactly. I have other spells. And you know how, uh, time can't be trusted in there. I saw him in image. Though he was already gone."

While the Keperis mirrored shock, and Hibern's eyes narrowed warily at the mention of time being untrustworthy, Senrid's gaze shifted away at the mention of the enemies book. The temptation to steal it from Jilo had nearly been irresistible. Too nearly.

Karhin said with Colendi politesse, "Please forgive my lack of understanding. Who is Kessler Sonscarna?"

Jilo had drained the rice wine in two sips, which made him heady. He cautiously tasted the steep, then drank more. When the delicate, shallow little cup was empty, he said, "How much do you know about my country?"

Nothing good. Karhin said in an apologetic tone, "We've all heard regrettable stories about the former king, but we know little beyond that. I don't believe I've ever heard his actual name—someone said that Wan-Edhe is a title."

Jilo thought of all he could say, then chose the simplest explanation. "Wan-Edhe had most of his family murdered, except for one prince who got away—named Kessler, who ended up in Norsunder, and became a very powerful mage."

Senrid put in, "Kessler is also a military commander. He was also the one who defeated Everon last year. He didn't just command, he led the slaughter."

To Senrid, there was a significant difference between the commander who points his finger from a safe distance at the rear, and the one who leads from the front lines, but he could see in Hibern total disinterest, discomfort in Jilo, and polite incomprehension in the two Colendi, except for Karhin's unconscious wince of distaste at the word *slaughter.*

"So you brought the books because you cannot read them?" Thad asked.

Jilo's shoulders jerked up. "That's right." He turned to Senrid. "I don't know this script. Not Chwahir. But it reminds me of something you showed me, once."

Senrid took the books, flipped open the top one, and his upper lip curled. "Is this written in blood?"

Jilo looked uncomfortable. "I believe so."

Senrid's expression changed, his brows drawing together and mouth thinning. "But this script, I think it's Old Venn runes. . . ."

"What?" several voices exclaimed at the same time.

Senrid looked Hibern's way. Shock pooled cold in her stomach when her gaze met Senrid's. His pupils were so huge that his normally gray-blue eyes looked black. Then his lips moved in the transfer spell, and he vanished, causing a brief current of air to rustle Adam's sketch papers.

"That was . . . sudden." Karhin sighed. "I wonder what disturbed him so much?"

Hibern got up and straightened her robe. "I'll wager anything he's taken it straight to Vasande Leror." Hibern paused, and remembered Leander's nosy stepsister. More likely Senrid would ask Leander to come to him. "Leander Tlennen-Hess, as you probably know, studies Old Venn along with all the other ancient and dusty languages he so delights in."

"Oh, yes, he has visited," Karhin said, smiling at the memory of the handsome, green-eyed Leander, another teenage king.

"I'm sure you'll be hearing about anything they discover. Thank you for the refreshments," she added, remembering her tutor's words about politeness. She let herself out and whispered the transfer spell.

Inside Thad's room, Jilo stared at the space where Senrid had been. "He took the books."

Thad said, "Maybe you ought to follow him? You know the magic to transfer to his land?"

Jilo shut his eyes, sorting his emotions. He hadn't known the books existed previous to finding them in that startling way. He could not read them, and had no clue to their content. And surely Kessler wouldn't go to the trouble of hiding them in that bookcase if he didn't mean to come right back for them.

Fear was a habit. He had to get used to trusting those who had helped him. "Senrid recognized the script. He'll tell me what it says." Jilo blinked, noticing the two Colendi looking at him oddly, their hands pressed together. He had no idea what that meant, but they weren't acting like enemies. He recollected what Hibern had said, Colendi politenesses being as foreign to Chwahir as they were to Marlovens. "The food. It was very good," he said awkwardly, and repeated Senrid's breach of good manners by transferring directly from that room.

Thad said over his shoulder as he opened his window, "Life! That was disquieting. And you were wondering why Senrid and Jilo don't talk about their backgrounds."

Karhin sighed. "I wish I could unhear all that. Those careless words about Everon were unsettling enough, but not as painful as those about a book written in blood."

"I suggest we walk below, and leave those words to drift on the wind. Besides, the bells rang long ago, and we ought to fetch Adam in for lunch."

Thad and Karhin ran downstairs, and found Adam and Little Bee in the garden, their upturned faces dappled with shadows of spring leaves.

Thad said, "There you are, the both of you! What have you been doing?"

"Listening for insects," Adam said, opening his eyes. "I counted six different kinds."

Little Bee wriggled with joy. "I got eight!" And he named them.

Then he laughed as Thad ruffled his hair. "Come inside. Lunch is waiting."

Four

EVERYONE BRACED FOR ONE of Detlev's lightning-strike reorganizations.

The last time he'd ripped through the Base, he smashed a carefully planned ambush against him that resulted in a courtyard of broken assassins and the scorched remains of a universally hated and feared mage. But as half a day turned into a day, then two, Detlev did not return from wherever he'd transferred shortly after Siamis's departure.

Dejain rarely left the command center. She maintained a cool front, listening to gossip and speculation, but her real interest was the steady stream of reports that arrived by magic in the transfer tray, to be identified and relayed by the duty mage.

When she spotted a report written in Ancient Sartoran, she used a carefully prepared token that dropped a stone spell over the duty mage. She plucked the report out of the tray, then waited with accelerated heartbeat for another report to appear as she watched the doorway and listened for the noise of arrivals at the Destination down the hall.

Come on . . . come on . . . At last another report appeared, and she snapped her spell away, watched the duty mage blink, rock a little in his seat, and then reach for the new report to log and send on, covering the fact that one had gone missing.

Then she walked around the room, looking at Detlev's huge map of Sartorias-deles on one wall, before she drifted out with her prize.

It was risky, of course. Whoever had sent it could easily be sending a copy directly somewhere else, or some other kind of code or signal might have been arranged as a failsafe. But chances like these rarely occurred: Ancient Sartoran meant Siamis, now sent off alone on an impossible errand, or Detlev, who was either in Norsunder-Beyond, or at his compound on the world they call-ed Five. At best, they might never miss the report. At worst, she had a little time.

You had better be worth it, she thought at the paper as she slid it into a pocket of her rose velvet gown.

As a defensive measure she made certain she was seen at Lesca the steward's, then down at the stable as supplies were transferred in, vital as nothing could be grown in the blasted ground outside the base for three weeks' journey in any direction. Nobody came demanding to know who took an expected message.

Dejain finally retired to her chambers — painstakingly warded — to translate the report. Sources on Ancient Sartoran were frustratingly scanty, especially on idiom. Her comprehension was imperfect, but this much she discerned:

> *Subject: magic books, writ in blood, runes*

> *Found by Jilo in Chwahirsland, left by Kessler Sonscarna*

> *In current possession of either Leander Tlennen-Hess of Vasande Leror, or Senrid Montredaun-An of Marloven Hess.*

Ice ran in her veins. Blood? Runes? That had to be one of the rare blood-magic texts left over from the days of the Old Venn.

Any books about the secretive, long-warded Venn blood magic were extremely difficult to find, in fact nearly impossible: Yeres and Efael of the Host of Lords did not share willingly. Dejain knew that one of her rival mages, Benin, was busy with some secret project having to do with blood-magery and the soul-bound. And here was either Siamis or Detlev showing an interest, for no one else had their minions write in Ancient Sartoran.

Dejain simply had to get there first. But she would have to act fast.

Marloven Hess was nearly impossible to get into without expending much effort, but Vasande Leror?

It called itself a kingdom but was in reality little more than a trade town surrounded by farmland and silk-worm trees, verging on a vast plain. Its young king had no claim to interest save as a friend to Senrid, whom everyone knew Detlev had marked for his own.

She threw the report into the fireplace, and smiled as it burned to ash.

Marloven Hess

Two long transfers in less than a turn of the hourglass really hurt.

Hibern stood in Senrid's huge castle, breathing the dusty air that smelled like stone with a whiff of horse, aromas of early childhood. Her stomach stopped trying to tie itself in knots as she glanced around the large, sunny room overlooking the academy that Senrid called his study.

Two boys looked up from either side of the desk: Senrid and tall, dark-haired, and green-eyed Leander Tlennen-Hess, another who'd ended up with a throne due to violence in the previous generation.

Leander's Vasande Leror was a kingdom only because of royal presumption in the past; as Dejain, far away at Norsunder Base had noted, in reality it was a tiny patch of land bordering huge Marloven Hess to the west. To the east and south lay the great Nelkereth Plain, where no humans lived. Vasande Leror's capital —also its single city—would be a market-town anywhere else. Governing it consequently took up very little time, leaving

Leander to his pursuit of history and linguistics.

"You could at least have showed me a page," Hibern said.

Senrid said, "I recognized Old Venn runes. At least I think it's Old Venn. Blood magic, written in Old Venn. Not something you'd know. Thought Leander might recognize the language."

"I just got here," Leander said to Hibern. "A moment before you did."

He sat in Senrid's chair, and bent over the ancient, crackling pages as Senrid said to Hibern, "How is Liere doing?"

"You know Liere," Hibern said wryly. "Working hard." And at Senrid's pained expression (of course Liere was working hard), she said slowly, "It's odd, actually. You know she remembers everything she ever heard or read." Hibern touched her temple, signifying Dena Yeresbeth, the little-understood mind abilities that Liere had been born with, first of their generation. "She has performed two very complicated spells that we all know of. And yet, though she has memorized the basics, she has trouble building the simplest spells."

Senrid wondered if Liere was badly taught, but kept that to himself. He didn't know anything about that northern mage school, except that he disliked the mages who headed it, a dislike he knew was thoroughly returned simply because he was a Marloven trained in dark magic.

He looked down at the page that Leander was poring over, slipped one of his throwing daggers from his sleeve sheath, and gently, carefully flicked the edge of a single letter. Dust flaked. He thumbed it, rubbed it between his fingers, and sniffed it. "Definitely blood."

"Then this is blood magic?" Hibern shuddered. "I thought they eradicated that nearly a thousand years ago! It's dangerous!"

Senrid wiped his fingers on his trousers and looked up, his lip curling. "Not arguing. I've some prime records about the nasty old Venn, saying among other things that Erkric the Evil's secret cadre of blood-mages had to use their own blood to write their spells."

Leander said slowly, "The sad thing is, from everything I've read, blood magic is a perversion of healing magic, the kind where they clear bad things *out* of a person's blood."

Hibern assented.

Leander went on. "These are definitely Old Venn runes, but the language? It is either a really obscure dialect or some kind of code."

Senrid tapped the book with the edge of his knife before he cleaned that, too, and slid it back into its sheath. "I think this book might belong to one of the blood mages trained by Erkric the Evil." He shook his sleeve down over the knife in its sheath, and over the white scar around his wrists from when he'd been a prisoner of the Norsundrians, right after he turned fifteen.

Leander shook his head. "Can't be. I thought the Magic Council of that time destroyed all their work."

"Maybe they thought they did." Senrid's brows lifted. "Sounds kind of comical, doesn't it, said out loud? Erkric the Evil. Did they really call him that, back in the days of Inda and Fox? Who would want to be called 'the Evil'?"

"It came later. Around the time the Venn were first defeated, before they were permanently confined inside their border," Leander said, refraining from pointing out that "Inda the Fox" was mostly legend, conflating at least three separate individuals who might or might not be even real. He and Senrid had been arguing about that almost as long as they'd known one another. "According to the archives in Bereth Ferian, during his lifetime Erkric was known as The Dag, which meant the leader of the Venn mages, who were called dags."

Hibern shrugged off the history. "Burn them." She pointed at the books. "Our ancestors were smart to get rid of that kind of thing. It's dangerous, volatile, and would draw all the wrong kind of attention. There's no use even looking at them."

"I don't agree." Senrid held out a hand over the second book. "Don't you see? Somebody filched those, maybe from Norsunder, and hid them in Jilo's castle. You could feel that place sucking your life out of you. I still don't know how Jilo survived."

"He has that onyx ring protection," Hibern said.

Senrid made a flat-handed gesture. "His ring kept him from being annihilated when stepping into that library. That's about all the protection he got. Before I visited, he'd removed a lot of the worst traps, but it was still deadly in there."

Senrid gestured again, as if pushing something away. "Right now that doesn't matter. Here's what does. Maybe Kessler Sonscarna, maybe someone else pinched those two books. Since we don't know who, or why, the best thing to do is find out what's in the books, so we know what we're up against. Like Keriam says, ignorance is never a successful defense."

Hibern crossed her arms, her eyes meeting Senrid's.

"I think I agree," Leander said slowly and reluctantly, poring over the page of the first book without noticing the silent struggle of wills at either side of the desk.

Senrid said to Hibern, "You think I'm going to be sucked back into using dark magic."

"You were," Hibern stated. "During summer. When we were fighting against Siamis and Norsunder on our sister-world. You and Jilo both used it."

"To break Norsunder's traps keeping that old mage prisoner," Senrid retorted. "You're not going to — "

"Save your breath," Hibern cut in rudely. "Spare me what I'm not going to do, because you can't hear my thoughts, can you?"

Senrid flushed. "Wasn't even trying."

Hibern said relentlessly, "And if you had been, you would have discovered I have been practicing the mind-shield. So don't try to tell me what I'm thinking. I know you and Jilo did the right thing by using your old training, but that's what I'm afraid of, that you'll keep having to use dark magic for all kinds of good reasons . . . until the reasons become convenient."

Leander glanced up briefly. "She's got a point, you know."

Senrid sighed. He'd been fighting that battle longer than either of them knew. But there was no use explaining that this Venn thing, whatever it was, didn't represent even half the temptation that Jilo's enemy book did, with its ability to track the transfers by magic of enemies. "For all we know these are somebody's diary."

"Written in blood?" Hibern crossed her arms, her black brows expressive of skepticism.

Leander had been turning over the fragile leaves of the old tome, careful not to touch any of the long-dried blood used for ink. "I love translation. It's never as simple as one word swapped out for another, it's more like breaking code." He gave Hibern a lopsided smile. "If I translate it, do you think I'll be sucked into becoming the next evil mage?"

Hibern rolled her eyes. "You both know any blood mage text is perilous. I can't stop you from messing with them, but at least can you promise me you'll do whatever you're going to do then get rid of them, or give them back to Jilo to get rid of?"

"That, I'll agree to," Senrid said, hands spread. "I don't want any Norsundrian mages to come nosing around here looking for them. Although I'd like to see them try. Even Detlev can't get into this city."

"Then we'll keep them here," Leander said absently as he began to copy out the runes on a piece of paper, careful to reproduce them exactly.

Senrid opened the second book, which appeared to have been written by another hand, but again the medium was the same blotty brown of dried blood. "Considering how fast it clots, it must be nasty to write in blood. Do you have to keep bleeding?"

"They mixed the blood with the same stuff painters use to keep it from drying," Leander said even more absently, causing the two Marlovens to give him startled looks.

Rather than ask how he knew that, Senrid changed the subject. "The only ones aware of these books are the six of us — we three, Jilo, and the Keperis. I think we should keep it that way."

"That reminds me. " Hibern flicked her palm up. "We pretty much chased Adam out. Didn't Rel vouch for him?"

Senrid said, "In most instances I'd trust Rel with anything, but it sounds like they just traveled together. I think we need to take time with newcomers. Find out who they are. Where they come from."

"I agree about the six of us and these books." Leander glanced up, his green eyes catching the light from the windows. "But that brings a new question, when *do* we share everything we know? There are several newcomers. My sister met one in Everon, where she went with the Mearsiean girls to help with the orphans. And Bena Dak, you remember from the other world? He's been up north visiting Arthur, and I guess he brought a mage student who's staying on to join the school up there. He had an odd name. Roo? Riu? Roy. That was it. Anyway, that's three new people right there."

"Bena Dak was vouched for by the Geth mages." Hibern's voice was short. "If he brought Roy, then we can assume he's trustworthy."

Her tone was so curt that Leander eyed her. "Are you angry about us taking the books?"

Like Senrid, Hibern gestured flat-handed, as if pushing his words away. "Not my business." She scowled down the length of her blue over-robe as one hand picked absently at the hem, then she raised her head. "It's the alliance. That is, I still think it's a good idea."

Leander laid aside his pen. "Hibern, is there something going on that I ought to know about? I thought you were the one who supported the idea most."

"No. Yes. It's . . . it's not that." She exhaled in a hiss. "All last summer, when we, the alliance, were up in Delfina Valley and then when we went to Geth-deles, we *weren't* allied. Really. Except on the surface. And I felt as if every failure was my fault, though there was nothing I could do. I'm going to feel that way, it seems, and it makes me . . ." She shook her head again. "I can't be at the center of it. I'll be there if needed, but I'm hoping that Karhin will take over as the center, if we even have to have a center. *She's* good at it. I'm not."

Hibern shook her head again, leaving Leander totally bewildered, but Senrid knew what she was talking about. So much of her sense of failure was due to her fool of a father, who'd disowned her, but there was no use scraping old scabs.

So he turned to Leander. "Are you really going to copy out that entire book?"

Leander looked at his paper, onto which he'd painstakingly reproduced three lines. "Yes. I think I'd better do it here. Senrid, you've got protective wards, and while I usually don't think those necessary, this is the exception."

Senrid said, "I've got a Venn lexicon in the archive." He thought of Commander Keriam waiting for him in his tower, and went out. "I'll send a runner with it. Now I have to get busy . . ." *Facing down my kingdom.* ". . . doing things."

"Doing things." Hibern gave Senrid's back a wry look as he shot through the door. When Senrid grew vague like that, it was usually to cover something bothering him. "I meant what I said," she said to Leander. "Send a message if you need my help, but if there's anything to report to the alliance, Karhin is the one to contact."

She gripped her transfer coin, braced for the wrench, and transferred home.

Colend

Karhin found Hibern, who seemed to know all the famous mages of the entire world, very intimidating—even more intimidating than Senrid. But she was central to the alliance, and so Karhin turned to her for advice.

She was at her most polite when Hibern arrived, which in turn Hibern found intimidating. How to see the real person behind the graceful Colendi gestures, the well-trained, modulated voice? The way Colendi spoke Sartoran was smooth and a little singsong. Hibern had come to utterly distrust her evaluations of people, but as they went through politenesses, she reflected that everyone liked Karhin. Even the Mearsiean girls, who could be . . . difficult.

And Adam was still there. Hibern could see him down in the village square, sketching a group of three young men, their arms intertwined. "He earns a living this way?" she asked.

"Yes. He says it is also good practice, until he can find another drawing master again."

"Who was his first one?" Hibern asked, and remembered Senrid's words about vouching for people. Hadn't Rel already done that? "Where did Rel find Adam?"

"On the border of Sartor."

"Is he a Sartoran, then?"

"He hasn't really said. Thad and I have both asked, but Adam is so diffident. One does not wish to trespass." Karhin made another of those graceful gestures with her hands, not quite a flutter, but describing an arc that Hibern was sure had meaning, and Hibern gave up.

"Why did you need me to visit?" Hibern asked with Marloven bluntness, leaving Karhin wondering if Hibern disliked visiting, or if Karhin had somehow erred.

Karhin pulled a note from under the neat pile on her desk. Hibern glanced at the sloppy scrawl:

> *Puddlenose of Mearsies Heili gave me your*
> *notebox sigil. Hold this for Rel when he comes*
> *north? Terry*

"I have a sealed note, which I have set aside," Karhin explained. Her freckled face shuttered into bland politesse. "I know that 'Terry' is King Tereneth of the kingdom directly north of us, called Erdrael Danara. We met once, when Senrid of Marloven Hess and the Mearsiean princess honored us with their presence. But this barely legible hand . . . among us, respect is shown by clear letters, well placed, on good paper."

Hibern had absorbed the Marloven prejudice against Colendi as frivolous and decadent liars, and had worked hard to overcome it. But she sent a sharp look at Karhin, and of course could not penetrate that polite front.

So she said, "You might not know that 'Terry' is a name the Mearsieans gave him, a nickname after one of them met him while a fellow hostage to the former Chwahir king. He was nearly killed in his kingdom's civil war. He tends to hide what happened."

Karhin looked puzzled. She remembered a glimpse of Terry sitting hunched over, his hair hanging in his face, more like a moping miscreant than like a king. She remembered specifically that he'd ignored their refreshments, and she had wondered after the visit if they weren't exalted enough for a king. But it would not be polite to say any of this.

Hibern saw her ambivalence as disbelief, and said bluntly, "During the civil war Terry was taken prisoner, and three of his fingers cut off. He hides that hand, I think out of habit. He also had a broken leg, left unset. His face was cut up, which is probably why he has that hair hanging down."

Karhin's flinch, her tight shoulders and turned-away face were plain enough human responses.

So Hibern eased her tone. "Well, those were the worst of his wounds, but by no means all. Anyway he's had to learn to write with the other hand. Some can do that easily, but he can't. The scrawl is his best attempt."

Karhin, much chastened at how very badly she had indeed erred in judgment, made a full peace bow. "Thank you," she said.

Hibern added, "You've got to remember that most of the alliance have had bad things happen to the older generation. Some caused by them, like Senrid's uncle, the regent, assassinating his own brother. He would have killed Senrid if he thought he could get away with it. So he controlled him by . . . severe methods, let us say, and then tried mind-control magic. It's a thing to remember when dealing with him."

Once again Karhin bowed. "And Rel?"

"He doesn't talk about his past, except to say that he grew up with a guardian, and knows nothing of his birth family."

Karhin bowed a third time, and by the time Hibern left, the alliance in Karhin's mind had ceased being merely an interesting diversion. She was unsettled at this idea that evidence of suffering somehow made the necessity for an alliance more real. Vital.

Nevertheless, she exerted herself to write a friendly note back to Terry of Erdrael Danara, indicating her happiness to do as he asked, and she copied it in her best hand on her very best paper.

Five

Mid-spring, 4743 AF
Colend to Everon

THE FIRST WARM SPELL of spring had set everything blooming when Rel stopped to visit the Keperis in Colend. He found Adam still there, earning a few coins by drawing visitors and sketching the town amid the splendor of matured window boxes and spectacular pocket gardens.

Flush with pay from leading a caravan of silk merchants up the river, Rel treated the entire family to dinner at the eatery across the square, entertaining them by describing a play he'd seen in Sartor before he'd left.

Afterward, as they walked across the square toward the scribe house. Rel said to Karhin, "May I ask a favor?"

She smiled up at his tall, strong features, remembering what Hibern had said about him. Rel had already been an object of fascination to her, but Hibern's words had added compassion, for family was vitally important to her.

"I would be delighted," she said.

"Send this to Atan in Sartor?" He held out a folded note. "To the palace desk?"

Karhin's warmth chilled a little. Atan. So easily Rel referred to Yustnesveas Landis V, the queen of Sartor, oldest kingdom in the world!

Thad caught up with them as Karhin slid the note into the inner pocket of her robe. "Shall we meet in my room?"

"For what?" Lisbet asked quickly, pressing between them. "What are you doing? I want to do it, too."

"We are going to practice our Sartoran," Karhin said. "You are most welcome to join us. We always need work with Sartoran verb tenses, especially the three conditionals."

Lisbet curled her upper lip. "Thank you, perhaps later."

She skipped off, leaving the alliance members to retreat up to Thad's room, as their mothers and Little Bee walked into the main part of the house.

Karhin watched Rel ahead of her on the stair. He was so tall, so . . . *artistic*. No, that was not the word, but grace, and melende, and beauty were not quite right. Though he had those, too. Even if he wasn't Colendi, but Karhin had learned that other lands had other words for melende, even if those were not quite the same: honor, style, nobility . . .

She stopped at the landing, and turned to Adam, who had been behind her. "Will you make a sketch of Rel for me? I am assembling a book of our visitors."

She wasn't sure why she added that last, but at least it was true. Adam had been sketching their visitors, beginning with Princess Kyale of Vasande Leror, who had demanded a portrait of herself as soon as she saw Adam's drawings. He kept most of those in in his bag. She wanted a book of her own, preferably with sketches solely of Rel.

She ran to fetch Terry's note. Conscious of what she had said to Lisbet, she spoke in Sartoran, and cast the verb in the time-conditional as she put the note into Rel's hand. "If the future brings my wishes to pass, Terry and I shall begin a correspondence."

Rel's face lit with a smile. "Oh, that's excellent. I'd like to see him making new friends."

Karhin's heart lightened to thistledown as they continued

chatting in future possibilities, to make her words to Lisbet true.

Before dawn, Rel departed for the north road at the same time the desk scribe relayed Rel's letter via magic transfer to Sartor at Karhin's behest, which meant there was no charge.

After a pleasant stay of three weeks, and an uneventful crossing of the Elgar Strait, at the close of the month Rel rode over the border from Imar into Everon one brilliant morning. The low hills fuzzed with green, the trees in leaf. Birds, butterflies, and little animals flitted and rustled about, adding color under the bright sky.

It was so beautiful that his first sight of the war damage was more shocking by contrast. Until he saw it, he had not known how much it was going to hurt to be back in Everon again. Everywhere he looked evoked memories of those desperate days fighting a losing battle, until he had to flee the burning capital.

His friend Harn was another shock, his brown, good-natured face marred by a vivid scar from his temple down to his jaw that unexpectedly brought Terry to mind.

Harn's mother welcomed Rel, but he could see the tension around her eyes and in her hands, an echo of the horror in people's faces as they fled the capital city the summer before.

"Ugly as I am now," Harn said, the other side of his mouth turning up in the smile, "this slash across my face probably kept me alive. They left me where I'd fallen. Must've thought I was dead."

Harn's mother said, "Come, now, Harn. If you go back to Ferdrian, who is going to bake my seed cakes?"

Harn laughed as he ran his finger around the rim of his ceramic cup. "Uncle Hanold would have something to say to that! Something loud about all the mistakes I make in measure and mix." And to Rel, "I told Ma that I'd ride to the capital with you. I'm as recovered as I ever am going to get, and when summer comes round again, I'll remember why I never wanted to prentice in the bakery."

Then his smile vanished. "Did you know there were only twenty of us Knights left whole? Twenty-one, counting the commander, who is only just recovered. Twenty-one, a hundred sixty still recovering, or who will never fight again, out of nearly six hundred. The numbers of those lost among our infantry aren't even so severe. But Henerek, who was once one of us, made the Knights targets."

Rel and Harn left at dawn the next morning.

Over the next few days they rode north until they reached the river, and then turned west toward the royal city, Ferdrian. Here they entered the wide swath that Kessler's Norsundrians had cut through the kingdom on their way to burn the capital.

In every village and town they met the sound of hammers, and the sight of work parties scavenging support beams and stones from ruined houses. Here and there they recognized in the pock marks left by arrows where the attackers had set fire to key buildings in a village center, and then lay up on high ground to enjoy the sport of shooting everyone who ran out. In other locales the Norsundrians had preferred to fight all comers, ignoring the young, the old, the infirm but once they had killed or maimed everyone who could lift a weapon, they had flung torches inside the buildings before they moved on.

Twice Rel and Harn rode through empty villages, the burnt husks of houses occupied only by birds or small animals that skittered away at the sound of their horse hooves.

Rel dreaded his first sight of Ferdrian, which lay in a pleasant valley alongside the river. Last he'd seen of it had been the clouds of smoke, the sheets of fire, the empty streets full of the fallen. But when they rode up the winding main street toward the palace, and the Knights' garrison and training yard adjacent, reality gradually replaced memory: the fallen had been Disappeared, the detritus cleared away. Life went on, amid the sounds of repair and rebuilding, now that winter was past.

The hurt came back again, almost as sharp as the days he'd run about trying to help people get out of the burning city, when they reached the Knights' garrison. The rows of dark, empty windows in the fine building with the stone carvings hit with shocking finality: so very few had survived.

Harn turned his horse toward the stable. Rel hesitated, unsure, but the decision was taken out of his hands.

Prince Glenn Delieth had seen them from inside the fighting salle. He bolted out, dark hair flopping around his ears, his narrow face alight with a rarely expressed joy. "Harn! You're back! And Rel?"

Harn swiftly dismounted so he could make his bow, which Glenn scarcely acknowledged. "Rel?" he persisted. "You're here to join? We need you."

Rel gazed down into Glenn's expectant dark eyes, seeing in the prince's high, tense forehead subtle signs of the anger that was always there. Hadn't Glenn had enough bloodshed? He hated himself for the thought. Glenn hadn't seen any of the fighting, but he *had* seen his father lying dead not five hundred paces from where they stood now, his honor guard surrounding him in death. Glenn's thirst for violence aside, no one would be immune from wanting to protect the city and the kingdom against such a sight.

Glenn, gazing up at Rel's deep-set eyes and seeing the way the light sculpted the strong bones of his face, gritted his teeth against a surge of jealousy and longing. He couldn't grow up fast enough. Even so, he knew he'd never be as tall or as strong as Rel, the perfect commander. Rel would be a hundred times better than Uncle Roderic, who was old.

Rel wasn't speaking. "I don't care about birth," Glenn said. "I mean I do. I think serving as a Knight is the duty of all born to rank, especially now. But it doesn't matter where *you* come from, or if you really are a sheep-farmer's ward. You're *good*. We *need* you."

Rel had never heard Glenn use the word *need*. He hesitated, reluctant to quash the hope he saw in the prince's face, and was saved from having to respond by the appearance of the Knights' commander, Roderic Dei.

Commander Dei's stocky body was thinner than Rel remembered, his gray hair, usually as neatly trimmed as his beard, lying on his shoulders. The circles under his eyes testified to lack of sleep, but his voice was genuine and hearty as he exclaimed, "Rel! Just in time. Would you accompany the prince? He is going to visit the orphanages to scout Knight candidates, and I'd like someone there with more experience."

Rel made no claims whatsoever to sensitivity, much less the mysterious mind powers afflicting Liere Fer Eider and Senrid of Marloven Hess, but he was sure there was extra meaning in that steady gaze. "I just rode in with Harn. I've nothing else to do." He forced that lie out—his father had waited this long to be discovered, he could wait a little longer—and was rewarded by a smile of relief.

Glenn also smiled, jutting his chin out in a gesture reminiscent of his father jutting his short beard in exactly the same way. It caused another pang. "Come inside, set down your things, and we'll get going. They're waiting for us."

Rel dismounted, hefted his travel pack over his shoulder, and detached his Sartoran sword from the saddle sheath so that the stable hands could lead the animal away. He lifted his hand to Harn, who send him a rueful smile before going off toward the Knights' garrison and all its empty rooms.

Rel followed Glenn inside the palace, startled to find fire scars and cracks in the walls. Except for the faintest tinge of smoke in the air, the place at least was scrupulously clean.

Glenn said, "Tahra wants it to stay just as we found it until we get Mother back. I think it a stupid idea. Norsunder'd never understand it as condemnation. But Uncle Roderic says there is nothing in the treasury, so I guess it's just as well."

While they walked and he talked, he wrestled mentally with the worry that accompanying Rel to the guest wing was not a princely action, much less kingly. Glenn shut down hard on his longing to be king. Even if it turned out his mother had been killed by the Norsundrians after she was taken prisoner, he wouldn't really be king until he reached twenty, and he wanted her to be alive. He did.

Glenn scowled. *Twenty.* He could not understand how Senrid and Leander could stay boys under that stupid Child Spell when they didn't have to. In fact, hadn't someone said that Rel did the spell, also? Who wouldn't want to be as tall and strong as you could get, as fast as possible?

They reached the guest wing, which was deserted, before Glenn said in a low voice, "You'll find some others from the alliance at the city orphanage."

"Who?" Rel asked, as he set his pack on a carved chest and laid the sword next to it.

"Remember Piper, the scribe who wrote for us to that brother and sister in Colend? Piper lost her position, as did many who were placed in noble families whose residences were torched. The scribes put her in charge of this orphanage as a teacher." As he spoke, Glenn eyed the sword that Rel had laid down, its beautiful, swept handle distinctively Sartoran-made. Because Sartor had relatively recently rejoined the world after a century of enchantment, that meant the sword was probably an heirloom. A royal heirloom. "Where did you get that?"

"It was a gift," Rel said, hit with an image of Atan's trembling hands, her low voice as she gave to him. He wished he were in Sartor right now.

"Besides Piper, the orphanage is being visited by those girls from Mearsies Heili," Glenn said, turning abruptly to lead the way out. "My sister asked them to come, I guess. You know we've a lot of orphans. A lot. Our treaty-allies didn't raise a finger to help us during the fighting." He took a deep breath, and forced the anger out of his voice. "But at least they did help get Everon through the winter. We would have starved without their supplies. Let's go!"

The orphanage was a long, low house set in what had once had been a well-kept park, on the outskirts of the city. The duchas who had inherited it had left it neglected, having no use for a secluded house far away from court circles. After the battle she donated it to the crown in an effort to cut her losses.

The neglected house had sustained a recent and vigorous spring cleaning, but the garden was left wild, to the delight of the collection of children now living there. The house was built of whitewashed granite, like most Everoneth houses of a certain era; the whitewash, scrubbed free of moss, had turned a flat shade of cream. A bank of windows overlooked the wildflower-dotted, grassy field that had once been a lawn.

CJ, born on the world that called itself Earth, and adopted Princess of Mearsies Heili, paused as a small child pelted down the soft green grassy slope toward the pond. The children she'd been playing hide and seek with stilled until they heard the child shrieking, "He's here! He's here! The prince is here!"

Game forgotten, the players popped up from long grasses and dropped down from trees to stampede toward the house.

CJ followed more slowly, scowling at the ground as she brushed her bare toes through the soft grasses. Maybe her wariness toward people with titles was part of the Earth republic's paradigm — but maybe it was just Glenn? She did work hard not to let the Everoneth kids see how much she disliked their royal prince.

Irenne flitted across the grass, light brown ponytail flapping down the back of her lace-edged pink dress. "Here comes His Crabbyship," Irenne said to CJ, rolling her eyes.

CJ gave the taller girl a pained look. She didn't disagree, and to scold Irenne for saying more or less what she'd been thinking would be a piece of hypocrisy that CJ would scorn. But she'd gotten herself into horrible trouble the previous summer for voicing too many of her unsought opinions.

"Well, this is Glenn's kingdom," CJ said. "And you know, at home, people like it when Clair comes around."

"But Clair is *nice*," Irenne retorted. "And no snob." Again, voicing what CJ thought but wouldn't say.

Another Mearsiean girl joined them, her curls bouncing, and her wide blue eyes round with anticipation. "I hope Glenn'll notice all the work everyone did," Sherry said cheerily.

CJ walked alongside her, congratulating herself on hiding her thoughts, when they reached the door leading to what had once been a ballroom, and was now a playroom with a marble floor.

CJ stopped when she recognized the tall, dark-haired guy with Glenn. The Perfect Rel! Here? Of all the rotten luck!

As the orphans who wanted to become Knights scrambled into their lines, Rel looked up, then hid a sigh when he saw the three girls. He'd endured a long, one-sided grudge from twelve-year-old CJ, whose stark blue gaze stared from the frame of her long, straight black hair. More like glared.

But then she called in a high, clear voice, "Hey, Rel. Didn't know you were in Everon." Her cheeks burned beet-red.

Rel controlled the urge to laugh at the effort she made to sound friendly, and he lifted a hand in greeting. CJ's shamefaced regret over that grudge was evident all the way across the vast room. One thing you could say about CJ, she was incapable of hiding what she was thinking—even if sometimes you wished she would.

Glenn ignored the girls after nodding to them. He had no interest in those Mearsiean girls whatsoever, and he found their total neglect of royal protocol irksome. On his world map, Mearsies Heili was about the size of one of his duchas' lands, full of farmers and the like. Its scant importance was apparent in the girls' common manners; even if CJ called herself a princess, she never seemed to remember the most basic tenets of protocol, nor did she remember to bow.

In fairness, he had to admit that she and her friends had spent these past weeks helping to clean and order these new orphanages. But as far as he was concerned, they were his sister's to thank.

He turned his back on them, and looked at the row of expectant Knight trainees, all eyes anxiously on him. Every nerve thrilled: *this* was proper protocol.

"Let's get started." He walked along the orderly row, eyeing each prospective candidate. They stood stiffly, gazes moving with him, and he reveled in the power of choice. Norsunder had tried to destroy Everon, but things were reverting to their natural order.

"You," Glenn said, pointing at a big, strong looking boy, after passing a string of girls.

Behind Glenn, Rel paced. Without having spoken a single word to Commander Dei, he knew that he was expected to mitigate Glenn's inevitable choice of the biggest, most aggressive-looking boys.

It was going to fall to Rel to winnow out the bullies, and draw in the most promising of the youngsters whom Glenn had passed over, those quick of eye and hand, eager and loyal. Girls as well as boys.

Rel quietly gestured to the three he'd picked out, two of whom were girls, and as they smiled and joined the chosen, he sighed inwardly, wondering when he'd get his chance to begin investigation of that mysterious letter of his father's.

"Welp, *that* was a piece of stenchiferous luck," CJ muttered as the three Mearsieans watched Glenn and Rel motion the ones they'd picked to get the practice weapons. "Of all the places in the world, Rel just *had* to turn up here, a million miles from either of our homes."

Irenne snickered. She'd learned that "miles" were a peculiar number of steps in the strange world that CJ had come from, but CJ had never been able to explain "luck" in a way that made any sense. It was hilarious, how so many unconnected things "caused" bad luck, but somehow the cause for good luck receded like a mirage.

Completely uninterested in Glenn, or the Knights of Everon, Irenne turned her head and sniffed the air. Ugh. More of that stodgy, tasteless acorn mush to eke out the dinner. Of late it seemed there was more acorn than wheat in the rolls, and only the barest hint of molasses to make them bearable.

She sighed. She was so bored. It had been fun when they felt needed — when everyone was grateful — when the Mearsiean girls could put on plays and make everyone laugh. But the Everoneth had their own plays, and games, and nobody was hailing the Mearsieans for being generous helpers anymore, though they did the drudge work just as hard.

Plus, none of these kids even knew about the alliance. What's the use of being part of a secret alliance against Norsunder if nobody knows anything about it?

"Maybe we should go home." CJ scowled. "I think we're done here."

Finally, Irenne gloated to herself. Aloud, she said, "At least Rel is good for something." She added another eye-roll.

CJ prickled painfully all over, sure everyone had heard that — that they would think the same thing. "It's not because Rel is here!" she whispered fiercely.

She hated the fact that all Rel had to do was walk in and *loom* at everybody, and they fell all over putting him in charge. Whereas a girl could work ten times as hard, and . . .

She caught herself up. "What I mean is, now that those kids all want to be Knights, I think it's time for us to go home. The alliance is about sniffing out Norsunder, and there aren't any here. And all the cleanup junk is done. So we aren't really needed anymore, and all the other girls have already gone home. And! I would think it even if Rel wasn't here. Okay?"

Sherry nodded solemnly, and Irenne flipped her ponytail back. It had been more fun when CJ loathed and despised the Perfect Rel.

CJ said, "Let's go tell Piper what I just said, and make it *plain* our going home has *nothing to do* with Rel, and we'll transfer back."

"I hate transfer magic." Irenne fingered the medallion around her neck, with its transfer magic worked in. "It hurts so much."

"Who doesn't?" CJ shrugged. "But it's better than weeks and weeks and weeks on a ship, and then a long, boring walk."

Six

Mearsies Heili to the Chwahir Border

IT WAS NEARLY MIDNIGHT in Mearsies Heili when CJ and her friends arrived back. CJ's ears popped unpleasantly, and she held her breath, bracing against transfer reaction, which made her feel like she had been shoved through a keyhole.

They found Clair asleep in their underground hideout. Her room being the closest to the surface, they heard a low, uneven rumble of a thunderstorm.

Clair heard the patter of feet in the short tunnel connecting her room to the main cave, and sat up in bed. "You're back!" she exclaimed.

She smiled to see them again, but CJ intuited that something was wrong. She waited as the other two traded off telling her everything they had done at the orphanage, coming to the end at last. "Then Prince Glenn came, and you know who was with him? Rel! We decided to come home, because they were all going to be busy doing that fighting stuff."

"I am simply dying for a taste of hot chocolate," Irenne declared.

"Let's go make some."

The two girls ran out, as CJ breathed in the warm, welcome smell of loam that meant home. Then she faced Clair. "Is everything okay?"

"I know it's stupid, but I've been worried. About Jilo."

"Has something happened to ol' Jilo the Pilo?" CJ asked, on the verge of a laugh. It still seemed weird that Jilo was no longer considered a villain, though he was a Chwahir.

Clair sighed. "You might not know this, but Kyale sent me a letter about Jilo, Senrid, and Leander and some mysterious books. Written in blood."

"Ugh. But if anyone can deal with that, it would be Senrid. He studied dark magic."

"I know. But if Jilo is involved, oh, I can't help thinking about him in Land of the Chwahir. How dangerous that place is, especially if Wan-Edhe comes back."

CJ shuddered, hating memories of the evil old king of the Chwahir, whose very name was such a threat no one in his kingdom had dared to speak it for ages.

"Isn't Rosey watching out for Jilo the way he did for Puddlenose in the bad old days?" CJ asked.

Clair smiled at the mention of the irascible mage who lived high in the mountains overlooking Chwahirsland. Mondros, called "Rosey" by Puddlenose and later Clair, was not a Chwahir, but he seemed to have made it his life's work to counteract by magic as much of Wan-Edhe's evil as possible.

"Maybe I'm being stupid to worry," Clair said, looking away. "I'd ask Puddlenose to make sure, except I don't know where he is."

Again CJ had the sense that there was still something bothering Clair, but for some reason it wasn't coming out yet. "He was with us in Everon, but he took off when Glenn tried to nag and guilt him into joining the Knights. So I think you should just go ahead and ask Rosey."

"I do hate to pester him."

CJ bit her lip. That was the first time Clair had ever mentioned "pestering" Rosey, who'd always made the Mearsieans welcome. Because something else was bothering Clair, she thought unerringly. But all CJ said out loud was, "I'll go with you if you don't want to go alone. In fact, if you want, I'll go look up his Destination in the book." Anything to get Clair to stop looking so worried.

Clair was not ready to talk about the real worry, of which she was half ashamed. She'd brought up Jilo's name — about whom she did feel concern — so now she felt committed.

The following day, the two girls transferred to Mondros's cottage high on the border between Chwahirsland and Colend. The tiny cottage had once been a lookout centuries ago, when the present sharp division between monarch and mages had been far more diffuse. The enormous tangle of rosebushes out beyond the kitchen garden on the mountain side of the little plateau was at least a couple hundred years old.

Mondros, a burly bear of a man with thick silver-threaded dark beard and curly hair, came out to greet them. He gave the girls a basket and sent them to gather roses, a game that he'd played with Clair and Puddlenose as small children when he'd first rescued them from Wan-Edhe years before. CJ watched Clair narrowly as they trod around the neat rows of growing herbs and vegetables in the garden, and approached the vast, thirty-foot-high tangle of red, peach, white, pink, and butter-yellow rose trees, with blossoms of all shades between.

When they returned, he'd prepared toasted bread with melted cheese and a bowl of fresh berries. As he began expertly stripping the thorns from the roses, the girls sat down to the waiting feast.

"So you're worried about Jilo?"

"I know it's not my concern," Clair admitted with averted gaze. "But I wonder how he's faring."

Mondros said, "Jilo is doing better than anyone expected. But there is still danger. Not only from Wan-Edhe returning, but from some within the army who have a vested interest in maintaining the harsh and unfair laws that benefit only them, and most of all from the toxic residue of Wan-Edhe's magic."

With a twitch and a whispered spell, he held out a garland of roses to Clair. Her smile was less forced as she settled it around her shoulders. "I always liked these." She fingered a cream-colored rosebud. The magic on the roses would keep them fresh for a time, until they got the garlands home and could put them in water. Her gray-green gaze lifted. "It seems odd to be here when Wan-Edhe is . . . gone."

"I wish he was gone for good," CJ muttered.

"As do we all," Mondros replied, working on a second garland.

"I never questioned why he'd attack us when we were small, but now that I think about it, why?" Clair asked. "My uncle — my aunt — Puddlenose, whose real name Wan-Edhe made sure was lost. We've never been a threat to the Chwahir on the mainland. We weren't a threat to the Chwahir in the Shadowland, though at least it made sense for them to try to take more land away from us, living under that Shadow the way they had been."

Mondros considered what to say as Clair went on: "I know when Mearsieans first left Tser Mearsies and came to our continent centuries ago, the Chwahir chased them, and built the Shadowland as an outpost. But *why* did Wan-Edhe attack us so much? His kingdom is so much larger and so far away."

Mondros said, "I think it began when Wan-Edhe first exiled his brother Kwenz there, then came himself to see what the outpost bordered. Have you ever stopped to consider how very strange it is that your white palace is the only one of its kind in the world?"

"I haven't traveled enough to know it's the only one." Clair shrugged. "As for the palace itself, I grew up with it. It just . . . is."

Mondros's thick black eyebrows knit over his deep-set eyes. He handed CJ her garland, and set about making his own. "Let me put it this way. Have you ever found it odd that no one else has ever come trying to explore that white palace, or take it from you, besides the Chwahir?"

Again the girls looked blank.

Mondros shrugged massive shoulders, raked fingers through his thick dark hair, and said, "All right, let me try yet again. I, at least, find it odd that some of your more discerning visitors, who have spent a lifetime searching for magical artifacts, never seem to remember how very strange your palace is — both in itself, and in the way that it, alone of all the palaces of the world, was built above two places of very old magic. In one of which apparently dwells a being one of whose forms is *lightning*."

"Hreealdar," Clair and CJ said together.

"But he's just a magical horse," CJ said. "Well, part horse and part lightning. And the 'he' is only a guess because he's so large. He doesn't actually have any, um, *parts* underneath. Why should anybody fuss about Hreealdar, when he doesn't even come all the time when *we* ask? It's not like you can tame him."

Mondros whooshed out his breath. "I think I've gone about this wrong. It wasn't until I followed Wan-Edhe over there to discover why he kept harassing your family that I discovered your palace, made of some impossible stone, and located directly above a Selenseh Redian, unlike anything else in the world. And yet the first few times I came home, I recollected it only as another light-stone building built on a mountain top, of which the world has plenty."

The two girls still looked at him blankly, waiting for the point—to them, the "impossible stone" was everyday, and the strange, deeply magical, sometimes time- and space-shifting Selenseh Redian was what they called a jewel cave.

He frowned, searching for plain words; he knew the girls were smart, and had had more experience of the world than many of their age, but they were young. Of course they didn't comprehend the magical realm as well as he. "I think Wan-Edhe found some magic that lets him see past a very, very subtle, and thorough enchantment. It took me some effort to see past it as well. That palace of yours is full of mystery, and Wan-Edhe wanted— *wants* — its magic for himself."

"But he couldn't even get upstairs," CJ said, her skinny shoulders shrugging up and down.

"Precisely. Don't you think that fact would serve as a goad to him? No one says no to Wan-Edhe and survives."

He faced the two pairs of polite, uncomprehending eyes, and gave up. "Something to keep in mind, anyway. Now, tell me your news. Where is young Puddlenose wandering these days?"

Once she and Clair were back home in Mearsies Heili, CJ made it four days before leaving the others in the middle of planning costumes for a festival, and transferred up to confront Clair.

She found her sitting in the library in her favorite chair, deep in one of the handwritten books that, from the gilt binding and the tasseled page-marker hanging down, looked like something from the previous century.

CJ stood there, fists on hips, a small, adamant figure in black and white and green. "You're still in that mood. Something's wrong, and it isn't Jilo."

Clair looked up, the candlelight bringing out the green in her hazel eyes. "I thought I hid my funk better."

"Why do you have to hide anything at all?" CJ asked, hopping up on the table, where she drew up her knees and put her chin on them.

"Because I feel guilty," Clair said surprisingly.

"Heh? You never do anything wrong," CJ exclaimed. *Unlike me.*

"I try not to," Clair said, closing the book. "But sometimes . . . we make mistakes."

CJ groaned. "Is this about the alliance, or about me being mean to Rel last summer? 'Cause I don't hate him, I *don't.*"

Clair shook her head. "I started to talk to Seshe."

A corrosive bubble of jealousy popped in the pit of CJ's stomach, but she ignored it. Everybody talked to tall, calm Seshe, oldest of the girls. She was smart, and she was nice. Really nice. Not just pretending to be nice so people would like her.

"But . . ." Clair got up and wandered along the shelves, running her finger absently over the books, ancient and new, each hand-bound and written by somebody's pen. "The truth is, when Puddlenose suggested you girls go to Everon to help with the orphans, I kind of hoped that Mearsieanne would meet up with you, and . . ." She shrugged. "She might come back home again, and stay. But she didn't. I wonder if that's because I've done something wrong."

"You? Wrong?" CJ exclaimed, hands on hips, always fierce in defense of those she loved most. "She's your great-grandmother, but she's still a kid like us. She's bound to fit right in! If she was a disgusting, grabby grownup . . ."

CJ felt a rant about adults coming on, but Clair's averted gaze caused her to gulp in a breath. "What is it?"

"What does it really mean, 'she's a kid?' Before she was imprisoned and enchanted by Norsunder for all those years, she had a full-grown son."

"By magic." CJ shrugged. "So? We already know the Birth Spell will work for kids."

"Not quite," Clair said. "From what I read, you have to have lived a certain number of years before it *might* work."

CJ grimaced. Maybe this had to do with that weird stuff about parallel worlds—an idea that, once explained to her, had made her cry all through a night, because if it was real, she couldn't save the CJs still stuck on some version of Earth. "Like the Birth Spell has brains, and counts your age? That doesn't make any sense to me."

"How the Birth Spell works, or chooses to work, makes no sense to anyone, and the magic books are full of theories," Clair said, waving at the library. "How about this. You know the anti-aging spell doesn't really keep us from aging. We just stopped short of the physical change from kid to adult."

CJ loathed any reference to puberty and what happened after. She grimaced, then said, "Okay, so she was not still thirteen in birthday count, and she had your granddad Tesmer, and he grew up, and then she was captured by Norsunder for over a century. But she got free, and she hasn't turned into a grownup, from what I've heard. So she can't be all judgy like typical grownups. Why are you worried?"

Clair spread her hands. "What if she wants to come back and be queen?"

CJ was all ready to exclaim *Impossible*, but she shut up.

Clair went on. "It was thinking about Jilo that got me thinking about her. He went to Chwahirsland after Wan-Edhe got grabbed by Norsunder, and walked in where no one else could go, and took over the empty throne. Though everything else is completely different, Mearsieanne walked in and took over the empty throne right here, when there was an impasse among what used to be the six governing families and their friends. Nobody was willing to risk being attacked by the other side."

"Just to clean up the giant mess left by the last throne-warmer." CJ nodded fiercely. "Mearsieanne was a compromise. That's what your Aunt Murial told us. Mearsieanne wasn't on anybody's side. And she was very good at organizing, and she was really popular on the cloud top, and, oh, I forget the rest. But nobody knows her *now*, and you're popular, and she seems to be busy helping out in Wnelder Vee. Why should she want to come back here and take over now?"

"Don't you see? Maybe I ought to offer the throne to her."

CJ was about to say, *Why don't you?* She managed to keep her lip buttoned. Clair didn't have a lot to do as queen of small, mostly-farm-and-forest Mearsies Heili, but what she did she seemed to like doing. Moreover, would she like being kicked out?

The urge to say, *You could join the rest of us in games! It'll be fun*, almost got past her. She squirmed, thinking that before last summer, she would have said it.

Clair looked down, speaking in an unsettling parallel, "The problem is not my happiness, but what's best for the kingdom.

And she might be staying away for a reason, like she doesn't want to face me. I'm scared I've disappointed her."

CJ squirmed again. She hated the idea that anyone would think Clair was ruling wrong. How could anyone say what was best for anyplace? Though grownups sure argued about it, as if *they* knew.

Clair gave a short nod. "I know what I have to do. Go to Wnelder Vee, and talk to her. CJ, that means you'll be in charge here. You're the princess."

CJ wanted to howl in protest. Not that "being in charge" meant any big changes. There was Clair's hermit-mage Aunt Murial to call for help if some villain tried a magic attack, and there were the governors and the guild leaders who handled political stuff in the six provinces. But someone had to sit in the white palace in order to contact all those people, if trouble did attack.

Everything was perfect in Mearsies Heili, CJ thought unhappily as she and Clair parted to sleep for the night. Perfect just as it was. Of course poor Mearsieanne didn't deserve to have been stuck in Norsunder for a century, *but*.

CJ tried not to think any more along that path. Clair wouldn't be happy until she got things settled with Mearsieanne. But CJ wouldn't be happy if everything changed.

Seven

Vasande Leror

ONCE LEANDER HAD FINISHED copying the first blood magic book — a process that seemed to take forever, as he couldn't always get the time to go to Marloven Hess — he returned to Vasande Leror with his copy and Senrid's lexicon.

He was impatient to begin translating, but his hopes were dashed when his stepsister met him, a tiny figure bristling with indignation. "You've been gone *all day*." Kyale greeted him in a put-upon voice, hands on hips. "I *hope* you don't intend to frowst in that study the rest of the night, because you *promised* to take me to the spring festival tomorrow."

Leander sighed. He knew she wouldn't go alone. "I remember, I remember," he said, and made himself set the books on his desk as he dutifully sat down to dinner.

After dinner, Kyale ran off to play with her cats and Leander retreated upstairs to begin his work. Mindful of his promise for the next day, he made himself lay down his pen at midnight and go to bed. But he slept badly, his mind full of Venn symbols.

At the first bluing of dawn he got up and tackled another couple of lines of that first page, getting a few letters transliterated. He designed some quick boxes in order to test patterns of letters in possible codes. It seemed like he'd only just begun when he heard Kyale's voice calling to her governess and maid for her breakfast.

It was time to keep his promise. He set aside his copy of the book and started out. He had not gone two steps beyond his door when his imagination pictured all kinds of dire things, so he retreated, swept up the copy, folded it, and tucked it into the inside pocket of his over-tunic, which he had sewn himself for carrying books to read at odd moments when nothing else was demanding his attention; he'd feel safer carrying the copy, as the thing was surely dangerous, whatever the code revealed. And maybe he could sneak some work while Kyale was busy dancing or watching festival plays.

The day almost began badly when Kyale discovered that the entire staff of the castle was riding with them. She scowled at the handful of servants, stable-hands, and guards, took a considering look at Leander's set face, then decided to regard the servants as an escort. A princess ought to have an escort, she decided.

Kyale's reward for that inward compromise was a thoroughly fun day of singing, dancing, acrobat acts, a roustabout, a hilarious Peddler Antivad farce by traveling players, and all kinds of good things to eat.

Twice Leander got a crack at that first page, tantalized by repeated patterns among the letters.

The sun rested on the low, green-covered hills dividing Leander's little kingdom Vasande Leror from Marloven Hess as Leander and Kyale rode slowly back to their castle.

Kyale's good mood faded as their ugly, four-square "royal castle" appeared on the horizon, looking exactly like what it really was: an old Marloven outpost.

Kyale started in about how grand Lilah Selenna's palace was in faraway Sarendan, and even Tahra's royal palace in Ferdrian, after being burned and looted by the Norsundrians, was more impressive than their horrible square castle.

"I know you're going to point out that we're a tiny kingdom, and that a huge castle would be too costly. I'm not stupid, you know! All I say is, people will respect you more as a king, if we could make the castle into a palace — more *royal* looking," Kyale said. "No matter how small we are, if you *look* like a king, people will *respect* you as a king . . ."

Leander felt like a duplicitous coward, but he was tired of an argument that she seemed to have an endless well of enthusiasm for, and he longed to get back to translating that code. He'd promised he'd return to Senrid's in three days with the result, and he'd already lost one day.

"Why don't you look through the drawings in one of the old archives for ideas?" he asked Kyale when she paused for breath, feeling like a worm because he knew he would never be able to afford to adopt any of them. But he had to distract Kyale so he could get some uninterrupted time. "I mean about the castle. Making it look better."

Kyale brightened, her silvery gray eyes reflecting the light of the sinking sun. "You mean it? I will," she exclaimed. "Finally!"

As soon as they reached the stable she flung herself off her horse, leaving the animal to the stable staff, and dashed up to the library, knowing precisely which books to grab. There were two of them, one centuries old, left by one of Leander's ancestors who had been a queen from faraway Colend, and another, a sketchbook made by Leander's great-grandmother when she traveled up north for the royal wedding of a cousin.

Kyale curled up on her bed with her cats, and gloried in the most impressive and fanciful of the drawings. So lost was she in reverie, imagining the future brilliance of the castle, she didn't notice some of the cats' tails twitching, or the two biggest ones leaping noiselessly out the window.

Leander remained behind to help the stable hands care for the horses. When they were watered, fed, curried, and bedded down, he was free at last to run upstairs to his study, his mind on old Venn runes, and letter combinations to try.

He got to his desk, quickly stashed the copy he'd made in its magic-protected hidey, then blinked in dismay at his desk. His practice papers were scattered carelessly. He was never careless. He couldn't believe the servants would touch anything on his desk — they never entered his study, even to dust.

He reached for the top sheet of the scattered papers in order to neaten his desk again. The moment he touched the paper, magic ripped him out of the world.

When it flung him back in, he tumbled into a granite room laced with the bitter-iron scent of dark magic.

Eight

Norsunder Base

DEJAIN REGARDED THE YOUNG as credulous and ignorant.

She had performed dark magic to halt the appearance of aging once her skin began showing the first lines. That magic required increasingly frequent, and strong, renewals as the years passed — and one still felt the effects of age if one was not careful.

She paused outside the chamber she had set up for her Destination trap, put her hand to the latch, and slowly opened the door, as inside the bare, windowless room lit by a single glow-globe, Leander started.

He watched the door ease open. Illusion, he thought as a pretty, blonde young woman in an old-fashioned peach-colored robe peered in, then beckoned. "Do you want to escape?" she asked.

Leander said, "Yes."

He got to his feet, and as she led him into a hallway, he said,

"Where am I?"

"Sh! They'll hear you," she whispered back.

In silence he followed her down the hall and around a corner. She looked about her with quick glances, but as the light from widely spaced glow-globes caught her profile, he sensed excitement but no fear.

Down another tiptoed hallway, then she pulled him quickly into a room with tables and chairs. She shut the door. "The regular patrol will be along in a moment. We'll wait until we hear them pass."

Leander said again, "Where are we?"

"Norsunder Base. You must be a friend of Senrid Montredaun-An." She was still whispering, as if someone crouched nearby, listening.

Bewildered, Leander said, "I haven't seen Senrid for days."

"They're looking for some books he got hold of." She eyed him earnestly, her pretty brows puckered but her gaze was steady and watchful.

His sense of alarm spiked.

"Do you know where the books are?" she asked.

Her voice, her attitude, the lack of fear in a fearful situation — everything reminded him of Mara Jinea, the pretty mage who had drugged and drowned Leander's aging father soon after marrying him.

Leander flushed with anger. "You're lying," he exclaimed.

Dejain dropped the false manner and eyed him with contempt. This could have been so simple! "Yes," she said. "And *you* are stupid, you and that Marloven boy, fooling about with things far beyond either of your comprehension. But he's hiding behind an army, and wards that would take half a year to break. So it's just as well we have you, eh?"

Sickened, Leander regretted having said anything.

She tapped a smoothly filed nail on the table. "One of the two of you possesses at least one manuscript in Old Venn. We believe that this is the missing volume of Erkric's journal, from the period he was gone out of the world. Where is it, and the companion volume of spells he brought back?"

"I don't know," Leander said.

Her smile turned nasty. "I guess this'll be fun after all! Let's find a way to jog your memory."

She opened the door, and in came a pair of tall, strong-looking men, and a mean-eyed fellow with a heavy jaw, from whom emanated a whiff of magic.

"Work room," the woman said.

The big men each took one of Leander's arms, while the third opened a door to a room empty except for what looked like a wooden support going from floor to ceiling.

The two pushed Leander to this square wooden beam, and the third took hold of his wrists, yanked them behind this beam, and closed cold iron shackles around each. Leander's heart crowded into his throat. He was in Norsunder — and all the horrible things you heard about were about to happen to him.

I'm sorry, Senrid, he thought: he'd lie as long as he could, but he had no illusions about how long he'd last under torture.

Dejain brought in a chair from the far room, set it in front of Leander, then moved it a little back. "I want to stay clear of the splash," she said with a big smile, enjoying the way the boy blanched.

Most promising. She detested blood and took no pleasure in the sight of mangled flesh; perhaps she could frighten him into complying before anyone brought out a knife.

She let the moment stretch out as she took her time in disposing her skirts neatly.

The room abruptly filled with a weird green light, which caused a faint burned-metal singe. Leander braced against the beam, sensing very powerful dark magic coalescing around himself. The stench of hot metal made him sneeze so violently he feared his nose would bleed.

Dejain leaped back. She'd warded this room herself! She cast a tracer — blocked.

She turned to the new mage, who was smart enough to cooperate with her as senior power, though she had no illusions about how long that would last. She'd already been betrayed by old Benin.

And so she finessed. "A test," she said in Norsundrian, as airily as possible. "Find out who made that spell, what it is, and a way to break it."

As soon as the mage was gone she waved the guards at Leander and said in Sartoran, which the brat had to understand, "Let's give him a taste of the rewards for stupidity, shall we?"

The bigger man's expression changed from the slackness of boredom to faint interest. He flexed his hand and made a fist as he stepped toward Leander, who couldn't avoid an instinctive recoil in anticipation.

But the blow did not land. He opened his eyes as the guard staggered back, wringing his hand. A nauseating stink of singed flesh made Leander cough, his eyes watering.

The first guard cursed, cradling his hand, which had turned an ugly, boiled red. The second guard advanced more carefully, and reached rather than swung. Then he snatched his fingers back. "He's warded. It burns like fire."

Dejain beckoned the men out of the room, leaving Leander to sag against the beam, his shackles rattling.

Outside the room, Dejain met the mage, who had been muttering tracers. He shook his head.

She snapped her fingers, beckoned, and they retreated to her ward-protected study. Here, she walked the perimeter, whispering a tracer that she had put together years before: a powerful spell designed to expose magical interference.

Nothing.

She and the mage sat down. She didn't remember his name. He was entirely unprepossessing, his only characteristic the bulges at either side of his jaw from a lifetime of gritting his teeth. He sat with the stooped posture of one who spent most of his time poring over books.

These young mages at Norsunder Base were all alike. Dissatisfaction with the constraints of light magic— ambitions thwarted— theories on power— they all arrived thinking they would be hailed with respect. Most scarcely lasted five years.

"Someone is interfering. Most likely it's Siamis," she said. She had no intention of mentioning Benin, who despite his bulk had a sneaking, slithering way of knowing when his name came up.

The mage worked his jaw, then said, "I thought Siamis was stripped of command. Reduced to a truffle hunter."

"He'll be working to take command back, of course," she retorted. "Let's show him how mistaken he is, which in turn will put you over the rest of the mages." When she saw his eyelids flicker, she thought, *Got him.* "But there is another possibility, that young Leander is in possession of some light magic protection."

"Light magic cannot make fire wards," the mage scoffed.

"Perhaps. But the world is riddled with hidden or forgotten magical artifacts," she said. "I have some tricks that might disclose such a thing, since it looks like the brat is untouchable, for now.

I'll deal with those. I want you to use high level tracers and go over every room. The hall. This wing, if you must, because we'd better find out who was able to get past my protections on the work room. Someone has a relay-window, and was watching."

His jaw muscles flexed as his eyes flickered around. That was one of the perennial worries of Norsunder Base: you never knew who might be watching through a magical relay-window. Despite all your care with wards. Annoying as this task was, he knew he'd better master it. "What if you don't find any artifact?"

She noted with wary approval that already he was getting the idea. Useful or arrogant? She would not tell him the dangers of intercepting relays. Let him find out.

"I expect that Leander's friend Senrid will leave his citadel looking for Leander, or at least the manuscript, if enough time passes."

"So?"

"So I want to prepare a suitable welcome for Senrid."

Four Days Later
Marloven Hess

Well before dawn, Senrid rolled out of bed into air that didn't make him shiver. He leaned out of his bedroom windows, breathing the scents of growing things.

All winter he'd confined his early morning practice to contact fighting and knife work. The spring warmth rendered unbearable the thought of confinement in the stuffy air of the practice salle. He called for a horse and, while the academy boys were all in the mess hall at breakfast, he rode around one of the far corrals, shooting arrows from horseback.

The exhilaration of spring, the excellent horse, the pull of the bow from fingertips to the middle of his back and then down to his heels locked in the stirrups, the satisfying thud of the arrow in the target put him in a great mood.

It didn't last. It was open interviews again, and he suspected the blacksmiths, at least, had not forgotten the vexed subject of what they insisted was a false war.

When he reached the interview chamber, he found it packed

with not only various guild representatives, but first runners from two jarls, and a slew of people who insisted on airing their opinions. Again.

This was worse than last time! Senrid wondered if he ought to invoke the authority of his ancestors by commanding this crowd to reassemble in the throne room. There was certainly a big enough crowd.

The first thing Keriam always said to each new command class at the academy: *If you demand respect, what you will hear is flattery, and what you will get is contempt. You earn respect only when they give it freely.*

Senrid imagined himself strutting to the throne, on whose edge he had to sit so he could get his feet flat on the floor, and almost laughed out loud.

No. They'd all sweat it out right there in that stuffy room, he decided.

Tradition required the jarl representatives to speak first, after which the guild chief, then the various guild representatives. By the time they were halfway through these, Senrid had heard enough repeated words and phrases to perceive a pattern — since the last meeting, people appeared to have convinced themselves that the previous summer, the boy king Senrid had ordered the entire kingdom into retreat in fear of a war that never happened.

Senrid's guts churned with anger, the worse because he knew that if Keriam stood behind him, with the captain of the guard (old as he was) or even Van Stad, the day watch commander, there would be fewer wry looks and sarcastic words. *They* had respect. Not evoked through their ancestors.

Senrid had already explained about the double invasions of Sarendan and Everon. The war in Everon had been especially terrible. But he knew that to Marlovens, he might as well be talking about the moon.

There seemed to be two alternatives: first, shut them up by ordering out the guard, which would be the first step toward a reign like his uncle's.

Second alternative? Give in. He could call the summer retreat a war game, which meant the crown would pay. They might even cheer him, call him generous, but he'd know the truth: it had not been a war game, and further, at the time he'd made it clear it wasn't a war game. So a lie to buy them off would . . .

His teeth gritted. It would confirm what they already were

half-convinced of, he was sure: that he was weak, cowardly, stupid.

He drew in a deep breath to control his simmering temper as his gaze ranged the secondary mementoes of his family's long rule on the walls over their heads. The great mementos, swords and shields and helms of battle, decorated the walls of the throne room. Here were the artifacts of treaties, and personal artifacts, except that empty frame alone on the wall directly opposite, deliberately left bare as a grim reminder of the sinister king who had ridden straight into Norsunder at the head of the First Lancers.

Senrid gave in to impulse.

Ignoring the speechifying cooper guild chief, he slipped a dagger from his sleeve, cocked his arm back, and threw the dagger over the heads of the gathering.

It hit the edge of the empty wooden frame with a thud, reverberating in the sudden silence.

At least he could still nail a target, he thought wryly as all heads snapped his way.

He got up from his bench, putting his hands behind his back to hide the tremble of his fingers. "You all know," he said, "that I sent the signal for the retreat last year, and it was carried out with admirable swiftness."

A quick murmur, some of it derisive — he could feel the "What do you think we've been talking about?" — then silence.

"Here is what you do not know," Senrid said, and nicked his chin at that empty frame. "The Norsundrian who all the legends insist suborned my ancestor Ivandred —"

A quick, shocked susurrus at the name *Ivandred* caused him to say, "Yes, I am naming the Unnamed. As I said, the Norsundrian who suborned him is called Detlev. It's an Ancient Sartoran name. From four thousand years ago."

All eyes followed Senrid as he walked down the center aisle. "The mages say that he usually comes out of Norsunder every three or four centuries."

He reached the back of the room, and stood below that bare frame with the dagger protruding.

"Every three or four centuries, until now. He's been seen more times in the last five years than he has for a thousand years. A *thousand* years."

Senrid jumped up on a table, and reached to yank his knife

from the frame, then he turned and faced the crowd. "What you also don't know is that the day before I sent the signal, he trapped me by magic on the cliff overlooking the border where Norsunder decimated our border force the day after my uncle abdicated. That battle, you might remember," he added acidly.

The silence made it clear that they did: at least half of them had to know someone, or be related to someone, who had died in that slaughter.

"Detlev chose that place deliberately. You can understand the implied threat as well as I can. And you know what Detlev said to me?"

Nobody spoke, but Senrid saw some stirrings here and there.

"He warned me that he'd be back when it suited him. His exact words were, *You will not see me coming.*"

Senrid paused. He had everyone's attention now. He wiped the knife blade on his trousers, and jumped down from the table. "So if you were king . . ." He forced himself to meet gazes as he recrossed the room. "What would you do? Sit and wait for them to pick the ground? I know what he wants. He doesn't want this land, except maybe to hand off as a prize. What would he do with it, start farming?"

Someone laughed, and several shifted and whispered.

"Norsunder wants the Marloven army, trained and ready to ride. We're the best on the entire continent. And if he could send his nephew Siamis to enchant my brains out and force me to command Marlovens to follow Uncle Detlev's orders, what are *you* going to do?"

Senrid saw in lifted chins and a few grimaces how much Marlovens distrusted talk of magic. It was generally regarded as trustworthy as water, that is, necessary to life but you couldn't shape it, or weave it, and it was useless in war except as uncontrollable catastrophe. "Marloven law is, you obey orders or die. So what *would* you do if I started issuing orders for you to ride over the border and attack Toth and Telyerhas, not for Marloven glory, but for the convenience of Norsunder?"

Senrid could see the quick reactions of revulsion in crimped upper lips and tightened shoulders. "Detlev said, *You will not see me coming.* There were two attacks in other countries, ordered by him. So I thought the best thing I could do is hide so he couldn't find me at all, and order the retreat."

He shrugged. "And Detlev didn't get me. Maybe he never

intended to attack this end of the continent. Maybe he was testing us, a kind of scouting foray, to see how we'd react. This I do know: he's been in the world again for a purpose. Norsunder is coming for war, we just don't know where, or when. Or really even why. We just know they're going to do it."

He reached the desk, and sat on the edge, swinging a booted foot back and forth, twitchy as a cat's tail. "So here we are." He gestured with the knife.

One of the jarl equerries spoke up from the back. "Senrid-Harvaldar. Are we to expect more retreats?"

Using the blade, Senrid made the flat-handed swiping motion of negation. "No. One result of those battles at the other end of the continent is, the magic that turd Siamis used to enchant kings . . ." He twirled the knife and grinned. " . . . no longer works. We at least gained that much last summer. The next time Detlev comes, it's going to be at the head of an army." Senrid pointed his blade up at the blank space on the wall. "Maybe his."

That sparked a wildfire of whispers. As Senrid sheathed the knife at last, he controlled the urge to listen on the mental plane, knowing that he might be sensed, because he was not very good at that skill. In any case, he could see a difference in their faces, and hear a change of tone, even if he didn't know what it meant. Maybe they didn't either.

The watch bell clanged from the castle tower, echoing belatedly across the city. Everyone got up to leave, still talking, and Senrid noted more than one reflective glance up at that frame on the wall where the Treaty of the Rivers, signed by Ivandred, had so briefly hung before his name became infamous by riding out of the world at the head of his renowned First Lancers.

This elite force still waited in Norsunder, beyond time, an awareness handed down through the centuries: there were no more lancer divisions, at least by that name. And everyone there was recollecting that. Senrid could see it in frowns and downward glances and tightened fists as they walked out.

Keriam was going to be disgusted with that stunt, Senrid thought as he eyed the huge gouge in the four-century-old frame. When the last of lingerers had exited, Senrid pulled his notecase from his pocket, though he knew nothing was in it. He had to check.

Again, nothing. Most unlike Leander.

He ran upstairs to his study, where he performed the

complicated spell that protected Jilo's books from discovery. There they were, safe but unreadable. He knew they ought to go back to Jilo, but he had to know if there was something in them that he could use as defense against Detlev. Despite his words to Hibern, the truth was, he would use any kind of magic, even blood magic, if it meant he could ward Marloven Hess from Norsundrian invasion.

He sighed. So what to do now? Leander could lose track of time when he was on the hunt for some obscure passage or historical record, but the third day of his "See you in three days" had been four days ago, which was negligent even for Leander.

Senrid scowled down at the books, reached for his pen to write another note, and then threw it down again. He'd written yesterday. It was time to check on Leander himself.

He impatiently cast an illusion to hide the books, though his study was protected by a webwork of wards, and even more powerful and ancient ones lay over the castle. Any runner coming into his study knew better than to touch anything. But he wouldn't leave them sitting in plain sight on his desk. Still less appealing was the idea of taking the books to Leander's castle, which had no protections worth consideration, either magical or military — not to mention a very nosy stepsister.

He came out of the transfer in the foyer of Leander's castle. He shook off the transfer reaction, then ducked into the old servants' hall, which no one used anymore. He listened outside the kitchen and the staff dining room, which Leander (and his stepsister, under vehement protest) shared with the rest of Leander's small staff. Senrid heard Kyale's high voice chattering to her maid, but no Leander.

Senrid backtracked hastily. There was only one place Leander could be: his study. Senrid knew that Leander sometimes fell asleep right at his desk if he'd been working all night.

He ran upstairs, mentally preparing a joke in case he found Leander snoring, saw the door slightly ajar, and stepped inside.

Empty.

He glanced down at the desk, recognizing familiar Venn lettering on a couple of the papers scattered about. He stretched out his hand to pick up the top sheet in hopes of seeing Leander's code-breaking progress, but when his fingers touched the paper, dark magic ripped him out of the world and slung him onto a stone floor.

A trap — and he'd blundered right into it!

A breath, a soft footfall, and a pair of men in Norsunder gray walked in. Senrid flashed his hands to his sleeves and whipped out his blades.

In the instant the pair separated in order not to foul one another's reach, Senrid saw they were trained as a team. He hadn't a hope, but he fought anyway. A slash, a whirl, a kick, then one swept his legs, and the second man slammed him down onto the stone floor so violently that one of his knives flew from his grip and clattered away. He whipped the other in a hard arc, slashing someone's arm.

The one he'd cut cursed heatedly and punched Senrid. His head thunked against the ground. The first guard slapped something metallic against Senrid's forehead. He smelled the hot-metal reek of dark magic, then a shocking pain in his head that took away the senses of sight and sound.

Senrid blinked desperately. A hard palm smacked him across the face so he saw stars. A few more smacks, as he tried vainly to fight, and he fell, curling up in a ball with one arm over his head.

No blows.

He forced himself to drop the habitual mind-shield, and to listen on the mental plane. A skull-splitting clamor of angry emotions nearly overwhelmed him.

Then someone spoke nearby, the voice an emotion-infused distortion on the mental plane: "You can play later. Orders were nail and bail."

A hand yanked Senrid to his feet by his collar, and another hard hand gripped his arm. He tried to yank free, and got another slap for his pains.

The two fell in step on either side of him. The man at his left said, "What is it with brats, anyway? Dejain starting experiments now?"

Right-hand voice laughed, and red-yellow intent flashed on the mental plane.

Right-hand opened a door, and Senrid was slung into space. He fell rolling. The door slammed — he felt the reverberation — and Senrid lost the mental plane in the immediacy of aches, pains, dizziness.

Senrid tried to concentrate on the mental plane. Liere could do it easily, but his head hurt too much.

He sat up and felt himself all over. His knives were gone. He carefully felt his eyes and ears. Normal to the touch, at least. It's just a spell, he told himself, as he fought the rising panic. Spells can be undone. Warmth at his throbbing nose and his upper lip: blood. But not bad. He'd been worse off.

He wiped his face on his sleeve, glad he couldn't see it.

All right. He'd walked straight into a trap. That didn't mean he should continue to be stupid. He had one weapon, his wits, and the best way to use those would be to summon his strength, and everything Liere had taught him about Dena Yeresbeth.

He sat cross-legged, put his head in his hands, and concentrated.

Nine

PRINCESS KYALE MARLONEN WAS furious and worried by turns.

She knew that her stepbrother Leander was up to something, just because he'd been pretending so hard that he wasn't, in spite of their lovely day at the spring festival. The fact that he was pretending at all meant that it had something to do with Senrid.

She hated the thought of Leander and Senrid being friends. That snot of a Marloven had an enormous kingdom full of people. Didn't he have any friends there? Why didn't he go spend time with them?

Here she was, having thought of a brilliant idea for turning the castle into something a king could live in — but she couldn't find Leander to show it to.

Nobody else seemed worried. They were used to him riding off into Crestel to talk to guild people, or riding to the forest to clear his head. Or transferring to Marloven Hess for magic talk.

She might as well go by herself to gather what she needed for her brilliant idea. The house that she had inherited had been built by a long-ago Colendi princess who had been a Marloven queen before retiring here. A few rooms still had the Colendi decorations that Queen Lasva chosen, carefully preserved or refurbished over the succeeding generations. Leander had even admitted that it was a beautiful house.

Why not duplicate some of its rooms in Crestel's bleak, boring old castle?

Kyale rode south to Tannentaun. There she paced through the house from room to room, looking at it with fresh eyes. Weird, how you forget things you once saw every day. Like this beautiful room that opened into the north side garden, with the viny things painted under the ceiling, and the furnishings with the viny pattern carved into graceful table legs and oval chair backs. She had also placed the pretty mirrored pieces behind the crystal sconces that reflected light in the rooms on the south side, which was gloomiest in winter.

The caretakers welcomed her, spoiling her with her favorite foods, served in the beautiful dining room. She stayed a day, then two — always expecting Leander to come looking for her.

When she tired of eating alone, and Leander hadn't shown up, she gathered up old sketches of the rooms and rode back — to discover that Leander hadn't been seen by anyone. A horrible thought occurred. Maybe Leander was mad at her and had decided to stay with Senrid for some reason.

That night, she prowled along the hall. Senrid had given Leander transfer tokens for him to pass all those magical wards in his huge, horrible fortress. Leander could transfer directly to Senrid's study. Kyale knew where Leander kept the transfer tokens: in a little box on one of the bookshelves above his desk.

Ordinarily, the last person she ever wanted to see was Senrid, but if he knew where Leander was . . .

In Leander's study, she clapped on the glow-globes, and glanced at the papers lying on the desk. She didn't touch them. Leander hated her touching anything in the study. She went to the bookshelf, and opened the old carved box with the little fox faces on it. Inside lay a dozen carved wood shank buttons that Senrid had put the transfer spell on.

She drew in a deep breath, bracing herself for the nastiness of transfer magic. Magic yanked her out of time and space then shoved in again, in a moonlit room with four tall windows: Senrid's study. Empty.

Senrid invariably sat up late, she knew that from that terrible time she had traveled around the kingdom with him before the regent was deposed. But he wasn't there now.

She clapped on a glow-globe. Unlike Leander's desk, Senrid's was scrupulously tidy, with neat stacks of paper squared away. Kyale put her hands out to lean on the desk so she could look closely at the papers for Leander's handwriting. She was startled when her fingers bumped against a hard edge —

Illusion magic blurred with a faint sparkle.

She snatched her hand back. Nothing lay on that part of the desk.

She extended a cautious finger, and felt something. The magic blurred again. With her touching the object, the illusion vanished in a twinkle, leaving her staring down in disappointment. It was only a couple of old books. Anything Senrid read had to be boring.

She jumped when the door slammed open, and there were two guards, both with hands on the hilts of their swords. "Where is the king?" one asked, recognizing her.

"Who cares?" Kyale retorted, her heart still hammering. How she hated Marlovens! She uttered the reverse-phrase, and the transfer token's magic hurled her home.

In Senrid's study, Commander of the Royal Guard Keriam arrived behind the aide he'd stationed to watch for lights in the king's rooms. "Was that the king?"

One of the duty guards said, "No. It was the princess from Vasande Leror." And he repeated the short exchange.

Keriam's mouth tightened. "We can assume that she knows nothing. Let be." He paused, regarding the young men before him. He'd trained them all, and hand-picked the guards on Senrid's floor. "Continue as ordered," he said. "Anyone else who shows up and asks about the king, send them to me."

Fingers tapped chests in acknowledgment, and Keriam left, taking the residence shortcut to his tower, where he sent a young aide to fetch Captain Indevan Stad, the day watch commander of the royal guard — and effective commander while Keriam was busy with the academy.

Keriam occupied his time with the constant flow of academy affairs until Stad showed up, a tall, lean, black-haired young man.

Stad saw his answer in Commander Keriam's tense face, but

asked anyway: "Still not back?"

"No." Keriam exhaled the word.

Stad glanced out the window at the rooftops of the academy, where until now the best and the worst days of his life had been spent. Then he asked, "I know the king can get around invisible. Or however magic works. He ever done anything like this before?"

"Never. I would have said previous to yesterday, he's always let me know if he's going to leave. This I will attest to, he's never missed appointments. That's four today, and two yesterday, after the open interview session before noon. He was definitely there."

Stad's sober face flashed a wry smile. "Still blabbing about it in the streets. Pegged that old treaty frame with a knife, and told 'em Norsunder is coming, with the Unnamed leading the old First Lancers."

Keriam dismissed local gossip with a flick of his hand, and went right back to how much Senrid had missed. "Five today if you count this morning's session with the sword master, left standing around waiting the entire hour."

"That's not like Senrid," Stad said. "No one got in." It wasn't quite a question.

"Not on foot," Keriam stated. He would never make any assumptions about magic.

Stad opened his hand in assent. He'd put in a season on the upstairs patrol, and he knew there were no blind spots. No one could have got in to make a snatch.

Keriam said, "My instinct is to keep his disappearance a secret. For now. And step up vigilance, in case this is part of some kind of attack."

Stad rubbed his chin. "You know it falls to me to take the guards out for the spring maneuvers. Should I suffer an accident so I can stay here? I could get the captain to send them out with Evrec, or even Marlovair, up at the city guard. You know either of them'd do well. Or we could postpone—I could find an excuse, like the horses needing some training, after spending all summer loose on the plains."

Keriam liked the idea of having Stad standing by. Most likely, he would one day become head of cavalry under Senrid's Harskiald, Retren Forthan, the supreme army commander—a title that had not been conferred for over two generations—and everybody knew it. Nothing would happen if Stad was seen to be in charge of the city and castle guard.

But ... "No," Keriam said reluctantly. "Would cause too many questions, and right now everyone's too busy to notice Senrid's absence. Besides, spring is for the city guard's war game. They all look forward to it. We can't postpone until summer because that belongs to the academy. Ah. One thing you could do. It's been a few years since the war game has been an attack on the city, that way we don't have to rotate them out watch by watch. We'll have them all here, day against night watch. Nobody will get by us."

Stad flashed a grin. "After what everyone's been saying about Senrid promising a war with Norsunder, they'd love that."

That settled, they parted, each to a busy day, during which they never ceased to worry about Senrid.

Ten

I MUST NOW RETURN to Norsunder Base and Dejain's two prisoners, who were as yet unaware of the other. . .

Leander stirred wearily, his eyelids gritty, his arms and shoulders aching so badly that every move sent pain through him like cut glass. He had no idea how long he'd been tied to that post, but it felt like years. At least he had the Waste Spell so he did not totally humiliate himself, but there was no cleaning frame to wick away the sweat and grime of being stuck in one set of clothes for days and nights. The glow-globes set in the corners of the white-plastered room never dimmed, and there was no window in that stuffy room, only two small air holes on opposite walls, so time was impossible to measure.

The door opened. An older woman in Norsunder gray entered. She looked at him indifferently as she set on the floor a small jug with a reed-straw in it, and next to it a bread end. Dry, from the looks of it.

At least the chain between the shackles was long enough to

permit him to wriggle around so he could get his face close to the floor to eat and drink. The last meal had been a boiled egg. That had given him something to do, figuring out how to peel it behind his back, then roll it so he could get his face to the floor to eat it.

When he was alone again, he crouched down, arms twisted painfully, and lipped the bread until he could get a good enough purchase to gnaw on it. Probably two days old, over-baked. But he'd tasted worse when on the trail.

The meals were intermittent, but at least he got them. Yes, he could be worse off—especially as Dejain couldn't touch him. He suspected that she was watching from somewhere, hoping whoever had put that protective ward over him would appear, or talk to him, or try to transfer him out.

Nothing.

Senrid knew what they were doing.

He had read too many records about prisoners of war, and ways they were treated, and he'd been a prisoner in Norsunder Base once before. This was an obvious tactic: no food or water, leaving him to fight his own fear.

He was alive. That meant they wanted something from him.

The worst threat was knowing that no one would look for him. Keriam, the man he trusted most, had no idea where he was, and would never think of magic. Hibern, who would, was far in the north busy with her studies. And what could she do, a student of light magic? Nothing.

Then there was Liere, but Senrid kept himself from trying to reach her in the mental realm. She was younger than Senrid, a bundle of worry, still haunted by her brief brushes with Norsunder. Even supposing he could reach her, which he doubted, surely the Ancient Sartorans like Detlev and Siamis would sense him in the mental realm, which would result in Senrid and Liere both being scragged.

The struggle against fear, without means to measure its duration, seemed endless. He worked grimly to hold himself to the moment. His strategy was clear: gather information any way he could.

It taxed his strength, and as tiredness pressed on him, intensified by his inability to see or hear, he was not always certain when he was awake or dreaming. Sometimes he dreamed he was awake, hearing the howl of angry laughter right outside the door.

He dug his nails into his flesh: if it hurt, he was awake. If it didn't, he struggled to wake himself, and he'd roll around on the stone floor to feel the reassuring grit, to smell dank stone and his own grimy clothes.

Then he sat up cross-legged, put his head in his hands, and reached again.

How did you judge distance in the mental realm? Everything was distorted, perhaps even the mocking laughter that sounded like crows, no, like boys his own age.

Did Norsunder have people his age? He'd never seen any, but that didn't mean anything. He recollected what he'd overheard after he was captured, *What is it with brats, anyway? Dejain starting experiments now?*

That seemed to mean someone else was experimenting with, or on, brats.

But that could just mean prisoners, a wretched thought.

He slept, dream-wandered, woke in a cold sweat, and grimly tried again. And again.

And again.

He learned very little from the minds passing by, each closed inside its skull casing, focus narrow on immediate things. Secret hates. Plots, petty games or covert revenge. Private passions that made him grimace with distaste. He touched the surface of these minds and then lifted away, occasionally aware of very powerful awarenesses whose focus was elsewhere. They seemed distant, but he did not trust his perceptions.

The first time he sensed one of those, he withdrew behind his mental shield. When he forced himself to venture out again, he tried to make a "tendril" the way Liere did so effortlessly. It felt more like his mental self was an out-of-control horse blundering around on ice. So he ventured slowly over the mindscape, which had no discernible distance or place, only these presences whose proximity he perceived as darting lights. The powerful minds were like lighthouse beacons. He didn't want them turning his way.

Very slowly, like ink poured through water, he gathered little clues from the warped jumble of others' images, others' hearing, others' voices and thoughts. Siamis was in Sartor; Siamis had crossed the border into the Land of the Venn; Siamis was in Bereth Ferian. Detlev was out of the world, the confusing image one of some kind of military compound set against barren mountains of a sort never seen in Sartorias-deles.

Senrid hoped *that* one was true, that Detlev wasn't even in Sartorias-deles. However, maybe physical distance meant nothing in the mental realm to one such as him.

Ignoring his growing thirst, Senrid persisted in drifting along the outer boundaries of the mental realm—confining himself to Norsunder Base as much as he could—sifting, listening, until he found a mage whose mind smoldered with resentment. Dejain—books — *Why won't she let anyone else have a go at the prisoner?*

Prisoner! Himself, or someone else? Then Senrid sensed two more minds approaching.

Coming for him. Senrid shut himself behind his mind-shield, and braced.

Fingers closed around his arm and yanked him to his feet. Even though he couldn't see or hear, he could feel the whirl of vertigo. It took all his effort to keep his feet under him as he was borne along, then abruptly the hands let go. He dropped with a splat.

He stayed where he was, and concentrated on the minds around him. In spite of his weakened condition, the mental effort had become easier.

". . . are you really going to cut him up?" That was a tenor voice, distorted by fear, anxiety, a desire for the delight of bloodshed, with an overlay of magical awareness: the resentful mage. "Everyone says he's got Detlev's mark on him."

"Then why hasn't Detlev claimed him?" Dejain's voice twisted snake-like, false-sweet in her own ears, hot with fanged anger on the mental plane. Fear bleeding underneath.

"Who knows why Detlev does anything? He could even be responsible for that ward." Image flash: Leander Tlennen-Hess, shackled to a wooden post.

Ah. Now Senrid had another big piece of the puzzle.

"No. If he interferes at all, it's directly," retorted a pompous voice—an idiot, Senrid, thought, because Detlev was infamous for oblique interference and long plans. "Besides, my spy maintains that he's still on Five."

Again, a flicker of that military compound against jagged mountains.

A small feminine hand patted Senrid on the cheek. He couldn't prevent a recoil. He scrambled backward, to jeering laughter on the mental plane. Thin fingers seized Senrid's hair above his forehead and jerked his head back. On the mental plane, the woman's voice trembled with red-yellow anger, desperation curling beneath as she said, "Let's try cutting him up a little. Leander? This is all your responsibility, you know. All you have to do is tell me where Erkric's manuscript and spell book are."

Dejain's fury was corrosive; Senrid had no defense against the flood of the speakers' emotions. His head ached excruciatingly, and he couldn't control the shivers of exhaustion, of anticipation.

"Here's the knife," said the angry tenor voice, yellow-green with reluctant fear. "You're on your own, Dejain. I'll help against anyone else, but I'm not crossing Detlev."

"Stash him," Dejain said in disgust.

Senrid's head rocked as Dejain shoved him viciously, and hard hands yanked him back to his feet. "But time is our enemy."

Vasande Leror

What little king business there was to do in Vasande Leror had been handled by big, glower-faced Alaxandar, who had once been guard captain. He'd rescued Leander after Kyale's mother tried to kill him. Now he was Leander's trusted steward.

Kyale made it her business to avoid him when she could. At noon the next day, when she went to get something to eat, she overheard him talking to the other servants in the kitchen. She started to back away, then heard the worry in his voice when he said, "Leander's not back. I guess if he doesn't return by tomorrow, I'm going to have to try to find these other mages."

Kyale grumped sullenly. Alaxandar was not only taking over ruling, he wasn't telling her any of these other plans. She was the princess! She loved being a princess, but she had to admit she didn't know a thing about ruling the way Leander did it. Leander's idea of kingship was so boring, blabbing with dullards like farmers and guild people about taxes and borders and rebuilding and mines, or studying protection spells. A princess, Kyale had always thought, was meant to be the center of an elegant court, leading the way at parties, and picnics. Wearing the prettiest dress in the equally splendid room. When laws had to be passed concerning boring things like guilds and taxes, she gave an order, and some scribe scuttled off to carry it out.

But that was when everything was fine. If something was wrong, it was her responsibility to fix it. Except nobody seemed to think of asking her.

Llhei's large, comforting figure was silhouetted in the upstairs hallway, supervising the cleaning. Kyale waited until they were alone, then said, "Llhei, am I important to anybody?"

"Everybody is important," Llhei replied, her worn, calm face concerned.

Kyale scowled. "'Everybody' doesn't mean anything. Am I worth anything?"

"You are to me," Llhei said to Kyale's mutinous expression, an unspoken *I mean anyone important.*

Llhei knew her difficult charge—none better. She smiled to herself, then said seriously, "I sense you're talking about reputation. Others value us for what we contribute to the betterment of life. For being trustworthy, as well as for our gifts."

Kyale sighed. Trustworthy. Reputation. She knew what it all meant: nobody thought Princess Kyale Marlonen could do anything useful, much less brave or heroic.

It was the job of a princess to be heroic, and right now that meant finding Leander. She just didn't know how.

She decided to ask a friend—another princess. Kyale wrote a long letter to Lilah Selenna of Sarendan. Gratifyingly fast she got a return answer, but all Lilah said was: *Did you check with the others in the alliance? You should really get help.*

Kyale sat down at her desk and tried again.

CJ of Mearsies Heili wrote back a long, funny letter about being stuck throne-warming, and promised to ask Clair— visiting on the other side of the world — if she'd seen Leander.

Princess Tahra of Everon wrote back, but her letter was short and typically weird, noting how many days since she'd seen Leander. Kyale didn't bother translating that into weeks.

She hesitated before writing to Hibern, who was nice, but she wasn't a princess. Moreover, she seemed to have retreated to her studies. No one saw her anymore, so what would she know?

Maybe it was time to investigate on her own.

Feeling long-suffering at the prospect of two more magic transfers (and those boys would never be grateful), she returned to Senrid's study in Marloven Hess.

Senrid still wasn't there. Kyale marched to the desk and felt around until her fingers bumped into the invisible books. They had to be about magic. Senrid certainly never read anything interesting — like about adventuring princesses — but he was *always* boring on about magic.

She opened the top one. She couldn't read anything. She knew Leander collected alphabets, so maybe she could find out what this one was.

She heard footsteps in the hallway outside the door, so she tucked the books under her arm and quickly reversed the transfer spell. Back in Leander's study, she rubbed her head with her free hand, and when the pangs went away, she threw the magic-spent transfer-token into the little box. Then, as a precaution, she picked out a new one and slid it into her green silk fringed sash.

That done, she frowned down at Leander's desk. Right on top lay a list written in the same letters that she recognized from one of these books!

She reached down to pick up the papers—

And magic seized her again, much more violently than the transfer spell to Senrid's, and flung her onto a stone floor.

Her head throbbed. Her body ached. She had dropped the books, which promptly turned invisible again. She forced herself to sit up, and groped around until she located them. With those seized fast under her arm, she got to her knees and then to her feet, her thick, hip-length curtain of silvery blond hair swinging around her like a cloak and tangling with her voluminous sleeves.

She stood in a bare stone room lit by a single glow-globe. No windows. It smelled musty and dank, with a sharp whiff of mildew.

There was a door. How had she not noticed it? But as she started for it, the latch lifted, and she jumped back. A young woman came in. She was pretty, with short golden curls brushing her shoulders. Kyale was relieved to see another human. But she did not trust pretty ladies. She had grown up with a very pretty mother who was about as evil as evil could get.

"Welcome," the woman said in a friendly voice. "What a lovely gown. I adore lavender, especially trimmed with green, and your lace is quite fetching. Enaeraneth, isn't it?"

"I think so," Kyale said. "My mother loved pretty dresses. Everything I have is left over from her trunks."

"She had exquisite taste. Who are you?"

"My name is Kitty," Kyale said, offering the nickname that no one ever used, though Leander at least tried to remember it. For once she left off the "Princess," until she was on surer footing; that sudden spell was not a friendly thing to do. "Who are you?"

"I'm no one in particular. Shall we go somewhere safer?" The woman looked right and left as if she did not want to be overheard, and on Kyale's cautious nod, she led the way down a plain stone hall to another room.

This room was not much different than the one Kyale had found herself in, but at least it contained a wooden table and chairs.

"Where are we?" Kyale asked.

"Some place we should not be." The woman acted like it was a secret between them.

Kyale looked askance. The woman didn't look scared at all, more like she was pretending to be scared. Kyale guessed the most horrible thing she could think of. "Some place having to do with Norsunder?"

"This is Norsunder Base."

Kyale's arms were crossed tightly over the books, under the lovely lace draped from the square neckline of her gown, over which her long silvery hair spilled. "So we can't get out?"

"Unless we escape." The woman smiled again.

"Escape," Kyale repeated. "But first I have a couple people to find. Have you seen two boys? The one I really want to find is named Leander. He's tall for his age, dark hair, green eyes."

"He is not here," the woman said in a conspiratorial whisper.

"The other is a splat-face called Senrid. Short, blond, disgusting."

"I'm not sure I would want to meet any disgusting people," the woman cooed.

"Oh well, he only is to me. And to villains. Not that I'm a villain," Kyale amended.

The woman smiled brightly. "Let me go and find out. I'll come back as soon as I can."

She walked out.

Eleven

AS SOON AS THE door shut, Kyale ran to it. She tucked the books firmly under her sleeve, and reached with her free hand. When she touched the latch, shock ran through her, icy cold. Magic! Kyale looked around. She remembered that the door had been behind an illusion, so she walked along the stone walls, her fingers barely touching them.

On the opposite side of the room, she discovered another door. Feeling clever she took hold of a handful of her skirt, and reached for the latch. It opened — no magic spell.

Beyond was yet another small room, this one with a bench. And seated in the middle of the bench, all alone, hands between his knees, head bowed: Senrid.

"Senrid!" Kyale exclaimed and when he didn't answer, she said more sharply, "Sulking because it's me who had to come rescue you idiots?" Though she knew that wasn't quite true.

No answer.

Irritated, disappointed, worried about Leander, Kyale

stomped across the floor and stopped directly in front of him. She snapped her fingers in front of Senrid's nose.

No reaction.

She stared. Had Norsunder turned him into a stone? No, she could see that he was breathing. His clothes were wrinkled, dusty, and splashed down the front and on a sleeve with brown stains. Kyale's stomach lurched in disgust.

She put her hand on his chest and pushed.

This time he reacted. He gulped in air, his eyes wide and flicking desperately around in all directions. He collapsed back on the bench, his fingers spread.

"That must have taken courage," he said flatly, with all his old sarcasm.

"Hey, it's me. Senrid?"

He closed his eyes, his lips pressed in a line as he concentrated.

His heart sank when he sensed a distorted view of himself seen through the eyes of . . . "Kyale, is that *you?*"

"Yes."

"Kyale?" Senrid repeated, still looking around, one hand groping blindly.

Kyale's blood turned into ice melt. Either she was as invisible as his books, or else he could neither see nor hear.

So she bent down and tapped her fingers on the top of his right hand.

He leaned forward, and whispered, "Can you hear me?"

She began to say yes, then took his hand and shook it up and down. The painful tension in Senrid's forehead eased.

"They are playing games with us," he whispered so rapidly she had difficulty comprehending the rush of words. "Except I think someone else is playing games with them. Her. Dejain is her name. Don't make the mistake of thinking her friendly, or trustworthy, because she's not. Understand me?"

Once again, Kyale shook his hand up and down.

"We walked into a magic trap. Her spells don't work on Leander. That's why we're still alive. She can't seem to touch him by magic, so she's keeping me for threat power. Or we would have been dead long ago. Got it?"

Another shake of the hand.

"I know she's somewhere around trying to listen by magic, so I don't know how long we have— "

Kyale tried to think of some way to write an answer on his

hand. Fingers! She took his hand with both of hers, forgot the books—and they thumped onto Senrid's lap.

The result was even more startling than when she'd poked him the first time. He jumped, felt them, and his face actually blanched to the color of old cheese.

Kyale had only once before seen Senrid that upset—when they stood on a cliff overlooking the southern border of Senrid's kingdom and Detlev cruelly forced Senrid to watch his warriors being decimated by Norsundrians.

"Kyale," Senrid whispered. "You didn't."

The books tumbled off his lap and landed on the floor.

Dejain, watching from her spy window opposite the bench, saw only the back of Kyale's swinging hair, and her wide, fluffy skirts. The vexing chit completely blocked Senrid from her view.

She left her magic chamber and hurried for the door, as inside the room, the books promptly vanished under their illusion.

Kyale was bending to pick them up when the door opened. There was Dejain, smiling prettily.

"What a sweet scene!"

"Wish I could say the same about you." Kyale's voice quavered as she straightened up.

Dejain laughed as she looked from one child to the other. They had nothing in their hands; what she heard must have been the boy's heels on the stone as this little brat railed at him. But she said, "You didn't what?"

"Didn't come to rescue *him*," Kyale said stoutly as Senrid stilled, his head turning slowly from side to side. "I came to rescue my brother."

"Then let us leave Senrid where he is, and we shall see if Leander will enjoy this reunion."

The woman made a dainty gesture. A couple of guards in gray jackets tromped in and each grabbed one of Kyale's arms.

Kyale had just enough time to glimpse Senrid stretching out on his bench, crossing his arms, and closing his eyes. Then she was yanked back to the room with the table, and through another door that Kyale hadn't seen. In the center of this new room extended a wooden pole from floor to ceiling, with Leander shackled to it. He looked grubby and tired, and she could smell stale sweat in the airless room, but otherwise he seemed unharmed.

Kyale soon understood why, when Dejain marched up to him, pulled a dagger from her sleeve, and rammed it with all her strength straight for Leander's heart.

Kyale sucked in her breath to scream, but gasped instead when the point of the dagger turned away as though it had hit an invisible wall.

When Leander looked up, he saw Kyale, and he flinched as if that dagger had smashed right into his chest.

Dejain turned to her. "Try it," she said, pressing the dagger into Kyale's hand.

Kyale promptly threw the thing on the floor.

Dejain whipped her hand around and slapped Kyale across the face, knocking her to the ground in a welter of lavender skirts.

"Ouch," Dejain mourned, wringing her hand. "I prefer my minions for such exertions, but you get the idea, don't you? And you, Leander. Detlev has his mark on Senrid, for some inexplicable reason, but no one cares what happens to this stupid brat. Except, presumably, you. Should you like to watch me carve her up, hmm?"

Kyale had gotten to her hands and knees, but not fast enough. One of the guards yanked her to her feet by the back of her gown, pulling her long hair painfully in the process. Angry tears burned Kyale's eyes as once again, the knife was gravely pressed into her hand.

Trembling all over, she extended the knife, but slowly, hoping that the same magic would prevent her from touching the thing to Leander.

It did—the point slid away as if it had encountered glass, and clattered on the stone floor. The guard bent and picked it up before Kyale could gather enough wit to grab it again and use it to defend herself.

"What artifact created that ward?" Dejain asked.

To Kyale's surprise, the woman was addressing her. Oh, of course. Leander hadn't answered, and she couldn't make him.

"I don't know," Kyale said as rudely as she dared.

"Then it's time to get Leander to talk," Dejain said, and gestured to one of the guards. "Cut off one of her fingers. We'll throw it at Leander and see if it touches him either physically or emotionally, shall we?"

Sparks glittered in front of Kyale's eyes as she pulled her hands tightly to her waist—where her thumb grazed a hard knot. The transfer token! She could get away!

Not without Leander, she thought as a wooden-faced guard

reached for her.

Greenish light flashed, and the man's hand slid away as if he'd run into window glass.

Kyale backed up a step, then another. Both guards lunged at her, but they couldn't reach her. Somebody had put a spell on her! She stuck out her tongue so hard that the roots hurt.

Dejain frowned, looking around as if she could sense whoever it was watching from a magical window. Kyale ran around in a circle, trying to reach Leander.

"Get Senrid," Leander yelled, his voice cracking. "Get Senrid!"

Kyale made a break for the door, slammed through it, ran through the table room, and burst into the room where Senrid sat on the bench, his hands on his knees, his feet planted apart as if he meant to leap up.

Kyale grabbed hold of him with one hand, and with the other, pushed the transfer button onto his palm. She glanced back over her shoulder, whispering "Hurry hurry hurry," forgetting he could not hear her.

The door slammed open, the guards spreading out, hands wide as they slowly closed in, wary of more magic spells — it had taken Dejain three increasingly dire threats to get them to come at all.

Unaware of them, Senrid fingered the object Kyale had pressed into his hand. He knew that shape: it was one of his shirt shank buttons, with two spells on it, ostensibly for Leander to shift to Marloven Hess, and then to return. But with the addition of three words, Senrid could use the token to shift two people.

Muttering the emendation spell, he plunged his hand to the floor between his feet, and closed his hands around the books. With his other hand he clamped his fingers around Kyale's wrist, and transferred them both, a heartbeat before the guards closed in.

Their hands snatched air.

Senrid and Kyale jolted painfully to the floor in Senrid's study as if a giant hand had swatted them straight into a wall.

Senrid shuddered with relief. He couldn't hear, but he knew the familiar smells of paper, ink, old books, the spring air of home with a strong whiff of horse.

Dizziness and nausea whooshed through him, and he sank to his knees gratefully.

"I've got 'em," Senrid whispered from the floor, the books gripped to his chest. Then he lifted his head, staring sightlessly upward, and said in a low voice, "Kyale, I appreciate the rescue, but if you had left those books there I would have sent you back to fetch them. You should never have touched them."

"You left Leander behind!" Kyale screamed, then remembered he couldn't hear.

She reached for one of his hands, ready to spell out insults on his palm, but Senrid clawed shaking fingers through his filthy hair. "Kyale, we've got to get rid of them before . . ." *Before that woman tries to trade them for Leander's life.* Rescuing Leander would have to come after he regained sight and hearing, but first he had to lose these damn books. He knew Leander would agree.

He stretched out his hand, palm up, his fingers trembling so much that she saw the gesture as a plea, and not as a command, so she touched his disgusting, grimy and sweaty fingers. She shuddered as he closed his hand around hers and transferred.

It was, to her, another long transfer, every bit as terrible as the previous two. She came out of it with a pounding headache, and discovered herself in a forest.

CJ of the Mearsieans was walking along a forest path, kicking leaves. In his desperation, at the limits of his strength, Senrid used dark magic and fixed on her as a Destination. That was dangerous. Deadly, if the target person was in a confined space, or carried certain kinds of deadly wards.

The wild surge of air from transfer magic startled CJ, knocking her onto the grass. "Kyale? Senrid?"

Senrid sank down, entirely spent.

"CJ!" Kyale exclaimed, shuddering with residual transfer reaction.

"What are you two doing here?"

"Ask this slob," Kyale said, jerking her thumb at Senrid, who sat there, head down, one hand stiff at his side, the other clutching two thin books. "Well, except you can't, because he doesn't hear. Or see. We just got away from Norsunder Base."

"Kyale," Senrid said, turning his head from side to side. "Are we with CJ of the Mearsieans?"

CJ's annoyance vanished. She scrambled to her hands and knees, took Senrid's hand, and shook it up and down.

Senrid sighed with relief. "CJ, get Jilo. Don't have the strength to transfer there." And he did not want to attempt Chwahirsland without being able to see or hear.

"Oh, please, no more transfers," Kyale said. "I feel sick."

"Come on, let's go inside," CJ said— to no reaction from Senrid. So she plucked his sleeve, tugged, and he got slowly to his feet.

Kyale trailed, complaining about Senrid having left Leander behind in favor of some stupid books. CJ heard one word in five as she watched Senrid narrowly, and wished Clair were there to sort this mess out.

CJ kept a slow pace for Senrid's benefit as she led the way to the cave entrance, and down the tunnel into the Mearsieans' underground hideout. She pushed Senrid toward the pile of brightly colored pillows scattered around a yarn rug worked in rainbow hues.

Senrid sank down gratefully, saying in a cracked voice, "Water." He clutched the books against him.

"Get his water, Kyale, will you? I have to figure out a way to send a message to Jilo. There's corn bread in the basket, if you're hungry." She vanished.

Kyale entered the little kitchen annex, which Clair had fitted up with magical aids, like the stone jug that transferred water from the nearby stream. Kyale poured out a cup of water, took it back, and pressed it into Senrid's free hand, then went back for a corn muffin. After a hesitation, she got a second one, which she brought back to Senrid.

When she saw the empty cup, she went back and refilled it, annoyed that she couldn't unload her feelings onto him. Where were the rest of the Mearsiean girls? The place felt deserted.

Senrid had devoured his muffin in two bites. Kyale split hers in half, grudgingly pushed one half into his grimy hand, and sat on the opposite side of the rug, nibbling at her muffin and feeling very ill-used.

Twelve

Chwahirsland

JILO RUBBED HIS EYES more forcefully, surprised when his fingers slid over his eyelids as if someone had squirted them with a gritty oil. He brought his hands away and blinked stupidly at the blood smears on his fingertips. His eyelids were bleeding. Could eyelids bleed? Of course they could, because it was happening.

I've been here too long.

He blinked, and his eyelids clung to one another stickily for a heartbeat, burning like fire. He reached for a cup of water. His cup was there, but it was dry. He did not remember drinking the last of it.

He performed the spell that brought more water from the well. He drank most of it, then dipped his fingers in the rest, and gently rubbed them over his eyelids. The cool water gave him a moment of relief, but the fire flared immediately after.

He sat back, taking a deep breath. He had a vague memory of

rubbing his eyes more frequently, each time with increased impatience, followed by the sting that he seemed never to escape.

He pressed his palms against the top of his eyes just below his brow ridge and rubbed. Had he thought that before? The chamber was always gray, midway between day and night, light and shadow. The air seemed to move slowly, laden dust, or ash, or stone.

Stone. His skull felt like stone. Stone . . . gray . . . something about gray . . .

A distant pang of panic came with memory. He brought his hands up before his eyes, and looked at his fingernails. They were blurry . . . gray.

The alarm was sufficient to get him to his feet, and carry him the few steps toward the access to the space-within-space, the heart of Wan-Edhe's attempt to create a pocket Norsunder. But when he perceived a human figure wavering in the diffuse light, he jolted to a halt.

He blinked rapidly, but the figure remained a blur, vaguely man-shaped. Jilo hesitated as the figure appeared to grow. No, it was coming closer.

A hand seized him by the wrist and yanked him through the access. His body endured the wrench, and then he stepped free.

His lungs expanded, and the sense of release was so intense he nearly fell. He gazed wit-flown into an obviously Chwahir face: pale skin, light blue eyes, short curly black hair. He was not much taller than Jilo, nor that much older, barely beyond the threshold of adulthood.

"Prince Kessler," Jilo croaked.

"It was you who removed the Venn books?"

"Yes."

"What," the young man said in a soft, whispery voice, "possessed you to hand off those books? The mage Dejain at Norsunder Base very nearly got them. She would have if I had not been watching her."

Jilo sank down onto a nearby chair, sick with horror. Numbly, he said, "It looked like Senrid's ancestral language. He's helped me. Knows as much magic as I do. Maybe more, in certain areas. I thought he could tell me what it was."

"You could learn the Venn runes, as I did. And keep your mouth shut."

"For what purpose?" Jilo prompted, fear lending him a little strength. "What's in those books?"

"Among other things, spells for mirror wards, using blood magic. The most powerful wards that exist, and the most dangerous to make. Anyone who discovers the books' existence will willingly murder to learn any one of those wards," Kessler said, casting an appreciative glance around. "You're not ordinarily stupid. I can see that you've destroyed an appreciable portion of Wan-Edhe's labors."

"I still have much to do," Jilo said, swallowing with difficulty. "And it's . . ." He touched his eyelids, then swayed as belatedly he realized his danger.

Jilo had always thought he was prepared for the inevitable, but now that death was here, a sick thrill chilled his nerves. Renegade Prince Kessler last summer had led a Norsundrian force in burning and killing across Everon.

Kessler said, "Spend too long in there and it will kill you."

Jilo blinked slowly, surprised to find himself still alive. Impelled by a heady sense of irony, he said, "Before Army Command gets me?"

Kessler said, "So you have been using the spy windows?"

"No." Jilo hunched a shoulder. "I meant to take those out next. After . . ." He made a vague wave toward the non-space he'd been attempting to dispel — de-spell — from within. "After that."

"Why would you destroy the spy windows?" Kessler asked. "Since you know half the upper command is conspiring against you."

"Only half?" Jilo flopped his arms in a shrug. "I thought they'd *all* come after me. Once they were convinced that Wan-Edhe wasn't coming back." He was so very tired and hungry, and it took effort to talk.

"Why are you doing it?" Kessler asked.

Why indeed? Jilo groped in the air in an effort to explain what he couldn't even explain to himself. "Because I hate Wan-Edhe. I like undoing his magic. I'm not good at anything else. He's got a Norsunder pocket in there. Do you know how he feeds magic into it? It's sucking out the lives of everyone in the castle. It was spreading to the entire city."

He gulped for air. "If you're going to kill me. Take Chwahirsland. Just do it."

"I don't want Chwahirsland." Kessler's laugh was voiceless, a huff. "I've better game. But Dejain, who will never be more than an organizer, thinks she'll gain power by going after the old Venn magic. I'll handle her. But you might want to use those books against your enemies. Because you're going to have enough of those."

"You mean enemies from Norsunder?" Jilo asked.

"*And* the rotten faction in the army." Another voiceless laugh, and Kessler vanished.

Jilo sat where he was, counting breaths until he could stand without black spots swimming before his eyes. He remembered that he'd ordered a meal to be waiting, and trudged to the antechamber, which seemed a very long way away. . .

The stale bread and hard cheese tasted like it had been sitting for a week, but chewing his way through it revived him enough to enable him to retreat to his room, where he touched the notecase out of habit. To his surprise, he found a letter in an unfamiliar hand.

Jilo, Senrid is here and needs your help. Do you know how to reverse a spell making people blind and deaf? CJ

Jilo looked around, feeling marginally better. He was going to need to sleep, but at least he could do this much.

He shuffled to Wan-Edhe's magic study, where he found the tall book he sought. It was the volume wherein the evil old man had recorded his magical experiments on people, Jilo included.

Mearsies Heili

Senrid longed for sleep, but he held himself upright, testing the world through scents. He was reassured by the dusty-puppy smells of other kids. He kept his eyes closed against the blindness, until a sharp pang shot through his skull, splashing glittering lights across his vision. Sound impacted his head, resolving into a girl's high voice and the nasal twang of a teenage boy whose voice was on the verge of breaking. Blurred sight resolved into familiarity: CJ and Jilo standing over him. He didn't see Kyale, for which he was grateful.

"What happened?" Jilo asked. He looked even worse than Senrid felt.

Senrid forced out the shortest report he could contrive, beginning with his own stupidity for blundering into the magical trap. "Then Kyale found the books on my desk and took them with her into Norsunder."

Jilo blanched, even though he could see the books right there in Senrid's grip.

"But I brought them along. Here. You'd better take them away again." Senrid thrust the books into Jilo's hands. "I think that hole into damnation Wan-Edhe made in your castle is the only place Norsunder can't get at 'em. There must be tracers on at least one of those books, because a mage at Norsunder Base seems to have come after Leander within a day or so after our meeting in Colend, then set a trap for me. Hibern wouldn't blab. Neither would Thad or Karhin."

Jilo nodded awkwardly.

Senrid said, "Whatever is in these books, those who want them are playing for very high stakes, and using the likes of us for markers."

"I know." Jilo breathed the words. He considered telling Senrid about his strange conversation with Kessler Sonscarna, but he was too tired. "Thanks."

Both he and Senrid had just enough strength to transfer to their homes.

Jilo stumbled to the archive, returned the books where he had found them, then went to sleep.

His dreams were troubled. On waking, he returned to the archive, and was not surprised to find the books gone again. A short note waited on the table, in Chwahir: *You had your chance.*

He would stake anything that was Prince Kessler's hand.

Norsunder Base

Leander's head throbbed. His shoulders ached from trying to keep his wrists still so that the shackles wouldn't abrade his skin any worse.

He closed his eyes against Dejain's angry voice as she alternated questions with increasingly dire threats. He had long ago stopped telling her he didn't know the answers to any of them, and tried not to think of what would happen when the mysterious ward wore away.

Abruptly she stuttered to a stop, her head turning sharply toward the door.

A faint whiff of singed metal made Leander sneeze. Dejain rushed out of the room, the pink ribbons on her gown fluttering, leaving him alone with the two big guards on either side, both with weapons in hand.

The inner door swung open and in stepped a slim, black-haired young man no more than half a hand taller than Leander, dressed plainly in sun-bleached linen shirt and black trousers stuffed into riding boots. Not Marloven. He was too pale, and the trousers did not have the tan stripe down the sides. The shirt laced in the front instead of buttoning with shanks. He carried a knife in either hand, and when he saw the two guards, he smiled as he settled into an attack stance.

Leander shut his eyes to a fight he could do nothing about; a grunting gasp caused him to open them as the big man fell, hand pressed to red staining his gray tunic. A feint, a short vicious jab and the second man sprawled dead across the doorway.

The young man left his knives in the dead guards and stepped up to Leander. He traced a sigil in the air with two fingers. Green glittered and Leander sensed a spell breaking. The man unlocked the shackle, which dropped to the ground as Leander wibbled questions that went ignored.

The rescuer slapped a transfer token against Leander's chest, and transfer magic shoved him out of Norsunder and into his study, leaving him gasping for breath, and full of questions that no one could answer.

One thing was clear: though this terrifying experience was life and death to him, it was only a game to that young man with the flat blue gaze who didn't even say who he was, or why he'd rescued Leander.

While back at Norsunder Base, Dejain reached her private study, to discover she'd been decoyed. She ran all the way back to the prison cell, to find Leander gone.

She lifted her skirts and stepped delicately around in a circle, staring at the two dead men. One killed quickly, the other, the big torturer, gutted and left to die in agony, a black-handed Chwahir knife lying nearby.

That was personal.

There was only one person who knew the lower-level flunkies, who had been one himself, and had been studying magic in secret: the renegade Chwahir Prince Kessler Sonscarna.

Dejain slammed out of the room, incandescent with rage. Kessler! She had never thought to lay tracers for him. Once he'd escaped the blood-knife bond on him, she'd thought he would never come anywhere near Norsunder Base.

Even worse, since it was undoubtedly he who'd freed Leander, surely he'd wrenched the location of the books out of the brat first.

She retreated to her private chamber, and paused, laughing. This fashion for using brats? She believed that children were essentially useless, but Kessler had liked them when they were smart and ambitious. She'd always thought that his worst weakness.

She could use that now.

In Vasande Leror, Leander gathered all his strength and cast a protective ward around his desk. No one would come near it until he had the strength to remove the dark magic from the papers. Then he would set up more protections . . . but that could wait.

He also sent a message to Senrid to report his safety. He was certain that Senrid had taken the books away—he would have himself, rather than let Dejain get them. But he also suspected that Senrid would be trying to find a way to come for Leander.

That done, he walked through his cleaning frame, which snapped away the grime of Norsunder Base and the grit in the cuts around his wrists. Though of course the spell did nothing for those cuts. He dug around for a pair of clean handkerchiefs, wrapped them around his wrists, yanked his sleeves down, then headed for the stairs.

He found small staff gathered in the kitchen, all faces worried. When they saw him, everyone burst out talking, exclaiming relief, and concern over how terrible he looked. He kept repeating, "I'm fine, I'm fine," though nobody seemed to believe him. To Llhei's shocked gaze he said, "Being home is a better elixir than any mere nostrum."

"At least you must eat. Then rest," Llhei ordered with all the firmness of moral authority.

"I'd love to do both."

The kitchen staff whirled about preparing him a meal as he told Alaxandar and the others where he'd been, omitting only the nature of the books, as that was still a guess. Better not to start rumors he couldn't prove, and that he wouldn't be able to stop.

"Where is Kyale?" he asked, as hot food was set before him.

"We don't know," Llhei said, her joy dimming. "We think she went somewhere by magic to seek you."

Leander shut his eyes. "The food had better wait, then . . ."

At that moment, in Mearsies Heili, Kyale was tired of a horrible adventure for which no one seemed grateful, and relieved that both Jilo and Senrid were gone. She finished her hot chocolate, then said to CJ, "Can you send me home?"

"You teach me your Destination, and I can do the spell," CJ said.

It was the last transfer of a long and terrible day. Kyale's stomach lurched, and her head pounded. She wanted nothing more than to go to bed, but she forced herself to start downstairs, mentally rehearsing a speech to get that sour-faced Alaxandar to take her seriously, when she paused on the stairs.

Familiar voices echoed up the stairwell. "Leander?" she gasped, and ran the rest of the way down, her fatigue forgotten.

It was Leander himself, surrounded by the entire staff. He looked as tired as she felt, but he smiled with relief. "Kyale! I was about to fetch a transfer token to go find you. Senrid?"

"He's home." Kyale was about to rant about Senrid, when she remembered those stupid books. It would be just *like* Leander to gang up with Senrid against her, as if mildewed old tomes were more important than her. "What happened to you? How did you get out?"

"Not by my own efforts. I was rescued by some enemy of Dejain's. His was the same magic signature that put the protective spell on me."

"That's creepy. But that spell?" Kyale said. "In your study. That made us go to that nasty place."

"Warded, and will be gone by tomorrow."

"Good," Kyale snapped.

Leander looked around at the circle of faces, trying to hide that sickening sense of being not only outmatched, but ignorant. He made an effort. "Come on, we were just about to have dinner. And maybe we ought to order your favorite dessert, Kyale. I think you're wonderful for trying to come to the rescue, but I hope you'll never do that again . . ."

Marloven Hess

On getting home, Senrid walked through his cleaning frame, stuck his head out to alert a surprised, relieved runner that he was back, then opened his notecase while he waited for Keriam, who would surely be on his way from wherever he was to give Senrid the trimming he deserved.

He discovered a note from Leander stating that he was home safe, and that he'd found and eradicated the magical trap. Senrid stared stupidly at Leander's note, relief making him giddy. The worst agony of the whole pointless nightmare was the inward wrestling between duty — staying put in Marloven Hess — and a different sense of duty, a personal one he couldn't explain, which was to return to Norsunder Base and free Leander. Somehow.

The study door opened, and Senrid dropped Leander's note.

"It was a magical trap," Senrid said, recognizing in Keriam's haggard face the long watches of worry. "No use in details. The result was, I was stupid."

Senrid stopped there. Keriam waited. Each was aware in his own way of the conflict of position and expectation: king and sworn man, boy and adult; the genuine affection that brought Keriam to guardianship, and brought Senrid to rely on it.

The sworn man could not question, the adult might question, the guardian had to question, and Senrid, sensing the conflict, forced himself to say, "I know my stunt in the last open interview was witless — I'm sure you heard all about it — as witless as my walking into a magical trap after Leander." Then he addressed the real question underlying everything. "But adults make stupid mistakes, too. Look, Keriam, releasing the Child Spell isn't going to make me into one of my smarter ancestors, and I do want to get rid of it."

"But you don't."

"I told you why. You know what one of those Norsundrians said? That Detlev is waiting. For *me*. For some damned experiment. What can it be, but waiting for me to reach manhood?"

"You don't think he doesn't notice you're not growing?"

"No one knows what he notices or doesn't. But think about it, he's been alive four thousand years. More than that. But he obviously hasn't spent them in the world. I don't think years mean anything to him — that is, the way they have meaning for us. He pops in and out of time, and I mean for him to keep seeing me as a boy, unworthy of his attention. That's what he said, when I was a prisoner the first time at Norsunder Base, *You are not yet worth my time.* I don't want to ever be worth his time."

Keriam gazed into Senrid's taut face, the circles under his eyes, the visible bruises under the grime. His heart contracted fiercely. He had no sons of his own — the closest was his grand-nephew, Aldren, who he rarely saw since he'd left the academy. He regarded the boys who came through the academy as his sons for eight seasons.

Senrid had become the surrogate son he'd never thought to have, the bond stronger because it went both ways. He sensed that Senrid, who trusted few, had come to regard him in light of a father.

But there were still their relative positions. He knew exactly who watched him, and why. Marloven history was full of sudden and bloody ends of regents or guardians who had assumed too much power.

So he said only, "The guilds have agreed to consider last summer as a war expense."

He watched the slight easing of the tension in Senrid's young face, and rejoiced at this small triumph.

"They did?" Senrid's voice lightened. "Already?"

"Yes. But the underlying cause of the debate was a conflict between the civs — including two jarls — and the guilds, who know exactly whose animals belong to whom. It seems that most of these enterprising citizens were trying to get the guilds to pay for shoeing their animals, and when they wouldn't, they thought you might be inveigled into it."

Senrid winced. "I did not see that."

And you didn't ask me, Keriam thought, but kept that to himself. Senrid was testing his authority, and it was right for him to do so. Keriam had to accept that the young king was going to make mistakes, but Senrid was a fast learner.

None faster.

If he managed to stay alive.

"I suggest a bath and some sleep. There's plenty to report, but nothing that can't wait until morning."

Senrid's eyes briefly closed, and Keriam wondered what emotion the boy had shuttered away.

A quick step, and Senrid was gone.

PART TWO

One

Everon

REL STEPPED GRATEFULLY OUT of the sheeting rain, and ducked under the lintel into a big room built around a stove.

"Thee-ann-ra!"

The first person Rel saw was Commander Roderic Dei's wife Seiran, now duchas of Valenn after the death of her cousin the first day of the war, and her father the old duchas among the last defenders. Seiran was chasing a naked baby around the stove.

Commander Dei, two steps in front of Rel, swooped and caught up the child, who shrieked surprise at the feel of rain-cold hands grasping her middle.

"Chilly, eh?" Commander Dei said genially to the toddler, who sucked in a breath to howl. "Serves you right!" He plopped the child into her mother's arms. "Bath time, Sei?"

"As you see. You may take over," Seiran added crisply. "I've a thousand letters to write." She handed the child back and marched through the door opposite the entry, her white-streaked brown hair swinging over her water-splotched linen outer robe.

Commander Dei indicated a bench. "D'you know anything about bathing brats?" he asked Rel.

"There's a first time for everything."

"I'll help." That was Carinna, Commander Dei's eldest, a quiet, coltish girl whose narrow face seemed more Delieth than Dei.

What had seemed a room full of very small children resolved, with Carina's help, into five. The three of them got her two small sisters, two cousins, and the cook's little one through the wooden tube, into sleeping gear, and carried up into the loft, where Carinna promised to tell them the story of Peddler Antivad and the time he was turned into a cat.

Her voice could barely be made out rising and falling softly under the steady beat of rain on the roof, as Commander Dei and Rel sat down near the stove. This was the first warm rain of spring, but they were wet, and the last trace of winter's chill lingered in the old stone of the cottage.

A servant brought in supper, welcome and hot, and set it on the bench. "Honor Seiran said you can empty the tub and use it for a table, for she's using the other for the queen's correspondence," the woman stated, and withdrew to the room beyond.

With an apologetic air the commander fetched the water-wand from the wall, waved it over the tub, and when the water vanished, he replaced the wand carefully while Rel rolled the tub over. It made a broad table, though one couldn't get one's legs under it.

As the two set the dishes out on it, Rel reflected on Commander Dei's once-beautiful home located along the main street below the palace. It had been smoothly run, elegant, quiet. But that noble house was now rubble, half the servants dead, others nowhere to be found.

This small circular house, built around the stove in a manner found all over the south, had been left untouched. Rel hoped it belonged to one of the voices he heard in the far room; he hated to think of another family gone, ripped to lifelessness by Norsundrian steel.

They ate in silence, then the commander said, "I thank you for your help, but it seems that Prince Glenn has tired of his hunt for future Knights, and his current intent — unless the queen returns —

is to pick his favorites among the candidates and form an elite guard around himself."

"Glenn wants to defeat Norsunder," Rel began slowly.

Commander Dei regarded Rel with weary patience. They both knew the truth: Glenn wanted glorious bloodshed. And Norsunder was his target. One could blame the war, and it certainly had done no good, but Glenn had always been that way. Neither of his parents had been bloodthirsty.

Feeling his way toward understanding, Rel said, "He's very angry about his father's death. To find the king lying there, among his defenders . . ."

"I understand the thirst for revenge," Commander Dei said. "He may very well be the king, soon, if his mother does not survive being a prisoner in Norsunder. And I understand his wish for an honor guard to keep him safe. Perhaps it'll be good for him. Discipline is always good."

Rel acknowledged that. "Here's what puzzles me. He grew up knowing that his mother had earned a Knighthood before she and the king married, but Glenn didn't want girl candidates. Though he accepted one or two when he saw their prowess."

"I can deal with that," Commander Dei said. "Half of those boys he sent me are already on their way back home. He knows that there's a winnowing process, and a high-ranking family name means little in the practice ring. Are there any you particularly recommend?"

Rel thought back. "Yes. The two sisters, black-haired, the ones with country accents. I forget their names. The elder rides like a centaur, and the youngest is very, very quick. They're quiet but they learn fast."

Commander Dei said, "I'll watch for them."

"There was another Glenn took a liking to, in spite of a foreign accent. His name was Luh, Lah . . Laban. Lah-BANN. He was particular about the pronunciation, objecting to the Sartoran LAY-ban."

"That pronunciation almost sounds Colendi. Except I've never heard a name like that from Colend."

Rel said apologetically, "Well, Glenn seems to think this Laban a runaway noble from Colend, or thereabouts, though Laban refused to talk about his background. Anyway, he seems quick, and on his first try-out he hit the target with both knife and bow every time. But on the second test, once everyone had shot, his skill wasn't nearly as good, for whatever reason. Maybe trying too hard. He does seem eager to learn."

"All right, I'll watch for him, too." The commander pushed away his empty plate and sat back. "So to you. You said you came to a purpose. Now is the time to speak."

Rel said, "When I first visited Everon, I always thought you recognized me. This was why you accepted me, and invited me to join the Knights."

Commander Dei's grizzled brows rose. "Of course I recognized you, and I'll go so far as to say that for the sake of your family I hoped you'd show half the talents you subsequently did. But that ended at your candidacy. I can assure you that your invitation to join the Knights was entirely a result of your own merit."

"My family," Rel repeated wonderingly, not hearing the compliments. Could it possibly be this easy? He was aware of a painful thought: if it were so easy, why was he so easily abandoned? *No suppositions.* "That's why I'm here. I'm on a search for my father."

Commander Dei's eyebrows rose even higher. "What? Is he lost, then?" Quick sorrow. "Was he fighting for us, and here am I, not knowing?"

Rel shook his head. "No, no. At least, I have no idea. I'm trying to find out where he is. *Who* he is."

Roderic Dei could not look any more amazed than he already did. "I thought you knew that!"

"I told you my background when we first met."

"I thought the shepherd's son from Tser Mearsies was a fiction."

Now it was Rel's turn for amazement. "A fiction! Why would I do that?"

Commander Dei made a large gesture. "Because of the Chwahir connection. Which was why I never trespassed with questions that I otherwise was eager to ask."

Rel shut his teeth on the impulse to yell *What Chwahir connection?*

The commander had seen his reaction to the word, and misinterpreted it as defensiveness. "There're so many who hate the Chwahir, hate anyone connected with them even tangentially. I hasten to add, I never counted myself among their number." He laughed. "How could I, with my infamous name?"

Rel said, "Will you begin at the beginning?"

Commander Dei paused, as hail roared on the roof overhead then passed as abruptly as it had begun. "What do you know?" he asked cautiously.

Rel repeated what Raneseh had told him. The commander listened closely, then shook his head. "What I know is little enough, but you shall have it. I met your mother through my sister, who I believe I once told you was a mage. She died in the battle over those evil Ancient Sartoran dyra magical artifacts, before Detlev appeared and forced Everon into enchantment for his own ends."

Rel said, "I remember that much. So my mother died in that battle, too?"

"No. She was murdered. Her maid, a Chwahir woman as well, insisted it was assassination, but if she said any more, it was not to me. I don't think I would ever have known even that much, except that this maid came to our house in the middle of the night, begging sanctuary. She was carrying you, an infant. It was soon after your mother was killed, you see. So I had you with me for a time, until your father reappeared."

Rel sat forward, wondering if he now knew the cause of his sense of familiarity with Everon. "Go on."

"There's so little to tell, I'm afraid. He helped us in the first battle— fought well, but when Detlev turned up and ruined our efforts with a few spells, he was off again, some said to his home on another continent altogether. "

"Did he give you his name?"

"We knew him only as Glenred. In fact, it was in honor of your father that the king chose an older form of his name, Glenn, for his son. Glenred saved Berthold's life at one particularly tight spot. Glenred was a big man." Commander Dei touched his chest and shoulders. "Strong, brave, gallant . . . very well trained. Spoke with an accent. I knew that Glenred was a false name, as was his wife's. Glenred made it clear that they had been on the run. They vanished, and I knew nothing until the night the maid showed up with you."

Commander Dei paused, memory bringing back that late night, the rain dripping the way it was now, only cold, with winter coming on. The maid, her clothes blood-splashed, her black Chwahir eyes huge in her pale face as she whispered, *Her last command was to entrust the babe to you. Will you call him your own, if his father cannot come for him?*

Commander Dei had said, *And you?*

I will follow the assassin back to the homeland, and he who gave the order, and I will kill him if I can.

The commander sighed. "Her words, so low-spoke I almost couldn't hear them, carried all the, oh, the resonance of a vow. What could I do but agree? Though at that time I wasn't married, and lived in barracks. It was in fact because of you that I dared to approach Seiran." Commander Dei smiled reminiscently.

Rel waited, and presently the commander blinked away old memories and glanced up. "But scarcely were we married, and you accustomed to us, and beginning to learn words — you were already friends with the horses, small as you were — well, your father turned up one day, grief-stricken, took you away that very day, and I never saw him again. When you turned up all those years later, I knew you at once, for we'd had you nearly a year. But when you claimed to be a shepherd's son . . ."

Commander Dei drained his spiced wine and set down his cup precisely in the center of his plate. "It was clear enough that whatever the story was, it had no happy ending. So I left it to you to speak, or not, as you chose."

Rel pressed his hands on the tub's rough underside, as if catching the prickly grain against the pads of his fingers would make that heady sense of unreality feel real. Chwahir? Old battles over magical artifacts? Detlev?

He looked up. "Did the maid also use a false name?"

"I don't know. But when your father showed up that day, he asked if Iog Shunsu had brought you. I can hear him as if it were yesterday."

"Iog Shunsu," Rel repeated. "Iog, that sounds like a Chwahir name."

"Is it? I'm not surprised. All I know about her is that she was born in a small fishing village on the estuary of a great river. Well, if you go searching, I hope you find her, or Glenred." Commander Dei hesitated, not wanting to sound discouraging. That old story was bleak enough. "I'd give much to clasp his hand again."

"Thanks," Rel said.

Two

Norsunder Base

DEJAIN WAS NOT GOING to let the prize of the century slip away.

Her spies reported that Kessler was holed up where no one could find him.

That was because they did not know him the way she did.

She called in one of the soul-bound and gave him exact instructions. She had kept notes on all her magical workings from the time she'd aided Kessler in his mad scheme to replace all the kings of two continents with his own people, chosen by what he deemed to be merit. Among those notes were all the transfer Destinations she'd set up for Kessler's summary recruitments, such as a certain dell near those tiresome Mearsiean urchins' underground hideout.

It was easy enough to put her soul-bound there, and have him wait.

More dangerous was Siamis, who was moving around in an

unsettling way. No one seemed to know where he'd gone, but rumor put him most often up in Bereth Ferian. Which made sense, as a delve into the archives had furnished the information that the Federation of Kingdoms up there, and their mages, had bound the Venn magic onto the Arrow, whatever that was. But the northerners had successfully suppressed the actual identities of the mages, as well as the Arrow.

Dejain needed to act before Siamis returned to Norsunder Base either triumphant, in which case he'd be deadly — or empty-handed, in which case he'd be in a deadly mood.

Only one bit of relief: Detlev was still gone, and as yet seemed not to have missed his spy's report. But she could not count on him staying safely in Norsunder-Beyond for another century or two of real time.

As she worked, occasionally she checked her soul-bound minion through her scry glass. The soul-bound warrior's patience was unlimited, as his will was suborned, but Dejain's was not. Her anxiety had smoldered into anger by the time that stupid Mearsiean brat *finally* turned up.

Mearsies Heili to the Northwest Wilds of Drael

Unaware and unsuspicious, CJ had diligently remained in the white palace every morning in case anyone wanted an interview, but no one had. As a succession of days passed, earlier and earlier she found excuses to transfer to the forest below for ever-longer rambles in the woods.

One morning she decided to skip it altogether. She ran about as a fresh spring breeze rustled the leaves overhead. She remembered this dell as the place where they met the horrible PJ. Over there was the great hollow tree, her third favorite place for hide and seek games. That oak there was where Clair's cousin Puddlenose had first arrived, dressed as a girl as he ran away from a band of Chwahir . . . and here was the nasty place where the gang was scooped up by Kessler's snatch-and-grab team when he was looking for kids to —

The old habit of wariness had relaxed. She was still lost in memory when a footfall crunched a twig behind her. She had just enough time to whirl around, gulping a breath to yell, when a clammy hand closed on her wrist and dark magic flung her to the stone floor of a castle that smelled like dust and mold.

Dizzy and nauseated from the joint-twisting wrench of dark magic, CJ knew she was in trouble. The faint metal singe of a dark magic transfer was replaced by the dank smell of moldy stone.

She had time to take in one shuddering breath before someone grabbed her arm, catching hanks of her hair, and yanked her to her feet. Tears blurred her eyes as she was thrust out of the transfer chamber and into a room, where she sprawled on the stone floor. She scrambled up, flung her hair back — and stared aghast when she recognized Dejain's golden hair and pretty features.

Dejain said, "You are going to Kessler to retrieve two books."

At the sound of Kessler's name, CJ blanched. "I hate him," she retorted, her voice thin with rage. "I won't! He's even more evil than you are."

"'Evil,'" Dejain drawled scornfully as she gazed down into angry blue eyes. She recognized herself nearly a century ago, and loathed the tiresome brat the more for it. "No one here is the least impressed with your self-righteous fatuity. I know you. I *was* you, once." And as CJ's eyes widened, and she scrambled to her feet to strike a belligerent pose, Dejain smiled. "Except that I was far smarter. Someday you'll be standing right here, probably listening to some fool blather lighter idiocy, and you'll want to . . ." Irritated by the obstinate jut of that childish chin, she gave in to impulse and slapped the brat across the face with all her strength.

The sting hurt Dejain at least as much as it did CJ. Dejain suppressed the urge to wring her hand, staring with satisfaction at the red finger marks on the brat's face. *How* she abhorred the young, so ignorant, yet so utterly full of themselves.

"Now, shut your mouth and listen. Because I don't care if you end up dead. I'll just fetch another of you." As CJ backed away, gaze flicking at the door, Dejain signed to the guard to flank her. "If you make me exert myself, I'll take great pleasure in watching him break a few bones."

CJ stilled, her heart beating in her ears.

Dejain said, "Kessler is untraceable. I am going to attempt to transfer you directly to him. Yes, I know you know how very dangerous that is, which is why I would never attempt transferring myself."

She paused to enjoy the dawning awareness of helplessness in the brat's face. "I'm wagering he'll be curious enough to permit you access, but if he doesn't, I'll know not to try that with the next one of you brats I catch. I want those blood magic books. I am going to have those books. Either he gives them to you, or tells you where I can find them."

Dejain signed to the guard, who grabbed CJ by the arms.

Dejain carefully lifted a dagger from a side table. She enjoyed the way CJ's face slackened with terror as she recognized the greenish glint along the edge. "Yes. You know what this is: a blood-binding spell."

As she spoke she advanced deliberately, and though CJ stamped her bare toes on the guard's booted foot, and writhed, Dejain gripped the handle and slashed down, slicing the knife along CJ's arm.

She watched as blood beaded up, staining CJ's white sleeve.

"Excellent. I now have access to you by magic. And I will visit you every night, at the traditional eleventh hour, when you are weakest and our magic strongest, until you have accomplished my will."

CJ held her breath against a sob. She wouldn't break before this horrible woman, and give her the satisfaction. She *wouldn't*.

"You cannot do magic," Dejain went on, "or it will mirror back and destroy you. If you survive Kessler but do not do what I want, I will make you pay for it. If you run, I will make you pay for it. Bring me what I want, or at least news of where it is, and I might choose to lift the binding."

She had expected to gloat longer, but the brat just stood there, fingers clutching her bleeding arm. Dejain's palm still throbbed.

Brats. They were next thing to useless, unworthy even as entertaining adversaries.

Dejain flung away the knife with its lethal spell binding CJ's blood: she had no intention of lifting the spell. She slapped her carefully prepared transfer token against CJ's head, and watched with satisfaction as the brat vanished, then she left the room.

She did not notice when the knife vanished.

Lightning.

Ear-shattering thunder.

Sudden darkness. When the rumbles died away, the angry stamp of footsteps on a hardwood floor sent horror burning CJ's nerves; lighting again, gleaming along the length of needles dripping blood, the snap of a belt, the slash of a wire hanger and the remembered white-hot burn against flesh. . .

"Shut up."

CJ covered her eyes with her hands and screamed over and over, "I'm here, I'm here, I'm not there! Earth is gone!"

"Shut. Up."

She knew that voice. It banished the nightmares of Earth, but replaced them with more recent and horrible memory.

CJ gasped, opening tear-blurred eyes. She gazed up from a mosaic floor in a wild riot of colors to a man sitting on a bench carved from dark wood in interlocking patterns. He was as familiar as his voice: medium height, slim, dressed plainly in a white shirt, riding trousers, military boots. Short curly black hair, blue eyes in a pale face. A Chwahir face. She stared in sick horror at Kessler Sonscarna, who of all the villains she'd ever encountered, she hoped most strongly never to see again.

"I—" she started, but terror choked off her voice.

Kessler sighed impatiently. "It's obvious what happened." He pointed at CJ's torn sleeve, dappled with drying bloodstains. Beneath, the flesh had already healed in the familiar whitish-silver line that reminded CJ of a slug trail.

"Dejain did it." CJ's voice trembled.

Kessler gave a crack of laughter. "She put a tracer on it, which she will now believe puts you some three weeks to the northeast. Her search ought to afford some entertainment, as that will set her hunters in Helandrias."

CJ gaped. "But the animals there hate humans!"

Kessler's smile was distinctive for its total lack of humor. "What else does she want?"

CJ scrambled to her feet. "I won't do her bidding. I won't! Or yours!"

"Shut up," he said again, getting up from the chair he'd been sitting on.

CJ's shoulders hunched and her neck turtled down into her early childhood defensive position. Rage burned so hot her fingertips tingled. "I hate you," she yelled. Rage was so close to tears, the gut-twisting sobs that never did any good, but she'd die before she'd let Kessler see her crying. She gulped in her breath.

"Tell me what she wants," Kessler said. "It doesn't mean I'll bestir myself to comply. But you're here, so you may as well spit it out."

CJ said sullenly, "Some book. Books. She called them texts. Some kind of nasty . . . blood stuff."

Kessler laughed again, a single short bark, and glanced at a window. Kessler knew very well what Dejain wanted—his window into her chambers still worked—but the question had been his own test. CJ had told the truth. Very well, on with the game.

CJ glanced outside, bracing against a threat even worse than the one before her. Startled, she forgot her danger for a heartbeat when she perceived a rippling ocean of green leaves. She was very high in a tower looking down over a vast woodland.

CJ clapped one hand over her wounded arm, rubbing as if she could get rid of that evil spell. The slice had already gone numb in a sickening way.

Kessler turned his head, and CJ flinched as Kessler held out a tightly wrapped scroll. "Dejain does not know that the texts came from Chwahirsland, but she might be able to figure it out. If you get this to Jilo before she gets there, you might be able to save his life."

"No!" She put her hands behind her, and backed against the wall, nearly stumbling over the hem of her green skirt. "I don't want it! I don't want anything to do with dark magic stuff, or Chwahirsland, or her!"

"No one," he said deliberately, "is interested in what you want." He uttered another of those short voiceless laughs. "Regard this as a test of the integrity you so loudly insist you possess."

The idea of a villain slamming CJ for a lack of honesty and morals was so gaspingly unfair that she forgot her terror. Hopping from one foot to the other, she yelled, "Oh, *how* I hate you." Her voice rose, shrill and thin. "You were going to make me kill Clair."

"You could have refused."

"And get killed?"

He lifted a shoulder. "So? It would've been fast. Everyone dies someday. And yes, I can see you're about to howl about how you'd like to see me die. Maybe you will. But not today." He threw the scroll at her feet. "Get moving. Do whatever you're going to do."

She sidled toward the door, mute with misery and anger.

He smiled unpleasantly. "You'll recall I know the blood knife spell. It should be entertaining, watching what Dejain has in store for you next."

A tide of loathing burned through every nerve of her body, but she forced herself to stoop and take up the scroll, because she feared what he'd do if she didn't. She dashed to the door. To her surprise it opened, into a circular stairway.

The sound of his soft laughter chased her down, and down, and down, past the point where his voice could possibly have carried.

All the way down, the walls gradually shifted hues across the rainbow, with contrasting colors in knotwork. The stone was bare in places, and in others moss and lichen covered the tiles. Wherever this castle was, it seemed nobody had lived in it for ages, or maybe they just didn't care about repair.

Her breath burned her throat and her legs had gone trembly by the time she reached the ground. She staggered away, falling to her hands and knees on a mossy slope as she glanced fearfully upward at that tower arrowed at the sky.

She knew that if Kessler wanted to splat her like a bug on a windshield, he could have done it in the tower, or on the stairs. But still, the urge to get away made her frantic. She plunged past weather-worn fragments of wall carved with the same interlocking patters she'd seen inside the tower, down the remains of a terraced hill, until she reached the comparative safety of woodlands.

She stopped, leaning against the rough bark of a maple, and moaned, "Why does this kind of stuff always happen to *me*?"

She pushed away from the tree as if she could escape that question, or escape the hard slap that never-quite-faded from memory, though she was far away from Earth and the sudden beatings. *If you pout I'll give it to you again*, that early childhood voice threatened, and she began to walk.

She stopped occasionally, scavenging fallen nuts and drinking from streams. When darkness closed in, she retreated under a very old tree with thick branches, pressed her back against the trunk, tucked her skirt around her bare feet, and ate fruit until she was full.

Then she curled up to sleep, never quite dropping deeply. Though it was spring wherever she was, unlike the autumn at home, it was still cold.

The rain began, at first soft splats among the leaves overhead, a pleasant sound . . . but they increased to a rustle, and then a roar. The tree protected her from the worst of it, but cold water dripped onto her. She shivered, fitfully dozing, until with a lance of pain up her nerves, Dejain struck.

Pain first, deep aching cold ramifying outward from the cut, flashing to heat. Sound distorted into shrieks, scrapes, bone-rattling thunder, and then the images: fire, knives carving helpless flesh, yawning pits.

I know what this is, CJ thought fiercely. I got through it once before. I can make it.

She remembered what Sartora, that is, Liere, had told them last year about making mind-shields, and tried to build a wall inside her head, though it was nearly impossible to concentrate because she was so cold, and everything hurt, and a yawning, gaping pit into terror and pain reached to swallow her. She backed away and ran, heedless of twigs and hedges, rough ground that tripped her. She scrambled to her hands and knees.

Where are my books. Where are you.

Frantic, CJ could feel the abyss slurping up the world around her, and she ran until the nightmare faded with the voice, then dropped onto some grassy ground and slept.

When morning came, she rose wearily and began to walk again.

Three

Erdrael Danara

NOBODY WAS THINKING ABOUT loyalty, ethics, or betrayal in the newly reunited Erdrael Danara, at least not Terry and Curtas whooping and shouting echoes up the rocky hillsides as their canoe shot down the white-water. Their paddles smacked water up in splashes, whirling with speed instead of grace.

Thump! The canoe hit a rock and shot up into the air.

"Hooo-ooo!"

The yell came from both boys, a whoop of joy and anticipation and maybe just a little dread, though the canoe, and their hearts, racketed along far too fast for dread to last longer than a pang.

Another rock!

Curtas's paddle whipped round and he shoved the handle with both hands, pivoting them around the rock. The canoe slid by, dropping into a hollow of rushing, whirling white water. Terry gazed in admiration at the swift expertise of Curtas's move.

Terry's face filled with water; he gasped for air.

They were out.

"Bail!" Curtas shouted.

They bailed as fast as they could as the canoe lugged. Terry—Tereneth Larensar, the new young king of Erdrael Danara—already knew this route, though no one had let their crippled king try it himself, until he met this new friend who'd said, "I'll take you."

The rough stuff was over. They bumped and splashed downstream until the water widened and the canoe slowed as spring-forested hills slid by. At last the river broadened into sedate respectability and the boys sat up, the paddles easy in their dip and pull.

The canoe glided into the mountain lake, meek and silent among the little sailboats and canoes skimming round and round the breeze-ruffled waters. The little palace built in the middle of the lake had been put there as an escape by a wealthy aristocrat centuries back. More wildflowers grew there than along any of the many lakes in this corner of what had been once, and was now again, Erdrael Danara.

As the canoe eased up alongside the dock below the palace terrace, conversation broke off among the adults on the decorated barge nearby.

"He's back! He's safe!" an old princess—who had survived the civil war, and astutely accepted being demoted to a duchas—trilled.

A clamor of voices rose, some exclaiming, some relieved, some hiding disappointment. These latter were observed by a languid young man strumming a lute. His eyes met those of a quiet young woman aft, dressed in the plain livery of the mountain guard, her capable hands on the barge's tiller.

They both watched the big, thick-shouldered count in the fine green robe, who frowned. "Your majesty. You must promise us never, ever to attempt such a foolish thing again! I cannot believe, after all our careful warnings, in spite of your affliction, you risked your life, and for what?"

Those who were more observant noticed the subtle tightening of Terry's pleasant features at the word *affliction*. It was too subtle to be called a flinch, though the sun-brown flesh ruddied around the long scar marring his face, and Terry held one arm close to his middle in a habitual protective gesture, as if the missing fingers on that hand still ached.

"A wager, probably," the duchas said, and laughed. "Didn't we wager against foolish things when we were young?"

"Not prompted by some no-name." The count's voice sharpened. "The king ought to heed his responsibilities. You must speak to him, Honor. As his last living relation."

"The king." "He." Even after a couple of years some of the aristocrats avoided the breezy nickname Terry that their teenage king insisted on using—so common sounding—rather than the old, distinguished Tereneth, traditional name of Danaran kings . . . when there was a Danara.

The duchas resettled her embroidered robe. "I shall. But young people, you know."

"He's now a *king*. And there's been far too much trouble of late for such unnecessary risks as riding a canoe down a cataract."

"But his friend Rel did it," another guest said genially. "Can we blame our king for trying to emulate Rel? We were all agreed that he is an admirable youth."

A youth, some recollected, who had refused the royal invitation to join Danara's elite mountain guard.

"If," someone else drawled, "we wish to lower ourselves to futile effort."

"Yes," the count said, swerving to glance with approval at one of the finest and fastest of the sailboats sliding along in the freshening breeze.

His son stood at the tiller, tall, broad, handsome, his gem-braided hair pulled back as he turned a haughty look at the boat filled with attractive young aristocrats from the three kingdoms now joined into one.

An older woman spoke quickly. "Perhaps we ought to exert ourselves. If we provide better entertainment, King Tereneth will settle down to his new dignity, and will not have time for these unfortunates."

They meant Halad, Terry's best friend and now adopted brother, who was half-Chwahir. During the bad old days, both had lost their families when Terry also lost those fingers, and very nearly his life. But Halad had sheltered the half-dead prince in the stable below the tailor's shop where he worked, fending off the searchers who would have killed him outright if they'd known. He'd bound up Terry's broken limbs as best he could, and his wounded hand, and shared his scanty meals with Terry while hovering anxiously through the sweaty fever and pain of Terry's slow recuperation.

They had mourned their dead families together, and later, when Terry survived the ferocious in-fighting, he never forgot the promises he and Halad had made one another.

Many approved of the friendship he'd begun with Senrid Montredaun-An of Marloven Hess; Senrid's birth was appropriate, and while the Marlovens might have an unsavory reputation, their homeland was safely distant. There was also no doubt that the mountain guard was far more effective, after a season with Retren Forthan of Marloven Hess, at Terry's invitation.

But then not that everyone was happy with that, either.

The lute player, scion of the next oldest house and almost as royal as the Larensar family, wondered how many like, say, Count Stithar over there, father of the stupid and selfish teenage Braer (who had tried out for the new mountain guard, assuming that his birth would waft him in, but failed to pass the stringent physical tests despite his brawny size), were still resentful that they'd lost what they regarded as the privileges of birth, privileges that had contributed to the civil war in the first place.

The lute player smiled.

He studied Terry, pleasant and ordinary in appearance, if you paid no attention to his limp, the missing fingers, or the scars. Terry had surprised them all with that decision to consult Senrid, but then he'd already shown he would do what he felt right. Including the choosing of friends, like that first friend Halad, and Rel the Traveler, and latest this wanderer Curtas, who seemed to have no background, just a very quick wit and a fund of good games to try.

Curtas (he didn't appear to have a family name), was medium height, ordinary of face and build, but moved with the deftness of someone who'd been trained since childhood. Not everyone saw that.

The two collapsed onto chairs in the corner of the terrace, and wolfed food with the enthusiasm of danger conquered. The aches would set in later, but right now the sun was warm, the breeze just right, and oh, did the food taste good!

"Wow," Terry said at last, eyes half-shut. "I had heard that the Snake's Teeth was the worst part, but I don't think so. Not half so bad as the Dragon's Throat."

"It was all rough," Curtas said. "And went by so fast I hardly remember any of it."

"You were *good*," Terry observed. "Saved us from smashing, there at the Deathgate. We might still be back there, swimming along with the splinters of the canoe. It was fun, and I can say that I've done it. I've dared the lightning." He smiled, then nodded his chin in the direction of the barge easing up to the dock. "Unless I miss my guess, we're about to get ear-banged by the thunder."

"The count?" Curtas asked.

The count approached, allies at either side, and in a jovial tone issued his warning. "Now my boy," he finished as he bowed low. "I realize it is not my place to lecture one above me in rank, but I am also a parent. And a count—my duty, one might say, being totally duties as well as taxes. So when I see you appear from the north end of the Lake, I realize that it might seem irresistible to one your age to live up to the challenges of that no-family fellow, Rel— "

As the count went on with his lecture—his modulated voice loud enough for everyone on the terrace to hear—Curtas wondered to himself if there was a kernel of truth in all that yammer: was Terry really measuring himself against the mysterious Rel?

Terry didn't deny, argue, or sulk. "You're right, Count Stithar," he said when the peroration was finished. "But I did it, I know I can do it, and I need never do it again. Once was enough. Enough," he repeated, gently, and with his ready smile.

The count eyed him uneasily, then bowed again and retreated.

Curtas sat back, eyes closed against the sun, effectively invisible to the courtiers who were in the habit of ignoring him anyway.

"You can't be falling asleep!" Terry exclaimed, and elbowed Curtas in a friendly manner.

Curtas startled them both by his sudden reaction. One hand rose in a block, the other coming up for what looked for a heartbeat like a palm-hand strike, but arced to his forehead to ward the sun. Then he sat up and yawned, catching a speculative glance from the lute player's pale eyes. "Sorry. I startled easily."

"Let's take a ride and dry off, shall we?" When they had gone around the corner, out of sight of the courtiers, Terry flashed a grin. "Interested in a little fun?"

"I hate fun," Curtas replied.

"I love torture," Terry said. "I'm going to force you to have fun."

Terry led the way up the terrace's steps past the new gardens, and straight to the tiled magic Destination room. They were each transferred to the capital.

The transfer chamber was in the old part of a very old stone castle that had sufficed for the middle kingdom since the splintering of the Colendi empire centuries before. Before that, Erdrael Danara had been united, though along different borders.

Now that spring had warmed the ground and cleared the skies, the hammering sounds, sharp-wood smells, and endless wagons of quarried stone indicative of new construction went on almost everywhere you turned.

The boys headed toward the quiet of the old part of the castle, with its time-worn carvings of twined leaves and animal faces over arched doors. Here they met Halad, who joined them in a room packed with books and maps.

Terry snapped his fingers, murmuring some kind of long-practiced ward. "No one can hear us now," he said, and to Curtas, "You told me before we rowed up the river that you've met Shontande of Colend. When I was a sprat, I was taken to Colend to meet the king and the prince. He was barely this high, wearing what looked like silk pajamas. But he was smart, real smart. I played with him while the adults were blabbing, and I swear, I think it was the first time anybody had played with him, he was so surprised."

"Have to feel sorry for him." Halad looked down at his hands.

"Exactly." Terry turned back to Curtas. "Anyhow, that makes you one of the very few who's met Shontande."

Here it is. Curtas said, "Remember, my two visits to Prince Shontande were very brief."

Terry sighed. "At least you got past his guardians. Nobody except Colend's court gets to see him. Ever. I hate that. I did try to write to him once, but it went nowhere—I don't know if the letter vanished at my end or his. And nothing's changed since then. I mean, here I am a king, but King Carlael seems to think that Colend is just too exalted to heed us here."

"Or he's as crazy as they say," Curtas said. "Shontande really isn't."

Terry grimaced. "You can stand the idea of a twit being kept prisoner by his own people, supposedly for his own good. But not someone you know you'd like. Anyway, I thought, maybe

Shontande could use some allies — and bring his own influence to help with the direction the alliance is going in." Terry paused, looking at Curtas expectantly.

"Alliance?" Curtas repeated, palms up.

Terry leaned forward, his face earnest. "Well, the alliance is mostly, though not all, young rulers. United against Norsunder. It started as an exchange of information, though these days Prince Glenn of Everon seems to want to make it a military alliance. I don't know Shontande, of course, but Colend has never had an army. They're experts at negotiation. We could use that influence to save the alliance, is my thought, anyway. If he'd even like to join. I'll give you an introduction to Karhin and Thad Keperi . . ."

.

Four

Everon

PRINCESS HATAHRA DELIETH OF Everon entered the huge room her brother had recently taken over as a practice salle, and her nose wrinkled. Eugh. It smelled like sweat. Why was boy sweat stinkier than horse sweat?

But she had two goals. She needed to get rid of the first one so she could get to the second, which she'd been waiting to do for days: present Clair of the Mearsieans to Clair's own great-grandmother, who had been locked beyond time before Detlev had found her in Norsunder and used her as anchor to the enchantment over Everon, when Tahra and her brother were small. As an experiment, it was said. All those lives ruined for an *experiment.*

At the far end of the Knights' practice salle, several Knights went through sword drill, leaving the middle for Glenn and his dozen or so friends, what he called (when they were alone) his

Honor Guard In Training. A flurry of clangs, clashes, and grunts of effort, then a boy staggered back, blood dripping down his arm.

A slow, derisive clapping from the corner collided with Glenn's shout: "Hold!"

Light slanted down through the high windows. Tahra flung the door open to the fresh air. Even if rain came in, at least it wouldn't smell so awful.

Tahra recognized Laban the newcomer in the slim boy of medium height who sauntered through the slanting shafts. The watery light gilt the sun streaks in his wavy dark brown hair. His vivid blue gaze acknowledged Tahra, but when she didn't speak, he turned to the group of boys.

"Now I don't claim to be any expert," Laban said, "but it seems to me that if you want to learn control, that means learning to pull the blade before you hack off someone's arm."

"I said I was sorry," came a mumble from Hanold Wemegan, newly a baras after the slaughter of his parents during the Norsunder attack.

Laban's sarcasm had stung, as usual. Tahra did not like sarcasm, especially Laban's sarcasm, but she knew Glenn liked it.

"He's right, Hanold." And, with a quick wave to the other, Glenn said, "Go get that wrapped up, Rauric."

The wounded boy — another who'd inherited the family title after the battle — started away, clutching his arm, then turned. "Do you still want me for practice?"

Glenn said kindly, "No. That arm's going to hurt. You rest for a couple days."

Hanold winced, looking down at the floor. "Want me to go with him?"

Glenn glanced at Laban, who stood, arms folded. Unlike the Everoneth boys, he didn't seem worried or upset. "No," Glenn said. "Let's get back to work."

Tahra said, "Wait."

Glenn shivered as cool air from the open door ruffled round them all. "Close that. We don't need to slip and crack our skulls on a rain-slick floor."

"It's not raining at this moment, and you need air in here," Tahra said. "And there are visitors."

"Who? You can entertain Clair, since she has no interest in defense," Glenn said impatiently.

"It's someone new. Terry sent him."

Glenn's long face sharply angled in the slanting grayish light. Tahra studied her brother's familiar features — so much like her own — thinking with that inward tightening of unhappiness that he could scarcely wait to grow up, for all the wrong reasons.

"They're in on it," Glenn said, waving his sword at the other boys.

Tahra understood that he wanted his followers in the alliance, especially Laban, though he was new, and no one knew where he came from. "He's noble-born," Glenn had said. "He carries himself like someone of rank. After one night I questioned him, and when I asked if his family was dead and his lands given to someone else, he didn't deny it." That was enough for Glenn to change his rules about 'only Everoneth' people for his future honor guard — his future personal Knights.

Tahra did not understand that about carrying oneself, as she was a princess, as high a rank as you could get, but she was still awkward and sometimes clumsy. And Glenn as often as not lumbered about. Furthermore, the person she admired most, Liere Fer Eider, the Girl Who Saved the World, was a shop-keeper's daughter.

Tahra also knew that she didn't like Laban. But Glenn did, so whatever her brother liked, she tried very hard to accept.

She said, "Terry sent this new Curtas with a message."

Glenn thought wearily that this Curtas had to be some lackey, as people of rank didn't run messages. He said, "Laban."

The boy turned, eyebrows lifted in question.

"See what he wants. If you need me, I'll come, but I'd rather finish the sparring."

Tahra waved at Curtas, who had waited outside the door. "Go in."

"Ho," Laban said to the newcomer in greeting. "Glenn sent me out. They have a practice going."

Curtas's expression mirrored Laban's as he said, "Terry told me about this alliance. I mentioned that I happened to have met Shontande Lirendi. Terry wants me to try to reach Shontande again, to recruit him, but said I ought to run the idea by Prince Glenn."

Tahra looked from one blank face to the other, and wondered, do they know each other?

Laban tipped his head. "I think you'd better come in."

Maybe not. Tahra knew she was terrible with people. She had

to plan out everything she said. Even her reactions, because she never seemed to feel about anything the way others did, and they all thought her strange for perfectly sensible things, like always getting out of bed with your feet placed at the same moment, to start the day balanced. And counting things, so you knew exactly what was around you.

She turned her back as Curtas followed Laban inside the salle. She'd done her duty. No one would notice her leave.

Nor did they. Glenn saw Laban bring the newcomer in, and lowered his point. In a few words, Laban repeated the message, and then indicated Curtas with a careless wave of his hand.

Glenn endured the usual tight pang of jealousy at the mention of Shontande Lirendi. That little Colendi snot got more respect and prestige than he ever would, just by existing. "A moment, please," Glenn said as he put his sword back in the rack. Why did duty always have to be this difficult?

Of course he wanted Shontande, future king of Colend, to be part of the alliance—but later, later. When Glenn was older, and had solidified his position as international commander of the alliance force.

At their single meeting, small as he was, Shontande had spoken perfect Sartoran, and everybody commented on his wit and beauty. Glenn didn't want Shontande showing up and every one of these boys following him because of his famed beauty and grace. It just wasn't fair!

Well, neither was it fair for Glenn's father to be dead, his mother missing, and the kingdom so wasted they couldn't repair all the damage to the royal castle.

But it had happened.

And that's why there was the alliance—and it needed to be shaped into something that could *defend*.

Glenn forced himself to smile. "Great," he said to this Curtas. "Great news. Please do."

The others crowded around the newcomer, drawn by the power of the Lirendi name.

"What's he like?"

"How'd you get in?"

"What's he say about affairs in Colend?"

Laban canted a glance his way, then said in that derisive tone Glenn enjoyed so much, "Is he as mad as his father?"

Glenn suppressed a grin, and waved a hand. "Now, no pokes

at our allies. Save that for Norsunder." He hated his own hypocrisy, but he couldn't be seen making any denigrating comments about an ally, and a fellow prince. It was more kingly to be generous — to be seen being generous.

Curtas shrugged. "Seemed sane enough to me, young as he is. But our meetings were brief. Why did I try it? Wager. How did I get in? With difficulty."

That Shontande was effectively kept prisoner only added to the Lirendi mystique.

"Well, bring us back a report, all right?" Glenn asked, deciding the talk about Shontande had gone on long enough. "Oh. Did Terry give you transfer tokens?"

"Yes, he did. Wanted me to get your approval first, because of this alliance," Curtas said.

"It's a good idea to recruit another ruler," Glenn replied, pleased with this evidence that Terry — a king in his own right, and not just a crown prince — was accepting a subsidiary role, exactly as Glenn had planned. "Though Colend is not known for its military presence, I'd be happy to help with that. Tell him."

Curtas left. Glenn turned back to his group, expecting to see them impressed. And so they were, except for Laban.

Glenn could see it in those blue eyes, the winged brows that could express so much with a twitch. Glenn was acknowledged leader by everyone except Laban. His air was polite, cooperative, but not the least deferential.

Why? What could Glenn do to get that blue gaze to express respect, admiration, submission? He knew Laban *had* to be a prince in disguise. Had to. Not of anywhere that mattered, for Glenn knew exactly who lived and who didn't of all the surrounding kingdoms' royal families. But his looks, no, it was more his manners, his language, the way he moved, he had to be at least a high-ranking noble if not a prince.

Morgeh Troiad, immediately to the north, was another young king due to trouble in his family. But Glenn didn't bother with him; Morgeh Troiad hated being a king, even of Wnelder Vee, which was forest, sheep land, and coast; he hated his royal name, Morgeh, given all the kings of his country, preferring his family name, Troiad, a name so old and so common that it was shared by merchants and the like.

He wanted to be a *bard*. The world was full of bards. Not everybody got to be king. Glenn thought he was an idiot.

Glenn kept his eyes on the last bouts as his mind ranged through all this familiar territory. When the midday bells rang, a shout of relief went up, but then the boys turned to him, and he waved a hand toward the door, pleased that they were beginning to make a habit of waiting for his orders.

All except Laban. He stood there staring out the long windows at the mist-softened old walls, cracked and ivy-lined, and beyond those the ruined walls of the castle, and beyond those the dismal buildings of a city struggling to survive.

Glenn said, "What's out there?"

Laban turned. "Your royal castle."

Glenn glanced out at the familiar rubble, made wet by the rain, and beyond the jumble of rooftops that made up Ferdrian. "Let's go."

Laban followed silently, and as they emerged from the salle, he trailed fingers along the stone wall bordering what once had been a fine garden. "It will be handsome when you get the repairs finished."

Glenn waved that off. He hadn't wasted any time or scant treasury on castle repairs. Defeating Norsunder came first.

"So when will you start?" Laban asked.

Glenn said impatiently, "My sister can take care of that. She has nothing else to do, and I have enough to do to regenerate the Knights, and scrape together some kind of defensive force."

Laban turned his head and studied the half-ruined wall, to hide the visceral cramp of contempt. Now here comes the sword-waving, he thought.

And Glenn said, "Why don't you join in the practices? I know you're good, but everyone can get better."

"Oh, I'm not that good." Laban waved a dismissive hand. "Had a couple bouts go my way, but skill? No, no. I leave that to you and your Everoneth scions."

Glenn sent him a sidelong glance. "And so all the more reason to practice."

"But it's so fatiguing!"

Glenn laughed. "Never mind. Let's summon a page to order some lunch."

Five

IN WNELDER VEE, DIRECTLY north of Everon, Clair walked around the neatly organized garden, trying to argue herself out of apprehension. There had to be a perfectly good reason why Mearsieanne, her great-grandmother, missing for over a century, had not returned to Mearsies Heili.

When Clair first arrived at Wnelder Vee's Destination, she had found herself in a deserted courtyard, weather-swept, the stone mossy and broken in places. She'd discovered that this end of the royal palace had been abandoned for a newer wing, but even so, an old herald seemed to be left in charge of the servants, scribes, and the palace guard.

"The new king and the royal adviser are on tour of the kingdom," she was told when she asked a passing page.

The girl's gaze went from Clair's white hair to her fingernails. And then, when the page saw her ordinary hands rather than morvende talons, came the expected indifference. Morvende coming to sunsider buildings were rare. Interesting. Clair wasn't.

"Thank you," she said, and tightened her middle against what CJ called chickening out. "May I leave a message? I am a relative of the royal adviser."

The page's brows rose. "The scribes will see to that. All the way down that hall."

Clair thanked her, glad that she had the Universal Language Spell on her. Though she'd learned Sartoran, the version they spoke here was almost unintelligible — she heard an echo of it after the magic-translated word. Odd.

Her determination had sustained her long enough for her to dictate a polite note to Mearsieanne, saying that she would stay with Princess Hatahra of Everon for a few days.

Then she'd transferred to Everon as Tahra's guest.

The days then slipped by, Clair thinking each day she woke that this would be the day she'd get a message, and before sleeping each night, she'd decided to give it another day.

And today, coincidentally on the heels Curtas's arrival, the message had come.

Clair circled the garden (so geometric, clipped, and trimmed that she thought it very boring) again, worrying. She'd thought carefully about what to wear, something she rarely paid attention to. Not too fancy, lest Mearsieanne think she was trying to be pretentious. Not her comfortable clothes, because she owed it to Mearsies Heili not to look shabby.

She'd picked a leaf green robe that matched her eyes, worn over the loose pants gathered at the ankle that had been popular off and on in Mearsies Heili for generations, and a top made of silk that one of the girls had embroidered starliss on, for a gift. And she added an ornament on a chain as a necklace.

It was a curiously shaped, iridescent object with a spiral pattern that reminded her of a shell. Puddlenose had given it to her, after one of his adventures. It felt smooth to the touch, and sometimes she sensed the tingle of magic, though it wasn't always there. As if whatever magic lay over it responded to tides, or the movement of stars, or something else she couldn't perceive. Maybe that was mere fancy, in the way that thinking it a shell was fancy, but she liked wearing it over her everyday medallion.

Tahra returned, her lips moving. She stopped with both feet planted, which meant she'd been counting steps again, something Clair had discovered irritated Glenn.

Tahra looked up, her long sallow face blotchy-pink with some emotion Clair could not guess at. But that was gone as Tahra smiled. "I handed off Terry's messenger to my brother. We can go now."

Tahra's palace, though mostly ruined, had an intact Destination that the conquerors had found too useful to destroy. The girls shifted to Wnelder Vee, where they found a herald waiting on a bench.

He stood up, bowing low. Clair resigned herself to the awkwardness of protocol. It still amazed her that Glenn got angry, not upset, but actually angry, if anyone forgot who was to enter a room first, and where they stood in relation to him. She was wary now, in case she was about to meet with more protocol expectations.

Her heartbeat quickened as they walked along a hall that looked a lot like Tahra's palace— lots of archways, patterns made by subtle variations in color in the floor tiles, matching the colors painted on the ceilings. She had no idea she was seeing an adaptation of Colendi architecture of four centuries previous.

They passed a couple of interview rooms filled with color; Clair heard light laughter, and glimpsed a couple of maids fluffing seat cushions as they chatted.

A footman sprang to open a pair of golden oak doors inlaid with redwood patterns of interwoven iris.

Music spilled out, a complicated melody that caused Tahra, appreciating the quiet and order, to perceive fascinating number patterns. To Clair, the music evoked sunlight on the mysterious waters of what the girls called the Magic Lake, and the beings in the water, who looked like rippling ribbons made of glass.

Clair's gaze lit on the player, who sat on a silken cushion set on a low dais: an ordinary boy whose lighter skin at his hairline, below the strictly ordered brown locks, were evidence that he usually let his hair flop as it would. Troiad was dressed like a king now, in two layers of robes, the rich embroidered silk heedlessly rumpled as he bent over his lap harp, fingers blurring.

Clair's gaze went past him to the girl seated on another silken cushion, below the dais. This girl rose, and Clair gazed in dismay at her exquisite robe of the finest white wool worn over an under robe of pale blue raw silk, both embroidered with patterns of lilies, starliss, and queensblossom.

Eyes shaped like her own gazed back at her, each recognizing their relationship in the other, great-grandmother and great-granddaughter.

As Tahra walked up to Troiad, saying something that Clair didn't register, she stared at Mearsieanne, who looked so . . . so familiar, and yet so strange.

Mearsieanne's lips curved. "Did I already tell you that my granddad said that *his* grandmother was white-haired? Most of the family was, he said, before they left the north and came to Mearsies Heili."

Her welcoming tone caused Clair to smile, an expression that transformed her habitual sober expression. That smile, so unconscious in that young face, hurt Mearsieanne worse than a blow to the heart. But she hid it, stretching out her hands and making her own smile as wide as she could. "Welcome! It is so wonderful to meet again, without the threat of Norsunder overhead!"

She took Clair's square, capable hands in hers and pressed them gently, feeling the strength of youth, the smooth, taut skin.

Clair barely touched Mearsieanne's hand. It looked as smooth as hers, but it felt fragile in a way that disturbed her.

Mearsieanne let go and opened her palm toward Troiad. "As you see, I have found myself duty-bound to help a reluctant new king."

Troiad looked up from his instrument, gave Clair a sweet, distracted smile that reminded her of Adam, the painter boy who'd visited Tahra and Glenn the week previous. And, like Adam, his gaze went diffuse and returned to the art that called him, sound instead of color.

"This is good practice," Mearsieanne said in a low voice. "Think of Clair not as another youth, but as a visiting monarch."

Troiad's fingers lifted, and the beautiful music vanished into the air, leaving Clair feeling bereft.

Troiad swung to his feet, and uttered an entirely conventional greeting as he scrupulously put his hands together. Clair self-consciously mimicked gesture and words, as Mearsieanne looked on approvingly, then Troiad performed the same polite greeting to Tahra, though he'd been chatting with her moments before.

He turned to Mearsieanne with an air of a dog hopeful of treats as she twitched her head and made a slight motion with her hand toward the far archway.

"Oh!" Troiad grinned. "Would you care for refreshment?"

Clair thanked him, and Troiad led the way into the far room, where servants waited with trays of fresh fruit, tiny almond and cinnamon cakes, and a cold sour-sweet drink that Clair didn't recognize, but liked very much. She counted at least three flavors of berry in it.

She was glad to occupy herself with the food as she tried to navigate the conversational waters. On the surface everything was pleasant — the good food, the soft, aromatic breeze carried in from the fruit-laden trees in the garden — but she sensed shoals she couldn't quite define. Mearsieanne guided the conversation from travel to food to music, Troiad cooperatively following her lead without any evidence of the pleasure he'd expressed with his music. Tahra added pronouncements ("It's exactly a week from border to border, if you ride a single horse, whereas it's a week from the harbor to the strait if you take a ship, and walking will take . . .") without really responding to what anyone else said, though she was trying in her own way to keep to the topic.

Tahra's conversational side trips didn't bother Clair. The Everoneth princess was always like that. Troiad didn't seem unhappy so much as quietly bored. But why was Mearsieanne talking to Clair like a visitor?

Clair was trying to figure out a polite way to talk to Mearsieanne privately, and trying not to resent the need, when a distant gong resounded, and Troiad looked startled. "Oh, the review!"

"We got a bit of a late start, did we not?" Mearsieanne said apologetically.

Tahra flushed guiltily, though her decision to turn Curtas over to the boys had scarcely taken the turn of the small sandglass.

Mearsieanne didn't want Clair there — the conclusion seemed inescapable, and though Clair tried to hide it while staring down at her hands in her lap, the hurt was there to perceive.

"We should go," she said.

Mearsieanne's response was prompt and apologetic. "We have been overscheduled since Prince Morgeh Troiad's return." She turned from Tahra to Clair, "Please, once our immediate obligations are over, I would so like to spend a day, just the two of us. I trust you are not returning to Mearsies Heili?"

Clair hesitated, unsure.

Mearsieanne forced herself to tell at least part of the truth, "I'm not ready to go home yet. I know it's stupid. But I just can't." She looked around distractedly. "At least until every sign of Detlev's failed experiment is destroyed. And that means restoring order here, where they tried to force me to ruin this kingdom."

She watched the puzzled hurt in Clair's averted gaze transform to instant, uncritical sympathy. "Oh! I didn't think of that — of course."

She turned to Tahra, who said with a hopeful air, "I like having visitors." She added in an undervoice, "Girl visitors."

Clair did not have to be back in Mearsies Heili, where life was so quiet. Tahra clearly wanted her to stay, and Clair sensed that it might be good for Tahra to have another girl to talk to. She could wait, because surely Mearsieanne would be finished in a couple of weeks.

Six

Drael's North Forest

UNKNOWN TO CLAIR, CJ was still walking. Gleanings from the forest floor, the running streams, and the warm clothes kept her going during the day. Dejain's torments at night left her shivering and enervated.

Where are the texts?

What did Kessler say?

Where are you?

CJ resorted to screaming, just as loudly as she could, "Nonononononono!" Hoping she'd break Dejain's ear drums.

Eventually it ended, she slept, then got up with the sun and plodded on, trying to figure out ways to defend herself against the next attack.

CJ had no idea how dark magic worked, except that it was dangerous as it used a lot of energy, which could burn you up like a lightning strike. CJ knew that magic wasn't the same thing as electricity on Earth, but it was easier to think of it that way. Light magic used low voltage, with a ground wire, and plastic cord between you and the wire. Dark magic was high voltage and bare wires.

Down south at Norsunder Base, Dejain smiled as she carefully swept the ashes onto a paper, and tipped them out of the window to whirl away on the wind.

That was the third Ancient Sartoran message intercepted. Unfortunately it was either badly written or in code, because the translation made no sense.

Either way, Detlev didn't receive it because he was still gone, some said to Norsunder, others to Five. "Trouble with his precious pets," was the word making its way through Norsunder Base, accompanied by smirks, useless speculation, and worthless predictions.

The best thing was, no one's eye was on Dejain. As well, she thought as she glanced at the time candle. That irritating Mearsiean brat was proving to be typically stubborn.

She turned her attention to task of discovering what she could about this Jilo in Chwahirsland.

Where Kessler had originated.

Colend

After a few days' leisurely travel through Imar, Curtas used his transfer token, which took him to the border of Colend.

The unknown person who had selected this place for a magic transfer Destination obviously chose it for the view. Curtas looked about the old stone square, sheltered on three sides. Ancient pattern carved into the stone floor. A cottage adjacent, against transfer into a terrible storm. The unknown runners who'd traversed this way for centuries had taken the time to make the place pleasant, here on Colend's northwest tip.

But Colend was supposedly like that, Curtas reflected. It was so utterly alien to his life so far that he allowed himself a half day there, just taking in the view.

With morning light came the reflection that orders were orders, and he started down the old, worn path that crisscrossed the mountains toward the gently undulating land below.

As he worked his way down the switchback, the sky-reflecting ribbons meandering over the land below resolved into rivers, branches gently but inexorably reworked over the centuries into smooth canals.

Late in the day his path gave onto a greater road full of travelers. By promising help with the horses, he caught a ride on the back of a wagon full of silk from Derven.

A few mornings later he reached the pretty little town called Wilderfeld.

He walked to the scribe and messenger shop in the square, and got in line. The place was busy; scribes each sat at slightly slanted desks, a rainbow of inkpots around them.

Curtas remembered hearing that Colendi never distorted their script by altering letter size or underscoring. Instead, they employed colors to convey emotions. He watched the scribes either taking dictation or else copying a badly written paper into a piece of art.

A scribe student beckoned, and Curtas said, "I am here to see Thad."

The student, who couldn't have been more than ten, gestured toward a red-haired boy Curtas's own age, who sat behind a low table, busy writing into a ledger with a steel-tipped pen.

Curtas waited until Thad finished whatever it was he was copying, and looked up. "What may I do for you?"

"Alliance," Curtas repeated, as instructed.

Thad flicked his eyes toward the back stairs. "I invite you to find my sister. If she's not in reach, I hope you will honor us with a wait."

Curtas reflected on the power of words as he wound his way through customers and pages racing back and forth with rattling papers. One word, and he shifted from outside to inside the invisible boundary.

An empty hall gave onto several rooms, only one of which was open. A skinny brown-haired boy, half obscured by furniture, used the square of light coming in the east-facing window by which to draw.

His subject was a slender girl with red hair. She sat across him on the other side of the square of light. She resembled Thad in more than coloring; she had to be Karhin.

At Curtas's step she turned her head. The boy on the floor sighed.

She said, "Sorry, Adam." To Curtas, "And you are—?"

"Sent by Terry," Curtas said. "Alliance."

Karhin's face brightened at the mention of Terry. "Oh, one of my favorite correspondents!"

Adam, he of the deft drawing-pencil, looked up, his wide-spaced light brown eyes mild and friendly; his smile deepened briefly, dimples flashing in his brown cheeks.

"Your name?" Karhin asked, distracted by Adam's smile. For a heartbeat it had been more than a polite smile, more like the smile of suddenly encountering a friend.

"I'm Curtas."

"I'm Karhin, and he's Adam," Karhin said in a brisk voice, as Adam returned to drawing. Doubt assailed her. Adam was always friendly, smiling as if he knew you. People liked that about him. "Thad sent you up?" she asked Curtas.

"Yes." Curtas pointed at the drawing. "Go on. I don't want to interrupt."

Adam finished a bit of shading, then turned an expectant face to Karhin. She resumed her pose, and for a time there were no sounds, except for birds scolding in the trees outside the window, and the distant sounds of business below and horses and carriages moving along the paved square.

Thad finally came in, his student's robe fluttering at his heels as he rubbed ink off his hands onto a besorcelled cloth.

"A new member of the alliance, eh?" he asked by way of greeting. "Are you like Adam, here?" Thad pointed at the boy sketching away, head bent. "A wanderer? Terry sent you why?"

Curtas shrugged again. "On a dare I managed to get in and meet Prince Shontande."

Thad whistled. "That's more than I've managed. And I've been trying to communicate with him through scribes."

"We both have," Karhin said, making the Colendi gesture, palm arcing down, indicating no success.

Adam kept drawing.

"Our conversation was very short," Curtas explained. "But I got back again, on his invitation, and we spoke a bit longer. He's very lonely. For a prince."

"You know his highness might not even be in Alsais," Thad said. "He's kept out in the big castle in the middle of Lake Skya a good part of the year. And it's well guarded against Norsunder getting to him, or the Chwahir, or the usurper Canardan Merindar of Khanerenth."

"How is it that you can get past the guards?" Karhin asked.

Curtas looked at those inquisitive blue eyes, and dropped his gaze to his hands. "I was trained as a thief. Didn't want to be one."

"Is that who dared you to meet our prince? Thieves? Were you to steal from him?"

Curtas had been taught to stick to the truth as long as you could, because lies proliferated, and you had to remember them. But sometimes you had to lie anyway. "Yes."

"Where did you come from?"

"Melire." Melire lay over the border to the west; Curtas watched them register the fact. Of course youths whose parents ran a messenger service would know their map. "Orphan."

Ready, and real, compassion wiped the smile from Karhin's face she put her hands together and bowed her head in a gesture of sympathy.

Curtas spoke quickly. "It's all right. I made a family with the other orphans." Then added, "Before I became a thief." When he saw a slight uptick in Karhin's chin, he shrugged. "Later, after I wandered and discovered other friends, a mage gave me the Universal Language Spell."

"Ah!" Thad grinned. "Like Adam."

Adam looked up from his paints with faint question puckering his broad brow. "Yes?"

No, Karhin was thinking, they didn't know one another. That smile was Adam being Adam.

Thad laughed. "I invite you to ignore us, and return to your drawing."

Curtas said, "I was told, and I believe I saw the evidence, that Prince Glenn wants to organize a military alliance."

"That's what we hear," Karhin said. "But we're not part of that. We try to keep everyone current with news others in the alliance believe must be shared."

Thad grinned. "Can you reach our crown prince again?"

Curtas spread his hands. "I'll do my best."

"Please take me." Thad put his palms together.

"What about your work?" Karhin asked, low-voiced, in their

home language.

"I'm always behind," Thad said with a shrug. "When I get back, I'll have incentive to catch up. But Karhin, do you really want others besides Colendi bringing in our own prince?"

"Well thought! You must go," Karhin said. "I'll do some of your chores." And to Curtas, in Sartoran, "Please take my brother."

Curtas shrugged. "Be glad to."

Seven

Limisde (Flower Day) 4743, AF
Elsewhere in Colend

ON FLOWER DAY THE year he was four, Shontande Lirendi, Crown Prince of Colend, stood outside the royal palace at Alsais, capital of Colend, as the aristocrats in the elaborate court dress passed through the Gate of the Lily Path. They were on their way to the King's Regatta along the canals, silks whispering, scented like a wind-tossed garden after rain.

The little crown prince stood the proper arm's length behind his father, who had startled him by turning around to whisper, "What year is this?"

But before Shontande could find words, his father's gaze blanked again. He fell silent.

Small as he was, Shontande knew his duty: he kept his hands together in the peace greeting, nodding to each noble, the depth determined by each person's rank. He had learned to keep his face

polite and blank even though the world seemed stranger by the
day. And he knew to keep his body still, even when a soft hand
drifted over his cheek or hair in a quick, furtive gesture, the same
possessive gesture he saw people use caressing or fingering jewels
and gems.

His father was still quiet when Shontande saw the nobles again
that evening, the first time he was permitted at the ball following
the regatta. As the last of the guests passed by, bowing more
deeply to his father by his side, his pale hair gilt by the light of all
the crystal chandeliers overhead, memory prisoned Shontande in
the past.

He was a baby, fresh from the bath, his nurse gobbling his
arms and his neck and his fingers, making him laugh. Kisses,
gobbles, his laughter, her laughter, and then, quite suddenly, like
a shock, the voice of his father:

What are you doing to my son?

Kisses, said the nurse.

That is not appropriate, not for the Crown Prince of Colend.

But all babies need kisses!

You will be gone by sunset . . . sobbing . . . the last caress . . Was
that crying her, or him? . . .

Slap. The sting of his tutor's hand against his face. *Your father
ordered me to punish you with pain when you do not pay attention, your
highness. Your mind must not wander.*

Furtive ruffles of his hair, strokes of his back, insistent hands
capturing his face . . . Intimate voices. *Oh, you're so sweet, you're so
beautiful, you're the most beautiful little boy in the world, let me just
touch your pretty hair, your sweet face . . .*

The images streamed through his mind and were gone, leaving no emotional trace.

Later, when he turned eight, he stood by his father a proper
arm's length away, at the entrance to the marble ballroom. Since
he was a child he was not permitted to stay for the Blue Night
Masque, last event of the social season. He was there to be seen,
and then his guardians, his guards, led him away to prepare for
the winter prison at Lake Skya.

The final guest arrived. The grand herald signaled for the
fanfare, which would commence the festivities. Shontande bowed
to the company. The company bowed back. Only his father was
still, gazing up at the steady flame on one of the candles, his eyes
reflecting the tongues of light, luminous as winter ice.

The crown prince's watchful tutor opened his hand, and Shontande walked obediently, thoughts in a continual stream. When they reached his wing, all those rooms below those of his father, he did not really notice all the packing going on. Instead, he walked right through and outside to the rose garden. Because the rose garden was private, because the night was warm, his watchful guardians let him go.

He walked to the wall, ready to be alone, when a boy came vaulting over.

Whup! Just like that!

He stood there on the grass grinning, not five steps from where Shontande lay, and said, "Bored?"

Shontande could have called the guards. But he didn't. He didn't think of threat, or danger. And wouldn't have cared if he had: at last, something interesting had happened.

"Yes," Shontande had said.

"I know some great games. Of course most need more people." The boy held up five fingers.

"No one's permitted," Shontande answered, because they understood one another from the start: 'people' meant people their age, and not the army of guards and heralds and servants who isolated Shontande from the world.

"Yeah, I can see that." The boy grimaced with sympathy.

"Why are you here? Who are you?"

"Oh, I made a wager with a friend I couldn't get in and talk to you. People are curious about you, did you know that?"

Shontande shrugged. He was used to being stared at. The only people he talked to were his tutor and servants and guards, and the only people he saw were the courtiers, each with their pre-determined words and smiles and bows, exactly like a play that never ends.

Oh. And once in a while, a very great while, he saw his father. No, his father saw *him*.

"Tell me about your friend who made the wager," Shontande had said.

"What do you want to know?"

"What you do. What you see. What you say to each other."

The boy grimaced again, and plopped down on the grass nearby, plucking up a blade in order to suck the stem. "You've got nobody at all?"

"I have cousins who are sometimes permitted to see me, but

they are seldom permitted to stay past a bow and formal greeting." All but Nashande, who couldn't seem to remember the
politenesses drilled into his head. He was funny, even when bragging about his horses and sword practice, and Shontande liked
him best of all. But the tutors and stewards seldom permitted
Nash to come.

"Well, I—"

"Your highness? Who is that you're talking to?"

The boy got to his feet. "Uh oh!" He gave a comical grimace
this time. "My name is Curtas. Shall I come back?"

Quick urgent commands from the doorway. The two boys
looked at one another, and Shontande said, "I can't stop them, I'm
sorry. Come back if you can."

"I will!"

Hop! Back over the fence, and when the steward and the head
guard rushed up, the steward saying, "Your highness, who were
you talking to? We must keep you safe."

Shontande said, "I am safe."

Shontande stood in the moonlit garden looking at that fence. He
remembered how afraid the head guard was, though he knew he
ought not to listen to the inner voices. But he had to know if they
chased the boy—if he got away.

Now Shontande crossed the garden so familiar that he didn't
see much more than the pale outline of blossoms, or the etching of
carefully tended roses against the stone. He stopped at the wall
and laid his hand against it. *They say my father is mad?* he'd asked
Curtas when he came the second time, a year or so later.

Yes, Curtas had said with sympathy that Shontande could feel
in the mental realm.

Sometimes he's sane, Shontande had said.

Curtas had been interested, not bored, and just like that,
Shontande had wanted to trust him.

But then the sound of marching sentries, and once more Curtas
was gone.

Shontande bowed his head, heart-heavy at the prospect of the
dreary stretch of months ahead in Skya Castle. His tutor would
talk freely about history, but never about the now. Not with the
guards watching. What did they think? Mostly they didn't listen.
Shontande knew he ought not to trespass in their minds—he
would hate it if anyone did that to him—but it seemed necessary,

somehow. Or the world would slowly cease to be real, and maybe he'd go as mad as his father.

He shunted aside that old, familiar worry, and recalled Curtas's considering gaze, the decision that conveyed itself in the cant of his head before he spoke.

Shontande made a circuit of the quiet, still garden with its ancient roses planted by the hands of his ancestors, and tended by others. His tutors had told him that the center of the palace was the state wing, but Shontande was convinced the true center was this garden, that led one in gentle, interlocking circles, almost without your being aware. How many heirs had done their reading, thinking, studying there? Hoped? Dreamed?

Raged?

He drifted back inside, where everything was lit. The servants paused in their packing to bow as he passed. He considered finding a book, for he was not tired, but then a stirring at the far perimeters of his confined world alerted everyone in sight.

The silence, the profound bows, announced the presence of the king before the tall, slender figure appeared in the doorway, dressed in the royal blue made in a shade so dark it was almost his customary black. Unlike his court appearances, he wore only one jewel, the Lirendi Diamond, handed down in the family since the first king of Colend — and rarely worn since.

Shontande looked at his father anxiously, not daring to listen in that way that wasn't ears. When his father's mind was otherwhere it hurt to listen, a mental pain akin to laying your hand against ice.

But his father's pale blue gaze wasn't blank as he looked down into the great diamond, which reflected lights in his eyes, though no candles were lit in the room. That gaze was awake, aware. His father was back!

Carlael looked around at the servants who had set down trays or abandoned their tasks and stood, hands folded, eyes lowered.

"I require a private interview with my son," he said.

They bowed and filed out. The last one gently laid perfect rose petals in the tiny rice wine bowls, then bowed himself out, shutting the door.

Shontande hid an inward sigh. That was true authority, not the outward semblance that he must live with. He got the bows, and the silence, isolation but never privacy. He'd learned very early that "the king's orders, your highness" meant he wasn't listened to. Even when he knew that the orders couldn't be from his father, but from those smiling, glittering courtiers in the privy council, who issued orders in his father's name.

But then his father stood with his back to the door, his palms pressed to it, fingers wide and tense. As if he braced the door from opening again. Shontande's nerves prickled with the cold of the first snow of the season. "He is not here," his father whispered. "Let us speak quickly. While we can."

"He?" Shontande asked.

"Nightland's master of dark magic." The king's wide gaze ranged over the ceiling painted blue as a summer sky, the pattern of stars accurate. "They tell me that the Silver Feather season is nigh. Do we still have it?"

Shontande gazed back, unsettled. He groped for sense in the new subject. Did his father not know that the Music Festival remained in Colend? "It's still here. Though Sartor wants it back." Shontande bowed, hands against his breastbone in the formal peace as he anxiously scanned his father's face.

Carlael flung himself on one of the low, rolled-edged couches. "It's good we still have it. Though it seems I missed last year's." There was no emotion in his voice, but Shontande's skin crawled, for his father never left the palace. "Tell me what you saw and heard."

Shontande described, in minute detail, the two times he'd been taken to hear concerts. Always surrounded, though once he'd managed to hear a performance from the rose garden, some young singers from far away in the north. He described how their voices carried across the still waters, there under the starlight.

"I was told that they won the Feather for their category," Shontande finished. "And Nashande told me at the New Year's Firstday gathering that they've been hired to go all the way to Toar, on the other side of the world." His throat hurt with his longing at the very notion of traveling so far, so free.

"So you agreed with the judgment, then?"

"I did not hear their competitors," Shontande said.

Carlael lifted his long hand to brush back a strand of hair off his high forehead. "You cannot hear them all. No one can," he said. And faced his son, eyes narrowing. "Minding me of this advice. You will remember it, I trust. I have. One of the few things I do remember." A bitter curl to his lips, and then he waved a dismissive hand. "And I might not remember that I remember, come half a bell. So listen."

Shontande gripped his hands together. What age would the madness set in? Would he know when it came to him?

"One of these days I will be dead, and it will fall to you to choose the judges," the king said. "If the world is not burned. If you are still alive. Sometimes I am not certain . . ."

Brooding silence. Shontande never spoke first, ever. Just waited.

But his father did not slide back into that dream world behind the ice veil. "When you select the judges, you are never to give in to temptation to select friends, and even worse would be the sycophants who desire position. Understand?"

"Yes, sire. But I do not really know anyone in court. I only sometimes talk to Cousin Nashande, when I am let." That bit added at the end was a tentative venture toward asking for his freedom.

His father made that dismissive gesture again. "No matter. Pick twelve servants, or twelve people off the streets, then. Better that than faction leaders, or courtiers who will conspire together. The judges must never know of one another, or the festival will distort into a political brangle. Understand?"

"Yes, sire."

"Pick people who love music. You will see it in their faces. A cook who loves opera is a better judge of quality than a duchas who yawns behind a fan. Even if the duchas studied from a master for ten years, and the cook doesn't know which end of a wind instrument to blow. Alsais is full of music, everyone knows music. But the only judges should be those who love it."

"Yes, sire."

Carlael sighed, as though he had discharged a commission of lasting importance. He said then, "How goes your progress in magic studies?"

"My mage tutor seems pleased, sire."

"And you?"

How to say, *They will not permit me to perform anything beyond illusion?* He couldn't, for what if his father concurred, and therefore his experiments in secret would be deemed wrong?

"I have memorized most of the water maintenance spells, and I'm learning—"

"Never mind the recitation. You must learn the underlying structure. Not the pieces. That is why I wanted you tutored in magic. I wish I had been a better student, because it's difficult to perceive—" The king's voice drifted, and he frowned as he gazed into the diamond, down and down into the infinitude of reflected and refracted lights.

Shontande waited, breathing only, for what ended up being a measureless time. His father spoke suddenly, as if only a few heartbeats had passed. "There is another structure under it, a greater one, buried deep, and yet not buried at all."

He fell silent. Only the candles burned, and Shontande waited again, having mastered patience far beyond his years.

But this time there was no reward. The king looked around with the blank flat gaze Shontande dreaded, as though he had no idea where he was. He walked out with the diamond clasped between his hands, the unperceived servants bowing low in his wake, and the door shut behind him, leaving his son alone, in the silence, with his grief.

Eight

Everon

MEARSIEANNE, SELF-NAMED AND self-appointed Mearsiean monarch a century previous, disliked certain youths among the
Young Allies, and distrusted those who would listen to a Marloven, much less a Chwahir. Nevertheless this elderly person still
wearing the form of a girl functioned as influence during this part
of their history, and will perform a crucial action later in this
chronicle.

So she must be introduced here.

The first time Clair met Mearsieanne, it was during the anxious
flurry when Siamis had enchanted the world. Mearsieanne had
joined Clair and the girls in Murial's hermitage, and everyone got
along, but there was no question of ruling, as Norsunder held
power, however lightly. Mearsieanne had kept to herself how
appalled she was at the laxity of governance since her day.

The second time was that encounter in Wnelder Vee. Clair was so anxious she hadn't really noticed much besides her great-grandmother's beautiful dress, and her smooth but fragile hands.

The third time, both were better prepared.

Mearsieanne scolded herself, and resolved to face the truth of Mearsies Heili — and its young and popular queen — today.

Mearsieanne came to Everon alone. Jenel, Tahra's maid, daughter of the castle steward, conducted her with a self-important air to the best drawing room, the only one undamaged in the previous year's fighting.

Clair was there, wearing her good outfit again. Mearsieanne waited until the door was shut, then sighed. "I do not understand why the Delieths won't repair this place. The effect is so disheartening."

For the first time, she was speaking Mearsean. Her accent was quaint, old-fashioned in subtle ways Clair couldn't define. She looked at first glance like a girl, for she had never released the Child Spell and so had never crossed the boundary of puberty, but there was in her face and hands the subtle signs of age. Clair's eyelids burned with unshed tears, though she could not have said why.

Mearsieanne moved with care, her long, shining dark hair still youthful, as she gestured toward the door to the garden. "I cannot abide this dingy room. Since no one is around to be hurt by my preference, shall we go out into the garden?" She smiled. "That, at least, looks like it has been kept orderly."

"Tahra told me that the garden is the special province of the Sandrial boys," Clair said.

"Sandrial? Oh yes, the hereditary servants. 'Sandrial always serves Delieth.' I learned that when I met the former king and queen." Mearsieanne's voice lowered, sharp with anger. "I replaced Queen Mersedes Carinna for the duration of Detlev's little experiment. Did you know that?"

"I remember," Clair said, her insides cramping. "But I don't know the details. I knew it was something terrible, which was why I didn't want to ask."

"It had to do with magic and mind manipulation. Something to do with the subjugation and the hiding of a magical object called a dyr. I still don't precisely understand it. I do not want to understand it." Mearsieanne flushed with anger. "All I know is that it's being smuggled into Everon compounded the evil magic somehow, and undid all Detlev's work," she said acidly. "All praise to the evil dyr!" And then, as if she'd had enough of the subject, "Come. Tell me about home." She clasped her hands.

Clair said cautiously, "Is it painful to hear about home?"

"I thank you for asking. You are exactly as considerate as I remember." Today Mearsieanne was wearing a gown, green edged with gold and embroidered with white roses, the undergown white, embroidered with green leaves. "I have made my peace with being superfluous in my own home. It helps to remember that this is your time, that is, not just you — though I am increasingly delighted it is you — and that CJ was not a figment of my dreams."

Clair exclaimed in surprise, "CJ thought you were a dream as well! But she really did go into the past to meet you. She and Elian."

Mearsieanne's eyes nearly closed as she said in a soft tone, one of reverie, "She said I would walk into the palace and take the throne. She said I would even change my name to Mearsieanne, though I did not change my family name. And everything, everything she said, came to pass." Mearsieanne stopped and shot Claire a sharp look. "She and Elian went upstairs in the white palace, did they not? One of the rooms that always seems to change?"

Clair shook her head. "Those rooms don't stick people in the past. I don't think. At least, it's never happened to any of us, and we've gone in them sometimes, playing hide and seek. And nobody has ever walked out of them in outlandish clothes, or speaking of past or future, or anything. It's just that we can't quite keep track of them. CJ said she was on the terrace playing hopscotch, an Earth version of counting-stone, when she saw Elian . . ."

"Who apparently is related to us but from a twin of this world. Yes, I remember. She did come from one of those rooms." Mearsieanne gazed sightlessly at a shrub trimmed into a box shape. She would not admit to anyone her attempt to revisit the past to fix certain errors, which had led to her being trapped by Norsunder.

She lifted her hands. "I'm of use here. Morgeh doesn't want to rule, but the guilds and landholders each distrust the others, exactly as it was in my day. I've told Morgeh they are looking to him as the last of his family. When I left the tailor shop and went to the palace, there wasn't anyone left of the royal family, which was the problem. I used what CJ told me to frighten them all by my knowledge of things I should not have known." She shrugged.

Clair said, "Being queen of Mearsies Heili is mostly a matter of being a symbol, that's what Aunt Murial told me."

Which is what a hermit would tell you, Mearsieanne thought to herself. She sidestepped that subject. "I can teach Morgeh. He's a quick learner. I feel of use," Mearsieanne said again.

Clair said, "It's good. I mean, I'm so glad." That didn't sound right either, so she gripped her fingers together and blundered ahead. "If you ever decide to come back, know that you are welcome." She took a breath and made herself mean the words. "You are by rights the queen. If you think I'm not . . . if you think Mearsies Heili could be better served, I wish you would share your wisdom."

Mearsieanne lifted her eyes, searching Clair's gaze. Clair knew that Mearsieanne didn't have Dena Yeresbeth — that sort of thing was confined to Liere, and the Ancient Sartorans — but it felt almost as if Mearsieanne scraped the back of her skull from the inside, searching for the truth.

And she didn't say, *You are doing so well*, or even *Things are fine as they are*. She said, "I couldn't." But it was — at best — tentative.

Clair gathered herself inwardly, and once again forced herself to the truth. "I want what's best for Mearsies Heili."

"I truly admire that about you," Mearsieanne said. "We will have to discuss when . . ." She looked up sharply. "Transfer. Dark magic? A tracer?"

Clair had forgotten that Mearsieanne knew magic. She followed Mearsieanne back inside the Everoneth royal palace, Mearsieanne's skirt whispering over the clean-swept tiles as they walked to the other end.

They found Glenn and Tahra facing the new arrivals, Glenn curious, Tahra hopeful when she recognized Arthur, but her head dropping when she saw that the boy with Arthur was not Liere Fer Eider.

"Arthur," Clair exclaimed, and looked with curiosity at a tall boy standing beside blonde, cheerful Arthur. The newcomer had jug-handle ears, cowlicky dark hair, a blob of a nose and a lopsided smile.

"This is Roy. Here to study magic, from Geth-deles," Arthur said quickly. "Siamis has been lurking around Bereth Ferian. The mages told Liere and me to go away. Hibern has her. I came here."

"As well you ought," Tahra said sturdily. "That's just what the alliance is for!"

"We might have been followed," Arthur said apologetically.

Glenn made a movement, hand toward the hilt of a sword that wasn't there, and his sister forestalled what she feared would be an embarrassingly pompous declaration, saying hastily, "The alliance can hide you."

"We don't really need to hide so much as not to do magic. So we can't be traced. If it's really us Siamis is after. My mother thinks it's magical artifacts, not us," Arthur said with a rueful grin. "But I'm not sure that staying here would be right. I'd hate to be the cause of any more Norsundrian visitors. And my mother thought I ought to bring Roy. Doesn't seem like good manners, leaving a visitor from another world—our first mage student from Geth-deles—to find himself face to face with a pustule like Siamis."

Arthur glanced uncertainly at Roy, who raised his palms, hiding his regret at leaving Bereth Ferian even for a day. His task was to learn as much magic at the school as he could. But he appreciated Arthur's thought. "Here, you are at home," he said with a charming accent. "You know what it is best to do. On Geth-deles? We should take to the boats. Nobody finds you on the sea."

Tahra smiled crookedly. "Boats? Oh, I know just what you ought to do. And it would be fun," she added enviously.

Roth Drael

"CJ! Waken."

The familiar voice zapped lightning through CJ's nerves. Her eyes snapped open. She stared at a round face dominated by a pair of light brown eyes that looked gold in the diffuse light. Raggedly cut, unkempt dull blond hair, a coarse-woven, threadbare shirt—

"Sartora? Uh, Liere." CJ tried to swallow in a raw throat. She flushed. "How did I get here?"

She peered beyond Liere at two faces, one a tall teenage girl with black eyes and hair: Hibern. Next to her, a middle-aged woman whose messy brown hair was caught up on the side of her head with what looked like a quill pen. CJ recognized her: Erai-Yanya, Hibern's mage tutor.

"You are safe in Roth Drael," Erai-Yanya said. The calm in her unremarkable face, the hint of a smile in her eyes, soothed CJ's rising panic. "Some traveling morvende heard your shouting, and thinking you lost and in trouble, brought you here."

"I don't remember that," CJ mumbled.

Liere said, "You were in a nightmare. I fixed it. Sort of. So you stayed in a dream. You were very, very, *very* tired." She looked down, her shoulders hunched.

CJ sensed she was bracing for . . . something. Remembering how weird Liere was, she just said, "Thanks." And saw Liere relax.

Erai-Yanya reached with a forefinger, not quite touching CJ's arm. "You have been marked with a blood knife."

"Dejain did it," CJ said. "How long has it been? Is Clair all right?" CJ's fingers plucked at her arm. "Dejain said she'd get at the others if I . . ." She shrugged sharply, her throat closing up. She would not blub, and give Dejain the satisfaction.

Liere sat back on her heels, her chin on her knees, and shut her eyes. Presently she said, "I can hear Clair, a little. I think . . . I think she is on a ship."

"A ship?" CJ repeated.

"She is admiring the sunlight on water," Liere said.

"Well, at least it doesn't sound like she's surrounded by villains." CJ lay back in relief, and discovered herself nested in fuzzy, warm blankets, with another one thrown over her.

Erai-Yanya said, "What can you tell us?"

Out it all came, in a pent-up stream.

At the end, Erai-Yanya said, "I am very sorry that I cannot lift that blood spell. There are various types, and this is one of the most vicious. I would need the blade with your blood on it before I could attempt to break the spell. And your scroll—"

"It's not my scroll."

"—The scroll you carry is warded to a single person, which as you know from your own magic studies is the most difficult to break. But I was able to determine that at least a part of it is written in Chwahir." She sighed. "I wish we could get you to a Selenseh Redian. It wouldn't break the spell, but you would be safe, and unreachable by Norsunder's magic until we can solve—"

"I won't be parked like a good little kiddie, while Dejain goes after Clair. Or one of the other girls," CJ said fiercely. "Especially if you stick me in one of those creepy jewel caves."

"Creepy?" three voices exclaimed, Erai-Yanya warily.

Hibern said earnestly, "CJ, the Selenseh Redian caves are *never* evil. They close up somehow when Norsunder, or someone with evil intent, tries to invade them. That's why the one nearby — the reason this city was built here — is gone. Norsunder tried to take it, and it vanished."

CJ flushed, burrowing down further into the blankets. "I know what they are. We've got one. In the mountain. Under the white palace."

Erai-Yanya and Hibern exchanged looks, remembering that pretty marble palace on the mountain. Usually Selenseh Redians were located far from human concerns.

"I know they aren't *evil*," CJ muttered. "Not at all. But when you go inside, even though all the jewels are pretty, it's just, you feel all hot, and weird. Like you're snockered. None of us like going in it, except maybe Clair. Sometimes. And Dhana, but she's not really human."

Hibern left quietly while Erai-Yanya studied CJ, unsure what to do. The child was difficult, to say the least, and she needed help that Erai-Yanya had no time to give. Then she caught Liere's eye, and promised herself that when the greater threat was seen to, she would return to this problem. Before then . . . "Liere says she can help you in another way, and Hibern can perhaps get you situated." She absently wiped a strand of hair off her forehead as she got to her feet and walked out.

CJ watched her go, lips tightened a sharp sigh. Presently they heard the sudden *whish* of a transfer.

Liere said, "Why are you angry?"

"All grownups are alike. Kids get waved off like they don't matter, just because they're kids."

Liere's eyes rounded. "Oh, that's not it at all. It's just that someone has invaded Bereth Ferian's magic, and we fear with evil intent. That's why I'm here. I'm hiding."

"Oh." CJ grimaced. Get over yourself, CJ, she thought. "That can't be good."

Hibern reappeared, carrying a tray. "I've got listerblossom steep for you." She handed CJ a shallow little bowl.

CJ sat up enough to drink, sighing with pleasure as the herb smoothed the knots and jags of pain into silken ribbon. She lay back, enjoying the warmth. Enjoying the lack of pain. Then she remembered the threat. "What time is it?"

"Afternoon." Hibern set out plates, fresh bread, a shallow bowl of butter, some shirred eggs, and more steep. "Liere and I put you through a cleaning frame before we got you into my nightgown. Your clothes dried out, and they lie on that trunk. Do you want to eat first, or dress first?"

"Eat, thanks," CJ said, ravenous right down to the inside of her toes.

Hibern passed out the food, and CJ said thickly around her first bite, "What's this about magic and Bereth Ferian?"

Hibern said, "Someone who has the ability to break all the wards. And pass in and out without anyone being able to catch them."

CJ made a face. "That's even creepier than an attack, in a way." She'd studied enough magic to know that the bigger the ward, the tougher it was to maintain, unless dangerous amounts of magic were used.

And they had to be maintained. Even then, the magic could become unstable, when it did things it shouldn't to the surrounding area. Like Chwahirsland's border wards. But for one villain to break a ward over a city that an entire school full of mages kept maintained, that meant some very powerful magic indeed.

"He's been in and out twice," Liere said, her eyes enormous.

"You say he." CJ grimaced in anticipation. Kessler?

Liere whispered, "I think it's Siamis."

Hibern shook her head. "Erai-Yanya says that that's impossible. There are wards against him, ever since he returned to retrieve his sword from the deep archive. Those wards are intact."

Liere reddened, her shoulders hunching again. "I know. They think I'm imagining it was Siamis because he's so scary, and I'm always jumping at shadows. But Detlev is scarier, and I don't think it was he."

CJ was instantly ready to resent adults on her behalf. "But you can't prove it, so the grown-ups don't believe you?"

Liere gnawed a cuticle. "It's not like that. I can't even prove it to myself. Oh, the only way I can explain it is, I only see him there in a dream, and I don't . . ." Liere dropped her head, unable to explain how she walked in dreamscapes, sometimes knowing where she was and what she was doing, and sometimes helpless in the grip of dream symbols. And in waking, could not always be certain which was real.

"*I* believe her," Hibern felt it necessary to add when she saw Liere's miserable face. The truth was, she rather resented the senior mages' impatience with Liere. Oalthoreh had said dismissively, *She can't even master the simplest beginning spells, so how can we trust her in a matter difficult for those who have spent a lifetime in study?* "I believe Liere and so does Arthur, when it comes to the Moon-fire."

"The what?" CJ asked.

Hibern poured more listerblossom steep into CJ's cup. "The mage-archivists are pretty sure that the reason Bereth Ferian is built exactly where it is because of a magical . . . thing . . . we call the Moonfire. There is no written record, of course, but a persistent legend that all the magic students at the northern school learn about in first year. The word 'Bereth' isn't even Sartoran, they tell us, but some language in which the root word is 'burrd', which supposedly means moonlight, or something having to do with magic . . ."

CJ had stopped listening after "Bereth Ferian." Why was Clair on a ship? *Are they running away from Dejain, too?*

Hibern, mistaking CJ's unblinking stare for interest, went on helpfully, ". . . and it's thought to be a very old object of communication, maybe not even from this world, and maybe going back to the days of Ancient Sartor. Magic we can't reproduce, but under certain circumstances, the senior mages can see a sort of, oh, call it a reflection of the magical beings living in this world. Like moonlight. Sometimes they are clear as glass, or as . . . complicated as a hole into another time or place."

That caught CJ's attention. "You mean, like ripples in water? Dhana's people are like that. They live in a kind of lake, below the jewel cave, uh, the Selenseh Redian."

"They might be related," Hibern said. "But we can't say for certain. Evend, you remember, the mage who used to preside over Bereth Ferian before Siamis's enchantment, did his master's project on the Moonfire, which he thought dates back to the end of Ancient Sartor —" She saw CJ's fingers rubbing restlessly along the silk edging on the quilt, and forced herself to stop. "Have I lost you?"

"Um," CJ said uneasily. She knew she was being rude.

Hibern's passion was mysteries such as these, the more ancient the better. She felt the urge to say defensively, *I was only trying to distract you with something interesting*, because she knew it would sound accusatory. Well, it kind of was. "Anyway," she plowed on determinedly, "there's a lot more that no one really understands, but the important bit is, if it's that ancient, then it might have to do with that Dena Yeresbeth stuff, and the only person who understands that is Liere. Which is why I believe her about Siamis, even if no one else does."

Liere sent her an odd look, grateful and worried at the same time, and pressed her thin fingers together before raising one to begin gnawing her ragged nails.

CJ said, "So somebody messed around with that moon thing? And that's bad?"

Hibern said slowly, "We don't know for sure."

"I think he's looking for it," Liere put in. "But I don't have any evidence. Just those dreams."

"Ugh." CJ shuddered, and gulped a bite of shirred eggs. "And if it *is* Siamis, he might be after you next. For revenge."

"Indeed. So they sent me here." Liere whispered this last, and CJ intuited that Liere felt as squirmy as she did, fearing she sounded like Princess of Pomposities. Louder, "They sent Arthur off, and also Roy, the magic student from our sister world, as a safety measure. Nobody wants anything to happen to a visitor."

"So that's Bereth Ferian's news. Back to you, CJ," Hibern said. "From what you describe of the mosaics, and the interlocking patterns, Kessler Sonscarna might have taken control of one of the ancient Venn castles that's been abandoned ever since the Venn were forced behind their border."

CJ rubbed her arm, wishing she could use transfer magic. But until the horrible Norsunder mark was removed, any magic would send her straight to Dejain's clutches. "I've got to get to Clair, or at least warn her. But it'll take me months to get away from here! Can you send her a message?"

Hibern said, "I can, and will, but I was going to say, it shouldn't take you months. A few days will get you to the Fereledria, the border mountains —"

"The equator, I know," CJ cut in.

"Then you should know that if the beings who live there, the ones we call the Geres, can sense that that dark magic spell on you is not of your making, then they might be able to do whatever it is they do so you'll take two steps and find yourself on the other side of the mountains. From the Wnelder Vee side, it's at the very most a week's sailing to the strait." She grimaced. "First we have to get you through at least one night."

Liere had been watching CJ steadily. "And that's where I think *I* can help."

Nine

NO MATTER HOW MUCH CJ yearned to slow time, the eleventh hour arrived.

When Hibern's time candle burned to the third mark before the white of midnight, CJ hadn't counted sixty under her breath before Dejain struck.

A single heartbeat after CJ got hit with dizziness and the magic-evoked memories of pain, some kind of window shut down in her mind. The dizziness vanished. The pain died away.

Liere was there, in her thoughts: *This magic is trying to pretend to be Dena Yeresbeth. It tries to find your memories of different kinds of pain and put you there again.*

CJ thought back: *It works.*

Liere: *It isn't real, what she's doing to you.*

CJ: *I know. Feels real.* She couldn't prevent a spurt of resentment that Liere could make that window thing so easily.

Liere: *I've been doing it all my life. But CJ, you can make it.*

CJ: [scorn]

Liere: *You're hearing me so clearly. It's like with Senrid, when we first met. I think your Dena Yeresbeth is waking.*

CJ: *My what?*

Liere: *Just like Senrid. You don't trust yourself.*

Liere showed CJ her own memories, sensing things. Intuiting. CJ, highly embarrassed, tried to stop Liere, but it felt like trying to shape air. Then, as suddenly as Liere was in CJ's memories, she was gone.

Another heartbeat, and Liere had formed a blank plaster wall around them. Her thought came clear: *See the wall?*

CJ: *Of course I can. You just made it.*

Liere: *If you can see it, you can hold it. You're not using your eyes, you're using your mind. It's just as clear as looking at a wall in the day and remembering it as a wall. You can do it.*

And she faded away.

CJ scrabbled frantically, and remembered she didn't have hands. She didn't have eyes to see that wall—

She was alone, she couldn't find the floor, she was falling—

"Open your eyes."

It was Liere's voice, using a tone that shocked CJ's nerves. Her eyelids shuttered open and there were Liere and Hibern sitting side by side, two branches of candles behind them.

Vertigo caused CJ to clutch at the blankets.

Liere's voice was low, urgent. "Shut your eyes and see that wall. You can do it."

CJ clutched the blankets tightly to remind her she was not falling into a hole, and put all her concentration into seeing that white wall. Yes. She could see it. Was it real? A horrible moment of panic and then everything righted. It was like the first time she rode a bike, or turned a handspring: she could see the wall, and that kept it there.

She tried to see her own room in the Junky, cozy, small, her drawings on the dirt walls, the roots overhead, all keeping her safe and warm. Was it working? Was Dejain outside, like some kind of howling storm—gah!

If she tried to listen outside, the wall vanished. She scrambled frantically to see it around herself again. It wavered— she was losing— see it! And there it was.

After uncounted time, she sensed a release . . . The wall faded, and she opened her eyes.

"Dejain's gone," she said wonderingly.

"You resisted," Liere said. "That is a real mind-shield. You made one. If you see it being strong, it's strong. They can't get past it."

"Before I got it. When you told me to open my eyes. What was that?"

To her astonishment, Liere reddened to the ears. "It's . . . I don't have a good name for it. Senrid calls it a command voice. I hate that, because command sounds . . ." She shrugged and shook her head. "I can do it if I know a person's voice, their, oh, their range. It's kind of like how you hear a song, and then shape your voice to sing the right notes? Well, if I know someone's song, I can say something in it long enough to . . ." She clapped her hands lightly. "Get your body to hear *me*, instead of your thoughts. Or will. For a heartbeat."

"Wow," CJ said. "I don't know if I want to learn that or not."

Liere's smile was rueful. "Get some sleep. We can talk about it in the morning." A sudden, fierce yawn took her, and CJ perceived how tired Liere was.

She sighed, and snuggled into her welter of blankets.

Trying to grapple with the idea that she had Dena Yeresbeth, she slid into a jumble of dreams about being chased by shadowy figures shooting light beams out of their eyes as she shot back with a water pistol.

Liere padded back to Erai-Yanya's room. Cold tightened the back of her neck and her upper arms. She knew the cause was not the room, which was warm enough, but the shock of CJ's memories, which were in so many ways a lot like Senrid's: full of violence from her father, he from his uncle. Liere knew what it meant to be afraid, for her father had despised her, but his withering scorn and obsession with controlling every tiny detail of life had not engendered in her the bone-and-muscle deep anger of small children who live with a sense of imminent threat from those who should be keeping them safe.

She had to learn how to keep herself from feeling what they felt, for borrowing someone's pain aided no one. That was the horrible part about being the first of their generation with Dena Yeresbeth . . .

She fell asleep on that thought. In her dream she wandered on the mental plane, trying to avoid memory distortions of Senrid, then he was there, and she shared his sense of suffocation, the cold sweat of terror.

She jolted upright, sleep gone.

"Senrid," she whispered, fumbling for the magical transfer token that he had given her after their return from the sister-world Geth-deles.

She had not told anyone. She was too embarrassed to admit to the nightmares she'd endured after being Detlev's prisoner. It had been so comforting, knowing that if she so much as glimpsed Detlev or Siamis, she could touch that token, say Senrid's family name, and be pulled across the world to Senrid, inside his castle full of guards, with magic spells that kept out Norsundrians.

The spell, formulated specifically for her, brought her directly to Senrid. She was the only person he permitted instant proximity.

He sat up in bed, disoriented at the gust of air caused by transfer. Then he recognized the thin figure in ratty shirt and knee pants: Liere.

His throat hurt. He'd been yelling.

Even in the dark Liere's eyes were enormous. "Senrid?"

"Nightmare." He hated saying even that much. But this was Liere, who'd probably heard him on the mental plane. "I was there again. Norsunder Base."

He snapped his fingers, and the glow-globes lit.

The pupils in Liere's huge eyes were round and black. "Which time? When you were Detlev's prisoner?"

"No. The recent one."

"When you and Leander were prisoners." Liere flinched, hoping that she hadn't somehow caused Senrid's nightmare, after helping CJ. If only she knew more about how Dena Yeresbeth worked!

She hunched up, remembering CJ's unhidden awe at her control. But Liere knew she didn't have true control, not really.

Senrid got out of bed and reached for his clothes. Liere obligingly looked away, even though she knew Senrid didn't care who saw him dressed or undressed. From her limited experience, that seemed common to those who were used to a lot of servants around. But she had been raised differently, and so she looked down as cloth rustled impatiently. She looked up again when he began moving restlessly around his room, his bare feet slapping on the smoothed stone floor as he fastened up his shirt.

His haste was due to the chill caused by so many thicknesses of stone. The castle was seldom warm. But he welcomed the cold air. It helped to vanquish that sense of suffocation.

"I don't know why I keep dreaming about that time, and not the other one," he said. "It was so stupid. So pointless. I was scarcely even there. Compared to the first time."

Liere sat on the floor cross-legged, only her head turning to watch him as he paced back and forth. He was briefly distracted by noticing that she'd hacked off her hair again, making it look like a mad goat had chewed it, and her clothes were so threadbare they were nearly rags. It had to mean someone had been admiring her in Bereth Ferian, or something similar. He hated seeing her tied up in inward knots over something so trivial, but he knew better than to bring it up. It had never helped.

She said, "*Any* memories of Norsundrians would cause nightmares. I hate mine."

He waved a hand impatiently. Not to dismiss her fears — and she knew it — but to get to the real subject, the one he hadn't wanted to say out loud. "It was when Dejain blinded and deafened me. Feeling so helpless." A brief, nauseating sense of suffocation closed his throat, but he forced himself to stop the restless wandering, to stand at the open window and breathe deeply as the castle tower bell clanged once for the midnight watch change. In the distance the city bells clanged once, then fell silent.

Below in the academy where his future officers were trained, faint sounds of movement rose on the quiet air: the night patrol. He grimaced. "I'm glad I got extra masters," he said.

Liere was used to this abrupt jumping of subjects.

"The academy is a mess." Senrid whirled around, his fingers tense as he flicked his hands up. "It's like they never learned anything. And they only missed part of last summer."

Liere stayed silent, waiting. She had no interest in the academy, but she knew that Senrid cared about it very much.

"Keriam's right. We have to keep the seniors an extra year. Though some of them I long to send over to the Guard so they'll be bottom rank. Being another year at the top isn't any good for 'em, though I will say Marlovair is a whole lot better than he was as a. . ." He stopped.

Liere waited, suspecting that Senrid was working his way around to what had bothered him, and sure enough, out it came.

Senrid said, "I still don't know if it's a real memory, or caused by whatever magic Dejain used on me when she was playing around during my blindness. But I thought I heard boys laughing in the corridor there at Norsunder Base."

"Boys!" Liere shivered. "I think we need to get some hot chocolate." And as they started down through Senrid's enormous castle, passing the occasional alert guard on constant patrol.

Liere's instinct had been to get away from nightmares, but the subject stayed right with them.

They reached the kitchen, which had a minimal staff on duty for the night watch, and to get things ready for the bakers who would arrive well before dawn to get the breakfast breads into the ovens.

The night staff were used to the king appearing at odd hours, but since he never interfered with the rhythms of the kitchen, they struck fists to hearts and returned to work.

Liere pattered to the jug where milk was kept, and reached up to retrieve the stone jar where the ground chocolate waited. Not many here drank it; this was kept just for her. She loved that, knowing that there was a something just for her in this enormous palace. Even though the Marlovens seemed really strange at times — difficult to understand — she liked this feeling that she was welcome.

She knew a lot of people in other countries hated the Marlovens, but she liked the swooping, stylish relief carvings in subtle shades of gray and silver and white down the upper level halls, and here and there in the city: wheeling and diving birds, racing horses, wind-streaming banners. She liked the way the Marlovens rode, and she liked that there was no bowing, and nobody called her Sartora.

Senrid set a pan on the stove, snapped the firestick into flame, and left Liere to fix the concoction to her liking as he poured out some of the guards' coffee for himself.

They sat on stools at a corner of the prep table. "Were they prisoners?" Liere asked, because the tightness to Senrid's mouth meant he was still wrestling mentally with his uncertainty about nightmares and reality.

"I doubt that prisoners would be gloating," Senrid said. "It has to have been my own nightmare. Or maybe it was one imposed by Dejain, though I don't get why. Her entire strategy."

Liere still did not grasp what he meant by strategy, though he'd tried to explain it to her. But all the words he used to define it were so alien to her thinking. So while he talked about strategy and Norsunder, Liere sorted through her own memories, trying to determine if she had inadvertently caused Senrid's nightmare. But that awful business about boys laughing, that sounded like his fears about the academy had mixed themselves into his dreams.

She breathed easier: awful as his fears about the academy were, at least she could reassure herself that she was not the cause. And she'd achieved something by teaching CJ the mind-shield. It was just as Erai-Yanya had said when Liere first joined the magic school: *Young as you are, you will have things to teach us. No, I know you are about to say you are only a beginner, and we all appreciate that. But you ought to know that one of the best ways to truly know a subject is by helping someone else to understand it.*

"Young"' If Liere were to have a child by the Birth Spell, would she be teaching the child everything about Dena Yeresbeth, and would that cause her to know Dena Yeresbeth better?

She was surprised by the warm feeling behind her ribs at the thought of a child. Of course it would be like a sister, and a friend. Not like her own sister, Marga, popular and good at everything she did — so different from Liere in every possible way. If Liere had a daughter, they would love each other, because they'd be so alike.

". . . speak about that," Senrid said, and Liere flushed, aware that she'd missed the gist of his talk.

She shut her eyes, and caught the drift of his thoughts. "Maybe it's time to visit the alliance people," Liere said. "You know they all want you as a leader."

"No, they don't." Senrid drank off his coffee and blinked. "Yow, that was stronger than I thought it would be." He set the cup down.

"I don't get it," Liere said. "I thought you said that the alliance is a great idea!"

"It *is* a great idea." When Liere looked puzzled, Senrid said, "At least, the alliance we had before. Since we got back from Geth-deles, Glenn Delieth has been begging and pleading and scorning everyone into the idea of the alliance becoming some sort of international military force . With him in command, of course. Though there's no talk of logistics, or where this army is to be quartered, boring little details like that. And if anyone tries to raise another idea, he flings Everon's defeat in their teeth — as if that kingdom's suffering means no one dares to question."

Liere knew that was true.

"I might favor it more if I thought he knew what he was doing. But he doesn't. Take my last visit to Everon. I tried to bring up practical things like supply lines, and he waved that off. Then I noticed that Glenn's got his future honor guard dueling. Dueling! As if Norsunder's warriors will obey the rules of dueling! But when I tried to ask about different drills for mounted and for foot, he cut me off with all this fart noise about how the Knights of Dei have a long tradition of honor, they have to be living symbols or else they become savages like . . ."

"Like Marlovens?" Liere asked, not surprised. She never admitted it to anyone, but she hated being around Glenn, and Tahra's quiet adulation made her uncomfortable in another way — Liere was certain she would do something stupid to disappoint the grieved, difficult princess.

Senrid flashed a nasty, toothy grin. Then jerked a shoulder up. "I think he almost said it. But he didn't. He seems to think we're a kingdom full of Inda-Harskialdnas. I think he's more envious than malicious."

Liere grimaced, thinking of Tahra's painstakingly careful letters. "Tahra *doesn't* think the alliance should be an army. She wants us all to warn each other if Norsunder is coming."

"I know. Karhin and Thad think the same. But we're the minority. Many have backed away from the alliance altogether, meanwhile Glenn is collecting those who like his ideas. He's collecting boys — and it's just boys — not just from Everon, but from all over."

Senrid looked away, over the shining pots and pans hung on their hooks, waiting for the day's cabbage to be boiled. "All right, I'll take the nightmare as the prod of guilt. I know Thad and Karhin want to save the alliance from turning into Glenn's Army. I'm not sure what I can do. But as soon as summer is over and the academy goes home, I'll visit them."

Ten

Norsunder Base

DEJAIN STARED AT ELZHIER, the only spy she trusted, and she didn't trust her very far. "That has to be false information."

Elzhier's mouth twisted in amusement. "I assure you. Wan-Edhe of the Chwahir is somewhere in Norsunder. Some say Efael has him. Others say Siamis ordered the snatch, before Yeres took Siamis away into Norsunder for her own purposes. Remember when Siamis was there nearly a year?" *There* being Norsunder-Beyond.

"The real question is, why no one is using what has to be the biggest army in the world? Because my understanding is, Chwahirsland is all army and army support."

Elzhier spread her hands. "Maybe it was to be handed off to Kessler as a reward before he went renegade." Her mouth twisted again. "And, maybe no one wants to deal with Wan-Edhe's webwork of traps, just to run a ruined kingdom whose army has numbers, but training centuries out of date. No one, that is, except this boy Jilo."

Another brat! Dejain had assumed that "Jilo" was some Chwahir flunky. Maybe Detlev's spy had garbled the truth, and Kessler hadn't given this boy the texts at all, but the unknown Jilo had taken them. But that didn't explain why he'd turn around and give the texts to Leander and Senrid. Or, most important of all, why Kessler had protected the brats, if he'd been robbed of the texts.

No, she knew the answer to that. He was playing games with her.

Time to leave the Mearsiean brat to her bloodthirsty assistant, and pay a visit to Chwahirsland herself.

Elzhier, an arrogant woman no older than twenty, said, "I don't know much about magic, but I can tell you this, Dejain, you will have to physically walk over the border. The wards there are the worst in the world — a magic transfer would be deadly. Worse than here." She jerked a short thumb over her shoulder at the rest of Norsunder Base.

"There are no wards here against *me*," Dejain said.

The woman shrugged, and with a flip of brown hair, sauntered off.

Dejain waited until she was well out of earshot, summoned her assistant, and said, "Vasz, the Mearsiean brat is all yours. Have fun."

Vasz, delighted with the opportunity to experiment with the mind tortures through the jealously guarded bloodknife magic, got his chance at last — just to find magical torment from a distance much less interesting than he'd expected. No matter what he tried, the brat appeared to be asleep.

Off the Coast of Wnelder Vee

I will not recount the conversations that took place between Clair, Arthur, and Roy during those pleasant days sailing around the hundreds of tiny islands. Arthur recorded them all, enumerating the wide range of subjects touched on. He even kept a tally of books mentioned, both those he knew and the few he didn't. I think it is important to record that though conversation often turned into debate, there was never any malice, or even a covert motivation to outmaneuver the others. Though not every argument was regarded as convincing, no one ever went to sleep angry.

Then came a day when Clair, Arthur, and Roy went with a couple of Dtheldevor's crew in a small boat to explore an island covered with beautiful shells. Clair hunted all over for one to match the distinctive, iridescent one Puddlenose had given her (partly to prove to herself it *was* a shell). But nothing came close to the singular beauty or feel of the one she still wore.

By the time she decided it must have come from a different sea, the light had slowly become glare bright, causing a pang behind her eyes that she didn't notice, until Sharly the centaur said, "We'd better leave! Storm's coming."

No one asked how she knew.

Fast as they gathered aboard the pinnace, they weren't fast enough for the dark line of clouds coming on. Too soon they huddled together in a futile effort to hide from the howling wind and sideways cloudburst.

Clair peered over the hand she cupped around her nose so she wouldn't breathe in the warm torrents. Lightning flickered somewhere, the thunder reduced to a broken rumble beneath the roar of wind and pelting rain.

The brief light illuminated Arthur, almost unrecognizable with his blond hair plastered flat over his skull. Next to him crouched Roy, his jug-handle ears sticking out past his dark hair flattened to writhing worms on his forehead.

Clair saw Roy grinning, and stared in astonishment. He thought this storm was fun? Maybe it wasn't as dangerous as she thought. Surely he wouldn't look so thrilled if they were about to drown.

"Boats pay no attention to season. Weather." The word came out sounding like 'wessair' in his Geth-deles accent.

If he wasn't worried, then she wouldn't be either, but still she kept one hand clutched around her medallion in case she had to transfer, and pressed her back more firmly against the hull so she could watch the centaur handling the tiller.

Sometimes life was so very odd. At home, during the quiet round of days, she had never thought to find herself pitching on the water in the middle of summer thunder, aboard a boat guided by a centaur who was part of a privateer crew.

Sharly was pinto in her horse half, her body reminding Clair more of a deer in size and the smallness of her hooves, though they were not cloven. Her braided hair was the exact reddish brown of her spots and her tail.

Handling the sail was Joey Warren, a tall boy whose brightly colored clothes plastered down his lanky form were barely discernible in hue. As lightning flared, he grinned fiercely, the golden hoops at his ears swinging as he turned his head back and forth from mast to sail to waves. His body leaned out as he pulled on the sheet controlling the sail.

Smash! The bow thumped down, sending a froth of water splashing up into the greenish wave rising high above them . . .

Clair shut her eyes as the boat began another long climb, the timbers groaning.

Indecipherable shouts between Sharly and Joey caused her to sit up, looking around wildly.

She glimpsed towering masts sporting a scrap of sail. Dtheldevor's ship!

They rounded under the lee of the ship. Ropes dangled down.

"You go," Roy yelled to Arthur.

"I can't climb that . . ." Arthur yelled, peering into the nearly blinding rain at the rope swinging against the heaving tumblehome of the ship.

"Hang on. They pull you," Roy roared back.

Arthur gripped the rope, trying to get his legs to close around it, as he heaved and jerked upward. The ship loomed closer, and he braced for the impact that he knew would smash him, but somehow the rope spun away, whirling him helplessly. With a couple of hard jerks he rose until he felt hands grabbing parts of him and pulled him over to relative safety.

Clair was next, her lighter form battered by the wind — at first it looked as if she'd be smashed between the wildly gyrating mast of the boat and the ship. Her numb hands began to slide, burning, and reflexively she let go.

But a hand caught her wrist. Roy was there, his grip unexpectedly strong. He kicked them away from the curve of the bow. She dangled helplessly as wood struck the side of Roy's face. Dark blood rushed down, and in desperation she fingered her medallion out of her sodden shirt with her throbbing free hand and tried to transfer, but the spell would not compass two, and

Roy's grip made them two. She tried to summon Hreealdar, the strange being who sometimes came as lightning, but again, she could not manage the spell—either that or Hreealdar was gone.

Roy's grip tightened. Somehow, somehow, they were pulled upward, and over the rail, to where Clair fell trembling to the deck, her wrist throbbing, palms burning. She forced herself to her knees as someone shouted something at Roy.

"I'm fine, me. It is only a scrape," he yelled back, fingering his bleeding head at the hairline. "Ropes and ships, this we know in Geth."

"Come below, all'ez yeh!" Dtheldevor bawled. She was barely a silhouette in the sideways-driving rain.

Clair got her trembling limbs under her, and followed a long, dripping ponytail to a square hatch in the deck with a ladder leading down.

A short time later, they sat clean and dry below decks in the wardroom off the galley, a bandage around Roy's head, and across Clair's palms, mugs of hot pear cider with a dose of listerblossom in their hands. Now that they were safely aboard, the storm had blown out to sea, leaving the waters calming quickly, the sunlight winking off little wavelets as if to say, *Just kidding!*

Presently footsteps thumped down the ladder from the hatch, and there was Dtheldevor herself, tall as Joey, tough and brown as old wood, with a fierce grin below slanted black eyes. "So what will yeh?" she asked in her captain's deck voice. "We gonna keep sailing around the blast-damn islands, or is it you bums want ta go somewheres?" she bawled genially.

Clair stared at her, unsure what to say. So she waited for the others to speak, as she studied Dtheldevor in a way she had never considered before meeting Mearsieanne again.

Both had done the Child Spell at roughly the same age, fourteen or fifteen. Both had lived many decades before Mearsieanne was snatched beyond time. Dtheldevor was tall and strong, cat-muscled from years of adventuring on the sea. She had no idea how old she was, that much Clair knew. She cared less. Her face looked like a kid's face, unless you looked really close at the many faint lines, imprinted perhaps by the weather. Clair remembered Dtheldevor staying with them during Siamis's first attack, the smell of whisky that had clung to Dtheldevor's clothes, and she'd wondered what childhood and adulthood really were, aside from the mysteries of puberty and what they did to the body.

Arthur said, "Roy, you are the guest. Have you a preference?"

"This world, I know it not." Roy turned up his palms. "If we cannot study, I am happy anywhere, for what I value most is our talk on subjects of history and magic. On Geth, I am used to wind and sea."

Clair nodded, smiling. The past two weeks had been full of sunlight on water, good food, and even better talk. She had always liked quiet, scholarly Arthur. Roy, it seemed, for all that he'd been born on another world, was much the same.

But there were regrets, too. Clair had thought herself well-read. Her aunt had been insistent on that, but Roy's questions pointed up her ignorance, and she was learning as much from Arthur's ramblings about books as Roy obviously was. All the time she'd spent running around the forest with the girls, or listening to music, or dealing with kingdom affairs, small as they were, Arthur had spent studying. And it showed.

Maybe it was time to return home, now that she had met with Mearsieanne, and delivered her message about coming back to Mearsies Heili. But she really liked being out in the world, meeting people who would never even think of venturing to an out-of-the way corner like Mearsies Heili, where nothing world-shaking ever happened.

Arthur was saying, " . . . like did you know that they used to be required to live as hermits for ten years at least, or even longer, away from human concerns?"

Roy snapped his fingers. "Someone, ah, they told me." He turned to Clair. "Did not you have some relative who lives as a hermit somewhere? A very great mage?"

Clair smiled, thinking about how Aunt Murial would laugh at being called a great mage.

Roy asked with casual interest, "What are her areas of greatest strength with magic, this aunt?"

"You'd have to ask her," Clair said. "Hermits are hermits for a reason. That much I learned really early."

Roy shrugged, his gaze away to the north.

Clair was raising her cup again when, for the first time, she felt the internal ting of her notecase. She dug it out, and under cover of the others talking about summer weather, quietly removed the note.

It was not CJ's expected hand, but another, unfamiliar. Clair scanned to the bottom, saw Hibern's name, and read quickly. Then dropped the note in dismay.

"I have to go home," she said, half-standing.

"This Siamis, he attacks?" Roy asked with quick concern.

"No. Not him. Another villain. Named Dejain, used to be allied with Kessler. She's after some book or other . . . I have to go. I'm sorry." She said to the others.

"No apology necessary. Get yer carcass where it's needed," Dtheldevor said genially. "Just come back, if yer minded to sail agin."

Arthur had blanched at Kessler's name. "Let me know how things are," he asked.

"I will," Clair promised. She gripped her travel bag in one hand, her medallion in the other, and transferred home.

Eleven

CJ DISCOVERED THAT BY day, everything was just as Hibern had promised, and by night, if she took the time before midnight to really hold tight to her mental wall, that, too, worked as Liere had promised.

First came some forest folk with white horses that reminded CJ of Hreealdar, the horse-like being that sometimes turned to light. Only these were real horses, with white hair hides, who gave her a bumpy but fast ride straight south to the mountains. Even better, she didn't have to try to figure out directions, or even hunt for food.

They left her at the foot of the mountains, in the middle of a snowstorm that abruptly went from teeth-chattering chill to a magical warmth. She never remembered how she got there, but come morning she found herself on the other side of the mountains, in sight of a harbor full of bobbing ships, as promised.

Hibern had given her some coins. She worked her way down the trade ships at the piers, hoping she wasn't going to have to be rowed out to the ones parked in the bay. But one after another of all those going south, as soon as they heard Chwahirsland as her destination, refused.

At the far right were the older piers for smaller ships. The first was a narrow one with two raked-back masts. Though CJ had sailed on board Mearsies Heili's single defensive vessel, the *Tzasilia*, she didn't pretend to know much about them, but this one looked fast.

The captain was a young man. A lot of the crew looked like kids on the Wander. Hoping this would be the one, she raced up the ramp.

The captain was friendly enough when he told her, yes, he was heading south and into the strait as far as Bermund.

"I'm going to Chwahirsland," CJ said—words she had never thought she'd speak. "I can pay. *And* I'll work."

"Even if you were good as an entire crew, and offering a bag of gold, I won't risk my ship docking anywhere along the Chwahir coast," he said. "But I'll sail as close as I dare, at night. You can swim for it. It's summer. You'll make it."

CJ hated the idea, but it seemed this was the best she'd get. She agreed, and was welcomed aboard.

When she'd sailed on the *Tzasilia*, she loved handling the wheel if the weather was good, and didn't mind being a lookout, but what she got was cook's assistant. That meant all the chopping, scraping, and scrubbing, and then the cleanup, but at least they had a magic bucket so all she had to do was dunk and dry.

They sailed on the outward tide, and CJ's heart lifted when she discovered she'd guessed right. With all sail set high and low, the schooner seemed to skim over the surface of the water.

Convergence on Chwahirsland:
Dejain

Dejain discovered that there was no Destination for Chwahirsland. In fact Elzhier had told the truth: beginning any kind of transfer spell raised the metallic heat stench that warned of dire consequences.

She could not get a force there without losing time. Therefore she was going to have to go herself. She briefly considered abandoning the project, but she *had* to get those blood-magic texts. She might walk in, but surely she could force this Jilo out in a transfer — and if it killed him, she'd look for another way. The gratification of taking those precious, rare texts from under Detlev's nose, without him knowing, was far too alluring.

Convergence on Chwahirsland:
Rel

It did not take long for Rel to make it back to Erdrael Danara.

The first time he had ventured into Chwahirsland was after Terry, as a young prince, had been captured by Wan-Edhe, to brandish as hostage against counter-attack after his unsuccessful invasion of Colend.

Rel had been able to steal a uniform from the long wagon train of supplies and slip amongst the mass marching back. On that journey he had swiftly learned the language, he thought at the time by listening; now wondered if he had heard it a lot as an infant, and so it came back quickly.

Though Terry was glad to see Rel, and did his best to get him to stay, Rel's quest had changed from idle curiosity to intent. Under the cover of one of the regular summer storms tumbling slowly down the strait, he vanished expertly over the border, and made his way down toward Chwahirsland's capital, Narad.

On the surface, everything looked the same. Smelled the same, like fear sweat and moldering stone. But here and there, always on the periphery of sight and hearing, furtive conversations, restive whispers, signaled a slow but inexorable shift.

It was clear to Rel in every stealthy look, every murmur, that the populace all expected Wan-Edhe to come back, a threat nearly as pervasive as Wan-Edhe's actual presence. The evil old king had left behind a miasma of fear, dread, and hidden anger that Rel tasted in the bland food, smelled in the stale, magically-leached air, and felt in his pores.

Though all roads led to Narad, he intended to avoid the
capital. Assuming Iog Shunsu had told the truth about coming
from a fishing village, he needed to get to the coast, where he'd
begin systematically at the westmost river, and then, if he came up
empty, move back eastward.

But first he had to become part of the weave of Chwahir life.
From border outpost to supply outpost, he insinuated himself into
the expected patterns of Chwahir custom. Without a twi—the
group of eight age-mates that all Chwahir became a part of when
small—or family connections, a stranger had to be a recognized
part of the military routine, or at the best one would be regarded
as one of Wan-Edhe's countless spies whom no one dared touch,
but who seldom heard the truth. At worst, the stranger would be
surreptitiously scragged, out of self-defense. Strangers could only
bring dangers.

At each step, Rel tried to think ahead. At some point he had to
abandon the lies, or risk being mired in falsehood. But deter-
mining the right moment to make the change was the challenge.

By the time he reached a small village outside of the main bay
above Narad, one of many small villages that existed mostly off
fishing and gleaning sea wrack, he carried legitimate messages.

No Shunsu there. Nor at the next. Nor the next. Nor the three
after. He worked his way around the bay over three days, until he
reached the military outpost that served the bay. Tired and wet,
he rode slowly, glancing obliquely from house to house. They
looked similar in that all were repaired with sea wrack. Up close,
of course, every house was different— every wall was different.
Windows were small and high, to make it easier to look out of,
especially with no light behind one; likewise there was no way to
sneak peeks into small, high windows.

He had no idea how many might be watching him. It could be
all. The shoulder blade twitch of being watched galled him cease-
lessly, unless he sat with his back pressed to a wall.

He went to the duty desk and handed off the latest batch of
letters, and as he had at each village, asked low-voiced, "The
Shunsu family. Are they here?"

The outpost captain, a stolid man with salt-and-pepper hair,
instantly looked suspicious. Because he recognized the name?

Rel said, even lower, "Iog Shunsu once served my family."

"She's dead."

Rel was never very expressive, and he had been on his guard

ever since entering Chwahirsland. The outpost captain was accustomed to his fellow Chwahir, who all kept emotions hidden.
And so, though Rel reacted with no more than a fractional tightening of his eyelids in a wince, the slightest lengthening of his jaw,
the captain saw those subtle signs and his own lowered brow of
suspicion eased fractionally. He understood regret.

So he said, "See if her cousin will talk to you. He lives in the
second house from the end of that row."

"The horse is army," Rel said, and it was understood that the
army would house and feed the animal, instead of burdening the
inmates of that dilapidated house with no barn or corral attached

Rel lifted his pack, as a thin, sour-tasting rain began to fall
again. The ground was already soupy with sand-gritty mud, so his
boots were thoroughly caked by the time he reached that second
house from the end.

Outside the door, Rel said, "I seek the cousin of Iog Shunsu."

"Who asks?" The words came faintly.

"She was known to my mother."

Some muffled sounds followed, and then he was taken completely by surprise as the door was pulled wide, and an old man
said in an unexpectedly high, trembling voice, "Come, come
within, child. You have her eyes."

Rel found himself drawn into a cramped cottage kept scrupulously tidy. His army coat was spread before the fire, and a short
time later, a tiny bowl full of noodles was pressed into his hands.

He had learned by now that these noodles in thin broth that
tasted vaguely of garlic, shallot, and an herb or two were the
highest social honor; the ingredients were all supposed to be
reserved to the army, but people managed to scrimp and scavenge
for those rare, important moments.

As he looked down from the simple meal to his host, he began
to perceive that perhaps this old uncle might be an aunt? He had
learned long ago that women dressed as men in order to join the
army and help their families survive. A couple of these supposed
men had come to his aid in surreptitious ways on his long chase
after Terry and CJ when they were Wan-Edhe's hostages.

He suspected then that "the cousin" was a Chwahir deflection,
but he knew better than to give any sign.

His hostess's black eyes were rimmed with tears that she did
not permit to fall. They reflected back the fire as she said, "How
did you find me?" A widening of fear, a tense glance at the door.

"Is someone from there coming?"

Rel wasn't certain if "there" meant the capital or Wan-Edhe, but made a negating motion with his hand. "I am on my own. No one at all knows who I am."

"I am she." Iog inclined her head. "Why do you seek me?"

Rel briefly repeated what Commander Dei had told him.

"Ah. He misunderstood, perhaps, but it is as well." Iog stretched out gnarled fingers to the fire. "I did hunt down the assassin, before he could report your existence, or you would no longer be alive. I killed him by my own hand. But I could not touch the one who gave the orders."

Rel gazed at her in surprise. "Why would someone order someone else to murder my mother?" Then the obvious occurred to him. "That would be Wan-Edhe, I expect. The worst, most bloody-handed king on the continent. Probably in the world."

"We call him The Hate," Iog whispered fiercely.

"But what would he have against her?"

Iog let out a long, hissing breath of pent-up grief, her head shaking from side to side. "I can see you do not have it all, or it would be clear. Your mother was Princess Gwasan Sonscarna. She ran when Wan-Edhe commenced the second of his rage purges, against her generation, for conspiracy. To The Hate, learning light magic was a death sentence, but she had done that secretly: he had thought her attending a school for nobles, to perfect her Sartoran, and she really studied magic far north in Bereth Ferian, for three years. The Hate had some plan for marrying her to Carlael of Colend, to gain inroads in the south. But the Colendi, of course, would have nothing to do with us. She studied magic, and though the world knows that light magic especially is useless for war, The Hate still considered that treasonous. And finally, to cross the border against his will was a death sentence, for her, for her twi. It was my honor to serve as her twi-sister."

Iog paused, and then, as the drizzle drummed the thin roof overhead, until the watery light vanished, she told Rel all about her mistress's life.

The old, uncertain voice sometimes thinned with passion and long-suppressed anger and grief as Rel gained a picture of the lives of the royal children, who under Wan-Edhe's earlier days had begun life with the traditional twi specially trained to serve and protect their royal charge. Iog and her twi-sisters had been the last women so trained.

But as the years became more restrictive, the servants were forbidden to train in defense. Iog said with heavy irony, "*Breathing* was a death sentence, when he was in one of his rages. Ah, whatever happens, the writing of history shall be in our hands, and he and all his doing shall vanish." She made a violent gesture. "Except as a noisome smear, forever cursed."

The word *doing* in Chwahir connoted effort without effect, unlike *work*, a word that had (or once had had) such profound meaning that the word could be translated as *honor* in other languages. Work meant dignity, meaning, purpose, and as such was nearly as important as the noun that Rel could only translate as *art-in-sound*, a word Iog whispered with sidelong glances. It was a fundamental concept he had learned when trying to master languages; he'd realized that the Chwahir tongue didn't have tenses as did Sartoran-branched languages. Instead, they had measure words for categories of nouns, and words of completion, underscoring the importance of work. *Work hard* was both a greeting and a benediction between Chwahir. *I have troubled you with extra work* was a high compliment, an acknowledgment of moral debt.

Wan-Edhe had done his best to destroy all that, in his effort to force on his people the idea that their purpose was obedience to his will. And so art had been forbidden, as it did not serve his will, inspired disobedience, and interfered with preparing for the war that he meant to carry all through the southern end of the Sartoran continent, to the glory of the Chwahir.

She went on with her tale, describing how the princess decided to break altogether with Chwahirsland. "Though I fear my twi-sisters were murdered in interrogation, I still hope they heeded the note my mistress left them, and vanished. I was the only one to stay by her side. I know not whether any live or die — to search might be to draw their names to inimical eyes — and so I live here alone. Ah, but once again I digress. To what matters to you . . ."

She explained that they'd become accustomed to living on the run when she met Glenred.

"Do you know who Glenred was?" Rel asked.

Iog raised her palms in that brief gesture many Chwahir used, with a little shrug. "Glenared, or Glenereth, he had as many names as a king has coats. But she chose him."

"Were they happy?"

"Together? Oh, yes. Though there was always the threat.

Gwasan, too, lived under various false names, the last Nanas, daughter of a fisher. When it came to her she was with child, they dwelt in Everon, for the king had need of Glenred. But the Everoneth despise Chwahir, and there were many whispers about her. So when your birth was nigh, she left Everon. Glenred accepted that decision, but they could not resist sending messages back and forth in a private code. I do not know if he summoned her or the assassin contrived a false message: all I know is that late one night she said we must flee, yet still the assassin surprised us." Her lips thinned. "He was surprised as well. He was not expecting the babe. Or her to know how to fight. But I had taught her."

Iog looked down at work-worn, gnarled hands. "She pushed you into my arms, or I would have put myself between him and his knife. As it was, she was able to knife him twice before he stabbed her to the heart. When he stumbled off, she kept me there, saying over and over that I must get you to safety first. Those were her last words, *Get Rel to safety*."

"She named me? Rel is not a Chwahir name."

"It is an adaptation of Ressler, a family name — there was a young nephew named Kessler, whom she had been fond of before she had to leave. She had tried to protect him, until it became clear that her favor harmed the little prince, for The Hate was exceeding jealous and threatened to kill him if she did not obey. So she pretended to turn against that boy, who she missed forever after."

She thumbed her eyes. "I digress. So very much to tell you! But to return to you, and your name. She did not dare name you for the nephew, lest The Hate discover, and discover her true feelings. Ress is the common short form of Ressler, but Rel is not unheard of. Glenred liked Rel. Said it was short and not distinctively identified with any kingdom, as he'd heard it in Goerael, and other parts of the world."

Her face crumpled, and she wiped away tears.

"After I left you with the Commander, as I could not find Glenred, I returned to Disappear her properly, and found the assassin's notecase. That meant he had not been able to report your existence. I followed the blood trail to where he had holed up."

Her mouth tightened. "After I killed him, I dipped a stick piece in his blood, and wrote on a paper, *It is done*. I knew how those notecases worked, as all the royal children had had them, and they were required to report where they were and what they were doing, and to answer instantly if *He* wanted them. I sent the paper and then threw the notecase into a lake. Then I returned here, and took on the guise of my cousin, who served the king's assassins. I hoped to hear of any further assassins sent."

"So you never heard again from my father?"

"I never saw him again. It took me three years before I could find a way to get a message to Everon, to discover that you had been taken out of the country, and neither you nor Glenred were to be found. I was content: you would live."

Rel didn't blame her for her lack of interest in his father. But he could not prevent a sense of sharp disappointment.

Then she surprised him by leaning forward, giving him a searching gaze, then saying in a low voice, "You could smite young Jilo, you know, and take the throne . . . until The Hate comes back. Though Jilo is well liked by many. I include myself among them."

Rel stared back, lips clipped tightly against expressing the depth of his revulsion at the idea. He hadn't even considered what learning his identity meant. He was Kessler's cousin to the second degree? That was an even more disgusting idea.

For that matter, why hadn't *Kessler* killed Jilo and taken the throne? *He probably will when it suits him.* "So Jilo doesn't call himself a king? That sounds like him."

Her eyes widened. "You know him, then?"

"We've met," Rel said cautiously.

Her chin came down, and she whispered, "I still have many of my old contacts. There is rumor some of the army captains will rise against him. Because he wants to better things for *us*." Her gnarled hand pressed to her black-clad bosom. "It is said, these captains do not wish to lose all their privilege, the best food, the best of everything, for doing little."

"Army privilege," Rel said.

"Yes. Come, then. It is late, and lights are put out early, as you must be aware. We still keep to the curfew, for no one knows when The Hate will return. You must bide here for the night."

"I would not want to put you out," he said, suspecting how very little she had.

"You must," Iog stated with calm conviction. "I would not dishonor Gwasan's own son, now found again, by turning him out into the night like some no-kin, twi-shunned spy."

Twelve

Chwahirsland

CJ FOUND THE SCHOONER'S crew friendly enough, but not exactly open about where they had been, where they were headed, and what they planned to do when they got there. She wondered if they were pirates, or privateers, which was what the *Tzasilia* had been before it became the Mearsiean navy.

Wondering seemed to make . . . others' thoughts come. Or something made their thoughts come. CJ was not trying to "hear" them. She wouldn't know how to, even if she wanted to.

It was unsettlingly like vertigo, how she'd suddenly see herself through someone's eyes, with a flash of emotions she knew she wasn't feeling. Irritation, avoidance, humor. She intuited in spite of these sudden, mentally loud intrusions, that the crew had some goal that they didn't want her knowing about.

That made her feel as if she had wandered into someone else's story, and not necessarily one she wanted to be in. By the time the few days of fast sailing had ended, and the captain woke her out of a sound sleep to say that they were approaching the Chwahir coast, she knew she wasn't going to find out what it was.

He kept his word. The weather was mild, and he sailed very close to the shore, close enough for her to see rocky juts in the moonlight. She had left her woodcutter's clothes behind as soon as she reached warm weather, so she didn't have any encumbrances except that disgusting scroll of Kessler's, which had so much magic on it she figured it had to be waterproof.

"This is where we part ways," the captain said.

CJ climbed over the rail, held on tight, remembering how much she hated high dives, then she held her nose and jumped.

What looked close from on board seemed a lot farther away when she was struggling with her sodden skirt dragging at her legs, but she dog-paddled grimly until she felt waves forming. She swam mightily to catch a wave, which buoyed her up until she was thrown upon the shore.

She climbed up onto the sand and collapsed, breathing like a bellows.

The air was chilly but not freezing. She made herself get up and start moving.

Chwahirsland.

The dank, stale brine reeked of Chwahirsland, forcing her back in memory, which made her shiver again. The stench reminded her of Earth smog mixed with sea air. There was never any fresh air in Chwahirsland — ever. Too much dark magic for that.

She made her way to an area with rough grass. By then her clothes were damp instead of wet, so she sat down and curled up. She didn't expect to sleep, but drowsiness stole over her, her dreams fitful until she jerked awake when a bug crawled on her nose.

Dawn. Definitely like smog, the sky a dreary brownish gray haze overhead.

She remembered that the evil king of the Chwahir was no longer around.

"Let's get it over with," she muttered in Mearsiean, got to her feet, and started walking along the river toward the ugly gray thing hulking like some big square monster in the distance: the Chwahir capital.

And so, as yet unaware of one another, Rel, CJ, and Dejain converged on Jilo in Chwahirsland's capital, Narad.

About half a day's ride eastward from where CJ trudged along the river, as thin clouds streaked the gray sky, Rel picked his way around the worst mud puddles and went to the outpost captain. After a restless night stretched out on Iog's floor before the little fire, he had made his decision.

Though he had discovered his mother's identity, his quest for his father seemed to have reached a dead end. There might be other angles to try. Perhaps Raneseh, after hearing what Rel had discovered so far, might furnish a hint, or maybe the man would see fit to end the charade himself. Supposing he was even aware of Rel's search.

In any case, his own quest had to be laid aside in favor of alliance business. He needed to warn Jilo about what Iog had said.

The outpost captain did not ask any questions. He gave Rel a sealed letter and a report to take to the regional commanding officer in Narad.

Thus provided with a legitimate reason to be in the capital, Rel rode half a day southward along the river. Narad loomed against the western mountains, gray mossy stone and unrelievedly ugly.

He had to break his silence at the outer gates to ask directions to the regional commander's headquarters in the enormous fortress, but he remembered how dull the populace in the capital had been, as if they sleepwalked through life.

He was surprised into wariness, even alarm, when the gate sentry looked at him suspiciously.

"The east is my regular route," Rel said. "This is my first time carrying in the west."

He watched the suspicious eyes take in his youth and the sealed messages. The man's face cleared, and he issued directions in a crisp voice.

It really had changed there. Rel marveled over that as he passed to the inner gate. If this was the result of Jilo's efforts, Rel was impressed. The air, the atmosphere, was still stifling, the sky still an ugly gray, but the people seemed more alive.

He found the correct office, handed off the two communications, and then, wondering how far he'd get, he said, "I want an interview with—" For the first time, he wondered what Jilo called himself. Should he say "the king?" He knew what a long, cruel shadow those words cast. Even laboring under the ugly spells laid on them, the army had employed indirect terms for their ruler, lest any kind of mention bring his notice.

"With Jilo," he finished, opting for the direct and simple.

An exchange of looks that he could not interpret was followed by, "That question must be put to the upstairs staff."

This shifting of responsibility was more like the Chwahir he had known. He walked upstairs, and asked the first person he saw. The fellow, no older than he, looked surprised, as if there was no rule for what to do with visitors. Rel wondered what would happen if he arrived in his usual clothes, without this guise of being Chwahir. Except that he was half Chwahir, he remembered with an unsettling jolt. It still did not seem real to him.

He was pointed to a barren stone anteroom with nothing but a bench. Rel sat down, and leaned back against the walls, his eyes closing . . .

Dejain remained in a state of helpless fury. It had been years since she'd been forced to travel without magic aid. She did not believe anything could be grimmer than the blasted land surrounding Norsunder Base, but Chwahirsland came close.

Though the time of year was summer, one would never know it except for the stifling humidity of afternoons, for the sky was constantly covered with ward-layered distortions that looked to the naked eye like wood smoke mixed with an indeterminate cloud cover.

Occasionally the clouds thickened to gloom, lowered enough to emit a thin, unpleasant rain that tasted faintly metallic, and other times they thinned to a glare, then coalesced into a clammy, unpleasant fog.

One of these fogs had formed in the river valley, making her feel she'd ride forever without getting anywhere. She loathed fanciful thinking, and tried to concentrate on immediate things: the chuff and suck of the animal's hooves in the mud; the pain of saddle riding; the dark face of the mirror she had carefully bespelled to warn her of any magical focus. The wards over this land were formidable, testament to Wan-Edhe's many decades of focus on making his citadel strong, stronger, the strongest.

Then one day the fog thinned and lifted, revealing the massive fortress that was Narad. She stared upward, impressed. Every line was evocative of power.

Her gaze took in the tiny sentries, like beetles, atop the towers, ever vigilant against . . . what? No one in history had ever displayed the least inclination to invade Chwahirsland. But then the dangers were probably always from within. She sensed the maelstrom of concentrated magic. It reflected in her mirror, inchoate. But curiously weakened at the center.

What she could do with this place!

She kicked the tired animal into a trot.

CJ slunk into Narad, shoulders hunched. People looked at her curiously. She began to suspect that her clothes were plain anywhere else, but here in Chwahirsland, the forest green skirt and her white shirt under the black vest were practically like a pink tinsel tutu with yellow pompons anywhere else. At least her hair was black, and her age kept the curiosity minimal.

No one came near her.

She lingered outside the inner gate, which was even more massive than the outer city gate. She debated hard, knowing she was chickening out of daring to enter that monster of a castle, when she spied an anomaly ahead: blonde hair amongst all the dark heads.

Instinctively she ducked behind someone pulling a cart. Snow chilled her veins when she recognized Dejain on horseback, gazing up at the towers while holding something in her hand that had the greenish glitter of magic on it.

CJ slipped around the carter and ran to the sentry.

She gabbled, "I am here for Jilo," and bolted inside before he could respond, her shoulder blades tensed against an expected weapon.

"I'm here," came Jilo's nasal voice. "Rel?"

Rel jerked awake as Jilo studied him in obvious dismay. "Why are you dressed like, um, us?"

"Long and boring story." Rel paused, eyeing him. "Are you all right?"

Jilo looked as if he'd been running for days, his hair lank and grimy, his clothing stale-smelling from across the room. But he was too pale for physical exertion. His fingers shook as he wiped his hair out of his eyes. "Excuse me."

He ducked out. Rel sighed and sat down again. Jilo reappeared a short time later, still pale except for two dull red blotches betraying his recent race up and down stairs, but his hair and clothes had been restored by a dash through a cleaning frame. He said, "I'm on this project. To dismantle Wan-Edhe's magic."

Rel pursed his lips in a silent whistle. "It took him decades to build."

"The idea is to set everything in motion so that it dismantles itself."

Rel began to understand what he was seeing in Jilo. That grayness in Jilo's complexion, the gnawed lips and dead nailbeds — this was the physical cost of living and working in the center of Wan-Edhe's lethally poisonous magic.

Rel drew a breath of respect and amazement. Now he was glad he'd come. "Jilo, it came to my attention that there might be some kind of conspiracy against you. Among your own —"

Rel stopped when Jilo waved a hand. "I know. But I don't want to know."

Rel gazed in surprise.

Jilo sighed. "It's the army captains. Well, two of the five. I think. And a couple of brigade captains who resent my taking some of the land out of army control and returning it to the people. And according to my uncle, until I told him not to tell me, at least one division commander." Jilo looked around, breathing deeply. It really was easier downstairs, now. But he didn't have the luxury of staying. "Come upstairs with me?"

Rel followed Jilo up to the third floor, and down the barren hall that smelled like mold, into what appeared to be a secret passage, in which the mold smell was quite strong. Jilo had set glow-globes onto stone protrusions along the moss-dark walls.

"These are Wan-Edhe's magic chambers. I'm trying to destroy all the wards here." He pointed at the floor. "Below me, off the throne room, he's got spy stones. I think he spent most of his time spying on his own people, the last ten years or so, always looking for the next conspiracy. I won't be that. I'm going to destroy those scry stones after I finish in here."

He shrugged awkwardly, gaze averted. "If they kill me, they kill me. I figured it has to happen."

"But —"

"You can say nothing lasts. There's no point. I know all that. Until they scrag me, I'm going to make life better for people like my Uncle Shiam. My cousins. Take apart Wan-Edhe's magic. It's *fun*." Jilo's voice ended on a defensive note as he backed out of the room.

"Jilo, I wasn't going to argue with you." Rel followed Jilo, thinking rapidly. One benefit of traveling so much was meeting all kinds of people, and finding ways to fit in, not always easy for someone of his size.

He sensed from Jilo's shuffling manner, the way he avoided meeting anyone's gaze, that Jilo would find direct praise merely painful. He wouldn't know what to do with it. But odd as he was, he was still a Chwahir. Praise of his work might be acceptable.

"I was going to say how different this city is from the last time I was here. I know this will sound stupid, but the people seem more alive."

Jilo's pale face splotched with color, and he actually smiled. "Yes, yes. They are, aren't they? But there is so much more to do."

His tone was anticipatory, not apprehensive, and Rel understood that Jilo had found purpose.

Jilo knuckled his eyes. "Time is . . . ah, well, it's different, but that is also getting smaller," he began.

That makes no sense, Rel thought uneasily. He wondered if he ought to put a question when they entered a long hall as a small black-haired, green-skirted figure dashed headlong through the iron reinforced doors at the other end.

"I *thought* I remembered right," she panted.

"CJ?" Jilo gasped.

Rel stared—he'd expect almost anybody else.

"*Rel?*" CJ stared back. "What are *you* doing here? Did *you* come to tell Jilo that Dejain is right outside the gates?" She jerked her thumb back over her shoulder.

"Who?" Jilo asked blankly.

Rel grimaced. "Kessler's mage. His ex-ally—"

"Kessler sent me," CJ said grittily, and plunged her hand into her skirt pocket.

At that moment, Jilo jerked as if someone had poked him, looked around wildly, then said, "Norsunder magic. Tripped a ward—"

The unmusical *bong* of a huge bell reverberated off the stone walls. From the halls outside came the rattle and clatter of footsteps, guards brandishing arms and running to defensive positions.

Jilo hustled downstairs in his peculiar flatfooted gait, his head bobbing from side to side, as CJ and Rel followed.

Below them, off the throne room, lay the antechamber that Jilo had mentioned, furnished only with a table full of scry stones, and a single stool.

Here Kessler sat, watching through one of the stones as the city brigade captain met the captain of northwest army and a division captain in the garrison command room.

The three men slammed the door and turned to each other.

"What's the alarm?"

"I don't know, but this might be our chance."

The youngest of them laughed. "And if it's a surprise inspection?"

"The little shit would never call one of those *here*. Whatever it is, we can turn it into an assassination. Then grab a few likely subjects off the street and execute them, and —" He extended his hand toward the royal wing.

Kessler smiled.

On the other side of the courtyard, unaware of either conspiracy or the secret watcher, Jilo burst through an iron-reinforced door and looked around wildly, unsure what he was supposed to do. That alarm had been set up by Wan-Edhe. Jilo had not known it was even there.

CJ thrust the scroll at him. "I think you better see this."

Glad to be distracted, Jilo took it. The much-crumpled and wetted paper crackled as he opened it. He blinked. "It's in Chwahir. And . . ." He looked up. "I don't know all the spells here. Who gave you this, and what is it supposed to do?"

CJ poured out the tale of her misadventures, as outside the gates, Dejain experimented with breaking the ward keeping her from entering the citadel. She had prepared some strong ward-breakers; CJ jumped violently as greenish lightning flared through the air, briefly leaching all color from Jilo, Rel, and the stone hallway.

CJ gulped and finished in a high, breathless voice, " . . . and so Kessler gave it to me. For you. I don't know anything more than that."

Jilo lowered the paper. "I recognize two spells. One is a transfer. I don't know the others. I don't know what they will do."

Rel said, "Remember what I said about ex-allies? Sounds as if you're caught in a duel between Dejain and Kessler."

"Bad stuff coming at us both ways." CJ's blue eyes widened as she fingered her medallion, then yanked down her hand. "I said I'd give it to you, but if you decide to burn it, I wouldn't blame you. But I don't know what to do about *her*. She might be here to kill me. Or you. After she gets those books she wants." As she spoke, CJ clapped her hand over the knife cut on her arm in a protective gesture.

Jilo frowned, considering. He immediately recognized that Kessler was testing him, though he had no idea to what end. "If it comes, it comes," he said more to himself than the others, and plunged through an adjacent doorway.

The other two followed, not knowing what else to do. They found themselves emerging onto a balcony that overlooked the main courtyard.

At that moment, below, Dejain held out some object and began muttering. Two sentries already lay either dead or stunned. The rest remained at a distance as a greenish flare scintillated around Dejain.

From another direction, a knife-wielding brigade captain slunk along the hall leading to Jilo's balcony.

Jilo began to read out the spells.

Rel, subliminally aware of approaching footfalls, put his hand to his sword. CJ hopped silently from foot to foot, looking anxiously from Dejain at the gate to Jilo, whose voice didn't falter. He, too, began to scintillate as power built around him. CJ abruptly held her nose so that she wouldn't sneeze from that burning metal singe . . .

"Done." Jilo whispered, and staggered.

Several things happened at once.

Lightning flared from the paper Jilo held. He jerked his hands away as the light branched outward, astonishing all the guards and sentries at their posts.

The lightning began to coalesce in weird streamers around Dejain, who touched a ring she had prepared against disaster. She vanished, and those streamers dissipated, but others strengthened as they tentacled up toward a balcony, and onward.

Behind Rel, someone screamed. The would-be assassin brigade captain lit up as a ribbon of light closed around him, then burst into a fireball.

He and the steel in his hand fell to ash.

The other two conspiring commanders flared, lightning-struck. The conspirator standing on the balcony, from which he had intended to take command, pitched over the rail, wreathed in greenish flame, and flared into ash. The other, lurking in the garrison command room, propelled himself through a window in his effort to escape the weird fire, and the flame got him as he hit the stones, leaving an ashy smear.

CJ yelped, "Ouch!" as white-hot pain seared her arm.

She yanked up her sleeve. Gone was the pearly line: her skin was red and tender, like a newly-healed wound.

She touched it tentatively, stunned. "Was that part of Jilo's spells? That means Kessler knew all along how to take away the bloodknife spell!" She reddened with fury. "Why didn't he take it away when I went to his horrible tower?"

"Where is that?" Jilo asked.

CJ flapped her hands. "I dunno, somewhere on the same continent as Roth Drael, that's all I can tell you.,"

Above, below, and around, the Chwahir stared at Jilo, from whom that lightning appeared to have issued. Jilo leaned against the door to the balcony, dizzy with reaction from that magic. He gradually became aware of Rel's urgent whisper. ". . . say something."

Jilo forced himself upright. He gripped the stone of the balcony, stiffened his spine, and pitched his voice to be heard by those below. "Alarm over. As you were." Then stepped back, stepped back, stepped back, and as waves of roiling darkness threatened to overtake him, he sighed, "I think I'm going to . . ."

As Jilo slipped to the ground in a faint, unseen by any of them, Kessler transferred away to where he could have his laugh out in private.

Thirteen

JILO WOKE TO TWO blurry faces bent over his. Both framed by black hair. Brown skin—not Chwahir. Vague alarm caused him to struggle upright, as waves of pain crashed through his head.

"Ow," CJ said softly, rubbing her forehead.

"The Norsundrian?" Jilo croaked.

"Gone." CJ hunched her shoulders as she cast a wary glance around. "This dump is still uglier than ugly, but it feels kind of different."

"Been trying to lift wards." Jilo winced. It hurt to talk. "It'll take a long time."

"Drink this." Rel held out a cup.

Jilo tasted the bitterness of willow bark, excruciatingly expensive in Chwahirsland.

Rel said, "I had some with me. I asked your people for hot water." His deep-set eyes crinkled in what for him was an expression of amusement.

CJ stared at Rel. She'd loathed him for most of time she'd

known him, simply for being big, competent, and in control of his feelings. She'd liked to justify her resentment by claiming that he didn't have any.

But he wasn't a hate object anymore, just a person, which made him seem . . . different. Like when his eyes crinkled like that under those heavy brows that looked threatening, but weren't, it kind of reminded her of someone, who? Someone she liked. No, it wasn't the eyes, it was that expression, a secret but somehow friendly inner laugh. Someone older.

Jilo—obviously unaware of any of this—sighed, blinking slowly. The wince in his expression began to ease.

"You are going to be getting a report when you leave," Rel said, the humor completely gone. "I've held off your people, but they're going to want a decision. Three of Narad brigade's captains are dead."

"Three."

"Yes."

"How?"

"Some kind of lightning strike. One of them," Rel added, "your castle-guard brigade captain, who I spotted right outside that balcony before he was struck. I think he might have been carrying a knife. But it's ash now."

"I bet all that was Kessler's doing," CJ said. "He was the one who gave me that scroll. Do you have some sort of deal with him?" Her face pruned into a very dubious expression.

"No." The word was an exhalation. Jilo swallowed the last of the willow bark infusion. "I don't understand what he's doing. But I thought, if he sent you all this way, then I should trust him. Even though it was strange, to send a message through you, and not come himself."

"He seems to be protecting you," Rel ventured.

CJ finished darkly, "For now."

Another of those unsettling inner jolts, this one sharp, as Rel wondered if Kessler knew who he was.

Jilo set aside the cup. "I should find out what other things that spell did."

CJ bounced to her feet. "And I think I can go home." She clutched her medallion.

"Don't!" Jilo said quickly. "Not here. There are safer places inside to transfer from."

CJ yanked down her hand. "Then point me out of this

stenchiferous castle."

Rel headed for the door. "I'll show you the way."

Jilo watched them go, thinking he should say something. "Ah, thank you," he called.

Rel half-raised a hand. "Think of it as a benefit of the alliance." He walked out, CJ following after a shifty backward look, as if she still didn't quite believe that no one was going to attack her.

Jilo waited as they continued on. He couldn't believe they weren't going to stop, turn, and demand something in return.

Maybe the alliance really did include him.

Time to get a meal inside of him, and he might as well begin studying the spells that he had just performed. He had so very much to learn.

CJ followed Rel to the stairway. "Did the alliance really send you?"

He glanced down at her. "I was here for something else."

"What?"

He'd forgotten how bluntly inquisitive the Mearsieans could be. "I was on a search for my father. Hit a dead end. But I overheard some rumors that I thought Jilo ought to know. Came to tell him, and you showed up."

They started down the main stairs. "I thought your father was dead, and Raneseh adopted you."

"He was my guardian. My father is alive, according to Raneseh."

"But didn't tell you why? Or who he is? Or where?" CJ eyed Rel, unwilling to voice her first thought: maybe the father was a villain. Second thought wasn't much better: maybe the dad had rejected Rel. Except who would reject the Perfect Rel?

And the third thought was most surprising of all. "You came to *Chwahirsland* to look?"

Rel took the time to check their surroundings, though there was no threat. He knew that her curiosity would probably be shared by other friends, even if they weren't quite that blunt. His first instinct was to regret having spoken. Perhaps it was a good idea to have some answer ready. He could practice on CJ. "The trail led here. But like I said, it was a dead end."

And then she surprised him. "If your dad was a prisoner of Wan-Edhe, or a victim, there's somebody who might know some more. You ought to go ask Rosey."

"Rosey?" Rel shouldered open one of the iron-reinforced doors, and they headed into the courtyard, where sentries in knots spotted them and broke up, going about their business. "I think I've heard that name before. From Puddlenose."

CJ didn't notice the furtive glances. Rel did, but pretended not to as CJ said, "Rosey—Mondros—is a really powerful mage, who was taught dark magic, and then he switched to our side, but pretended to be a friend to Prince Kwenz in the Shadowland. It was a way of watching over Clair, and Puddlenose—he rescued them from Wan-Edhe a bunch of times, but then they'd get trapped by Kwenz. Anyway, he—Rosey, that is—lives in the border mountains between Chwahirsland and Colend. I even remember the Destination, because Clair and I visited him right before Clair went to Wnelder Vee and Everon."

CJ paused, her thoughts running ahead. She had been so nasty to Rel on the other world that the alliance had nearly turned against her, like she was some kind of villain. Some of her friends had even been embarrassed for her.

She had to show them that she did not hold grudges. She could forget the past, same as anybody. "How about if I send you? Or if you feel funny going alone, I don't mind going with you to introduce you. His cooking is always delicious."

Rel was skeptical about the power and efficacy of this mage, given the terrible things Wan-Edhe had been getting away with for nearly a century, but he'd promised himself to follow any lead.

And he would not have to spend days riding out of barren, dreary Chwahirsland, where his mother's history was as bleak as the weather.

"Lead on," he said.

Fourteen

From Delfina Valley to the Border of Chwahirsland

TSAUDEREI HAD TAKEN OUT his old master's journal and was in the process of rereading the familiar words in hopes that something might gain him new insight, but his younger self's firm handwriting, glossed with notes from his long-dead tutor, merely stirred up memories of bygone days.

The reverie broke when his magical notecase alerted him, and alarm flashed through him when he recognized Mondros's impatient scrawl.

Norsunder magic, in Chwahirsland?

He lowered the note, frowning. He hated scrying, but it seemed this was the time, and reached for his stone.

The murky colors deep in the stone blurred as he whispered, then Mondros's worried face appeared, brushy brows meeting in a line as the mage concentrated on whatever it was he used for scrying. From the twist of his lips in the curly beard, he hated this method of communication as much as Tsauderei did.

"Is it Detlev?" Tsauderei asked.

At the other end of the communication, Mondros stared at his old colleague's face. Tsauderei seemed to have aged a decade in the few weeks since their last communication, but his eyes were alert as ever as Mondros said, "Unfamiliar magical signature attempting to cross the Chwahir border by magic transfer. A tracer alerted me to a particularly vicious ward-breaker spell with a Norsundrian signature. Unsuccessful, of course. Returned here to contact you."

Tsauderei whistled soundlessly. "Did Jilo invite a Norsundrian in, or was he being challenged?"

Mondros said, "Tracer suggests the latter—wait—"

Mondros paused, his gaze going distant.

Tsauderei, even after many decades, caught himself leaning his nose toward his scry stone, as if he could see past the discrete boundaries of the scry spell. He fought the inevitable dizziness until Mondros's voice startled him. He was losing control of the contact, for him a very prolonged one.

"Well. *Something* just happened. A cluster of powerful spells. But all I can tell you for certain is that the Norsundrian mage, whoever it was, is gone. Expelled from Chwahirsland. I need to find out more."

"Let me know," Tsauderei said, and gratefully relinquished the scry spell.

At his end, Mondros let the spell collapse to the flat polished stone surface, feeling a sense of relief akin to Tsauderei's. When the black spots in his vision faded away, he thumped his hands on his knees and muttered under his breath, "If that blast of spell-casting was you, young Jilo, it is time for a frank talk."

Then he set his scry stone gently in its carved box, and busied himself pulling together several sources, scattering four lines of possible magical inquiry over his desk before he noticed that he was overlapping another project.

He sighed, glaring fiercely at the mess on his desk.

This new problem had to supersede the old. Though he'd developed complicated spells for investigating magical layers in Chwahirsland's capital, it was time to find a way to get physically past Wan-Edhe's lethal border wards. He had to be able to get to Chwahirsland himself.

He was standing precariously on a three-legged stool, feeling along the top of his bookcase for an old tract he was fairly certain he'd thrust there to hide it, when one of his magic wards alerted him to a magic transfer — one he permitted.

He leaped down from the stool, walked out of his cottage, then stopped in his tracks as one figure appeared. Then another, swaying with transfer reaction.

The first was CJ's instantly recognizable short, slight form.

The second was a tall, broad-shouldered, black-haired boy whose familiar face caused Mondros to clutch at the door frame. His nerves flared with so bright a pain so excruciating that he could not catch his breath.

CJ blinked away the transfer reaction, eager to be praised for doing a good deed for Rel. So *there*. She just hoped that somehow word could get out without her having to brag, and sound like a pompous twit. Of course! If she told Kyale of Vasande Leror, she'd be sure to blab it all over.

Then CJ forgot Kyale, the alliance, and good deeds when she gazed in astonishment at Rosey, who stood half in, half out of his doorway like someone had taken all the stuffing out of him.

That inner earthquake sense that had jolted her ever since Liere had helped her out caused her to look from good old Rosey to Rel, who was waiting with his usual poker face. Weird, how they both had the same kind of eyebrows, though their eyes were different, Rel's so deep set, Rosey's deep, too, yeah, but narrower—

Another look. Another similarity, the similar shade of brown in their skin . . . the fact that she was looking for similarities, which meant—

The moment, for Mondros and CJ both, seemed suspended in time as the unheeded summer breeze rustled the branches of the fruit trees, and birds twittered unseen.

Rel waited, his curiosity giving way to uneasiness. He looked in a mirror so seldom that his own features were scarcely familiar to him, and not of much interest.

CJ tried to swallow but somehow a boulder had lodged itself in her throat. She squeaked past it, "Rel, I think . . . I think your search is over?"

Mondros's gaze shifted to her, his forehead creasing.

CJ felt the impact of emotions she did not comprehend, and with a wild glance between the two of them, she clutched the medallion around her neck, which she could now use to transfer home. "Um. I think I better . . ."

A last, horrible wrench, and she found herself on the rug in the underground cave the girls called home. The room was empty. The cave quiet.

CJ stumbled shakily to her room, clapped on the glow-globe, and fell on her bed. Her own bed with its forest green cover, and all her pictures on the walls, the tree roots overhead, and her little bookshelf. The quiet, the familiar sight, the smell of loam and pine and a faint trace of chocolate was so safe, so wonderful . . .

She was safe, she was home, everything was all right, that thing was even gone from her arm, leaving only the cut, which was merely tender.

She closed her eyes and listened the way Liere had told her to. She sensed some of the other girls nearby, dreaming in sleep. In the distance Clair slept, CJ guessed up in the white palace.

"I'm home," she whispered.

She was *safe*. Dejain couldn't reach her with that magic. Jilo wasn't an enemy. Wan-Edhe was gone. Rel was . . .

Rel and Mondros? Mondros and Rel?

She had always *hated* thinking about her family on Earth. She had a better family here, with all the girls. And yet her ribs shuddered, and a bowling ball of hurt erupted from deep inside her. She flung herself over onto her pillow, shoved her face into it, and broke into shattering sobs.

Fifteen

ON MONDROS'S PLATEAU, NEITHER he nor Rel noticed her leave.

"Rel," Mondros said on an exhalation of breath.

Rel's heart thumped somewhere far away, each sound isolated: birds, breeze, the rustle of grass. *Thud-whoosh.* "What did that mean, my search is over?"

Mondros brought his hands up, but the words were not there.

Rel shifted his gaze back to the man whose deep-set eyes were the same color and shape as his own, who was not as tall, but as broad through the chest— broader —who looked back at him as if he had been gutted with a knife.

"I . . . " Rel began.

The search couldn't possibly be over. This grizzled fellow in the mage's robe would hand him another clue. Would send him on another journey.

"Come inside." Mondros stepped back, the door wide, and added huskily, "Son."

So the search *was* over. Except Rel had expected anything but this bearded man in the mage robe, living in a cottage dwarfed by climbing roses, high on a cliff.

He let out his breath, and stepped into his new identity, one in which he had a living, breathing father, with all his own story to tell.

Rel stooped his head under the rough lintel, taking in the small cottage. It reminded him of Tsauderei's place high in the mountains above Sarendan: one room, a loft above, a kitchen alcove, and many, many bookcases. Only here was a big wooden table in the center space, covered over with books and papers.

"You're a mage? But . . . my father . . . I was told . . . you were a warrior named Glenred." Rel grimaced at how stupid that sounded.

"I became Glenred when I ran from home. As a boy I was sent to train in dark magic. The less said about your antecedents . . . my family . . .the better. Except for my cousin and his young son."

The words meant nothing to Rel, whose mind poked tentatively at the idea of "father," sore as a fresh wound. All his thinking had been about how to find him, but he hadn't considered what to do once the search ended.

Mondros discovered that his watery knees would not hold him anymore, and he sat down abruptly at the table, hands loose on his papers. He could not take his gaze away from Rel.

Here.

Where he had never really thought to see him. He had never believed this moment would come, or if it did, only after a great deal of preparation, and preferably somewhere else, somewhere neutral. Appropriate.

"Where." Rel's voice cracked. He swallowed and tried again. "Where was that?"

"Ralanor Veleth. Ever been there?"

"Never heard of it."

"It's midlands in Goerael, the continent to the northwest of us." Another breath, more unsteady than the first. The merciful numbness was wearing off. "Ralanor Veleth has somewhat the same reputation that Marloven Hess does on this continent." And when Rel didn't speak, "After I began life as Glenred, I met your mother Gwasan, who was also a fugitive. Mage student."

Rel made an inadvertent movement at the husky tenderness with which Mondros said the words *mother Gwasan*—no more than a twitch of one shoulder, the hint of a wince at the corner of his eye, but it silenced Mondros.

It was Rel's turn to fight for words. "Her — her story is still new to me. I found Iog . . . was it only yesterday?" He thrust his large hand through his hair.

"I've done my best to protect Iog," Mondros said.

"She said she hasn't seen you for years."

"That's how I protected her." Mondros couldn't bear to look at his son, though he listened to every shade of his deep voice, every subtle alteration in his breathing. "I was away on a task for Berthold — that is, King Berthold of Everon — when your mother was assassinated. You were safely with Roderic Dei . . . Well, the short version is, I knew that Wan-Edhe would be after you, too, if he knew you were alive. Iog had vanished. I had no idea what report had been sent back to Chwahirsland. I had two motivations: the need to protect you, and the desire for vengeance. The first took priority."

"So you took me to Raneseh."

A quick look. Seeing no anger in Rel, Mondros found the wherewithal to go on. "I trusted him. Knew him for a good man. He fought by my side in Everon, then eventually went home as he had responsibilities. I knew Wan-Edhe would never find him, as he knew no magic, so he could not be traced, and Tser Mearsies has its own protections. Then I set out on my quest for vengeance, to discover that there was a long line ahead of me wanting Wan-Edhe's death. An infinite line. And there were so many to protect. But no one to help. No, that's bitterness."

He inhaled again, trying to calm his thundering heart. To explain, and not to beg, to plead. "There are good reasons why mages swear not to interfere with governments. But right there in Chwahirsland there were so many to protect, and it was what your mother had risked her life to study magic for. She wanted to defend Chwahirsland against Wan-Edhe. She gave up her life for that goal." His throat tightened.

He paused to draw in a harsh breath, thumbed his eyes, and forced himself to go on. "So I took it over. I left the mage guild, and I did my damndest to interfere with Chwahirsland — I tried to save them, if no one else would. Given Wan-Edhe's poisonous mistrust, his mad fear of conspiracy, it was a duel I had to fight from a distance. And I lost. So many times."

Rel's own sense of shock began to fade, and he noticed little things: the tremble in Mondros's right hand, the subtle quirk in his lower eyelid that Rel equated with pain. He said, "I know a little. From Puddlenose."

"It was not only historic enmity between Chwahir and Mearsieans that prompted Wan-Edhe to interfere with those Mearsiean orphans. It was also spite. He found out that my wife had studied magic with Murial of the Mearsieans, and it was when he tried to get at her that he discovered the white palace on the cloud. You've been there?"

"I have. I've never seen anything like it in all my travels."

"Exactly. There is nothing else like it. Even the material it's made of is unique, except for some scattered ruins here and there on various continents. And a single tower in the heart of Sartor's capital."

Rel nodded slowly in acknowledgment, a lot of his own questions unexpectedly answered.

Mondros went on. "And though young Clair had educational guidance from Murial, that tutoring in light magic was useless against the Chwahir."

Rel said, "There was also that Chwahir outpost below the capital."

"Yes. I'd met Prince Kwenz when I was a boy, through my tutor. I prevailed on that to winnow my way into friendship, so I could sabotage Wan-Edhe's plots indirectly. It helped that Kwenz was no warrior by nature — which is probably why he was the sole survivor of the Sonscarna family, except for Prince Kessler, who managed to escape. If left alone I expect Kwenz would have been a scribe, or even a herald. He loved research. But he loyally served his brother by presiding at that outpost and in his slow, desultory fashion tried to conquer Mearsies Heili. He chose Jilo to teach magic to."

Rel said, "So that's where he came from."

"Jilo was the single great thing Kwenz ever did — though he probably never knew it. The two of them would sit in Kwenz's tower and delve into dark magic for days on end. They were alike in being scholars. Wan-Edhe, needless to say, despised Jilo. But." He drew a deep, unsteady breath. "We're not here to talk about Jilo.

He glanced up, and their eyes met, each searching for acceptance, for a sign of the emotion that each was so ready to give.

"Except we are. A little," Rel said, a bubble of laughter rising inside him, in spite of everything: he remembered how wise he thought he'd been, how confidently he'd told people who asked about his past that of course he was no long-lost prince, because royal families did not like mislaying relatives, even inconvenient ones.

His mother had died striving to make certain he stayed mislaid.

And his father. . . *What shall I call you?* "May I know your family name, even if I can't use it?"

"You have that right. I was born Mondros Glenereth. We were military governors. The family name has been disgraced, largely the work of the main branch of the family. They are nearly all gone, the family disinherited, but before that even happened I repudiated that name when I left home. So you can call me Mondros, or even Rosey, which was my evil mage persona when I rescued children like the Mearsieans, and young Terry of Erdrael Danara, from Wan-Edhe."

Father. Rel wanted to say the word, but couldn't get his tongue to form it. Not because he was angry, or resentful. He wasn't certain what he felt. But he was sure of one thing, his quest was done, and here was this man sitting before him, a vein beating high in his forehead, the sheen of tears gleaming along his eyelids.

"Tell me more," he said.

Sixteen

Mearsies Heili

CJ HAD CRIED HERSELF to sleep.

She woke suddenly, and though her room was underground, she sensed it was late morning.

She dashed through the cleaning frame, then hesitated, looking at her desk. That adventure had been a horrible mess, except one single thing, the last thing: Rel. She longed to brag to someone that she had solved his long search, because telling someone would make it really, *really* clear that she didn't hold grudges, and she *wasn't* a villain. Even if she'd solved it completely by accident.

She reached for a pen, then remembered that she was supposed to be in charge of the white palace! And even though she knew Clair was back, what did she think on coming home to discover CJ wasn't there?

She transferred up, to discover Clair holding morning court,

which in Mearsies Heili pretty much meant sitting alone in the
empty throne room in case a petitioner showed up who couldn't
deal with the guilds or the provincial governors.

Clair was reading, but when CJ dashed impetuously in, she set
her book aside after taking in CJ's puffy eyes and her nervous
hands.

"You're back!" they exclaimed at the same moment.

Then CJ said quickly, "Clair, I didn't dump this job, I really
didn't—"

Clair smiled with relief to see her. "I know all about it. Hibern
wrote to us. I'm so glad you're safely home!"

"I need to . . ." CJ rolled her eyes. "I mean, there's stuff I have
to tell you, but first, I was in Chwahirsland, and Rel was there, and
he's been searching for his dad, because you remember, Raneseh
was his guardian, and guess who the mysterious father is?" She
knew Clair did not like guessing games, so she went right on,
"None other than Rosey!"

"Rosey?" Clair repeated. "I don't understand that at all."

"Neither do I, but I kind of felt like asking questions would be
snouting in, the way they were looking at each other." CJ rubbed
her hands. "So now I want to let everybody know that Rel found
his long-lost dad, and I was the one who helped him. Nobody will
think I'm a villain anymore."

"CJ, nobody thought you were a villain," Clair exclaimed, hug-
ging her elbows against her ribs. She hated seeing CJ's red, puffy
eyes.

CJ made a terrible face. "Well, they thought I was a big grudge
holder."

"You do hold grudges," Clair said calmly. "But you got over
that one."

CJ sighed. "I know. You know what I mean, everybody probably still thinks I'm this nasty meanie . . ."

Clair was thinking rapidly. She wanted to believe that nobody
thought ill about CJ, or any of the other Mearsieans. But the truth
was, the alliance seemed to be going on around the Mearsieans,
and she wasn't quite sure why.

"Rel and Rosey," she said, resolving to think about the alliance
later. She sighed. "CJ, I don't think you ought to tell anyone. I
think that's Rel's place."

"But he'll never say I found his dad for him!"

Clair said, "Let's go to the kitchen. I now declare morning

court officially done."

There was no sound but the fall of rain outside the open windows as they pattered down the long hall. Unheeding the two ran past the softly blue and gray shifting shadows along the palely iridescent walls, to the warm golden-lit kitchen. Fresh bread had been set out in expectation of Clair finishing her morning court stint.

As they sliced the bread and slathered it with honey (CJ) and preserves (Clair), the latter said, "Pretend you're Rel. You've lived this long thinking you were an orphan, or maybe left behind for some reason. Then you suddenly find out you're not an orphan, your parent is alive and well. When you leave, do you want everyone knowing? Or even asking questions? Or do you want to think about whom you're going to tell, when, and how?"

CJ crammed bread into her mouth and groaned.

Clair said, "Did you really figure it out?"

"No. It was an accident. I was taking Rel to ask Rosey for advice, then I saw them — their eyes — they have the same eyes." CJ's shoulders slumped. "I left."

"Well, then."

"It doesn't count?" CJ's shoulders hunched anxiously.

Clair looked at her best friend, comprehending a little of what she felt: CJ's sense of worth had always been so low, scarred as she was from a childhood in which the most dangerous place had been home.

"It does count. It will always count, in our hearts, and I think in Rel's as well, even if he doesn't say it. You know how quiet Rel is."

CJ twisted her bare feet around the legs of the stool she sat on. "That's true."

"You and I will always know you did a good thing. Let the rest of the world find out when Rel is ready to talk about it."

"He'll never tell them about me," CJ mumbled, hunching up again. "He thinks I'm a creep, I'm sure of it."

"I don't think he thinks you're a creep," Clair said. If anything, she suspected that Rel found CJ funny at times, but she decided not to say that. Nobody likes being thought funny unless they were trying to be, CJ especially. "But it's his affair to talk about, or not."

"Okay." CJ sighed, relenting. "At least I'm home."

Clair sat in the stool opposite her, and put her bare feet up on the edge of the seat and her chin on her knees. "Now, I want to hear everything. From the beginning. And don't stint on the insults when the villains come in."

So ends Book Two of The Rise of the Alliance.
Here is a glimpse of Book Three . . .

RISE OF THE ALLIANCE III

THE HUNTERS AND THE HUNTED

Firejive

(gyve: to fetter, to shackle, to bind)

I will begin this chronicle with Detlev, who emerged from
Norsunder Beyond into the center of a violent struggle for power
at Norsunder Base. He stepped over the dead and entered the
command center, currently deserted as Dejain and Bostian stalked
one another elsewhere in the fortress.

He found out how long he had been gone via the accumulation
of messages in the dispatch tray. There was no sign of Siamis, nor
any report.

He reached the last, considered the lacunae, then sat down to
write a coded note.

> *Why was I not alerted about the blood mage text?*
> *Did any of you try to secure it?*

A short time later came the answer:

> *Jilo of the Chwahir was either given it, or was*
> *given the location by Kessler Sonscarna. Senrid*

Montredaun-An took it away. I wrote a report
immediately. I found out through gossip that
Kessler took the texts back, and I reported that, too.
Since we received no new orders, and information
was long after the fact, we stayed tight with
standing orders.

Detlev wrote:

Our relay is compromised. Reports to be made in
person, through you. Commencing with your
conveying these orders, face to face.

At the other end of the world, in a place of mutable time, occasionally — cruelly — some trick of light in a changing sky evoked in Siamis's memory the cloud ships of Yssel, the last of which he witnessed sinking slowly to a fiery death nearly five thousand years ago: dragon-ribbed keelson, spars of glowing crystal, and vast sails iridescent as wasp wings.

The glimpses into past times were never quick to last. The world had changed so vastly, and he was no longer a terror-stricken, bewildered boy. But echoes of those long-ago emotions sometimes lingered: astonishment, harrowing realization, the numbness of betrayal, and finally a long-smoldering anger.

"I will someday destroy the entire world," he had shrieked when summoned to the Garden of the Twelve early after he was taken, and all the Host had laughed but one.

Ilerian tipped his head, regarding Siamis with mild interest. "How will you go about it?"

Later, Detlev had said, "Existence will be far less painful if you say nothing to catch Ilerian's interest. But if that cannot be avoided, have an answer. And always have a plan. "

Siamis had scorned his uncle's too-late advice as he'd scorned everything his uncle said and did, until it was proven — excruciatingly, and lasciviously prolonged — to be true.

So his real training began. In Norsunder-Beyond, where time was nearly meaningless, marked by occasional and brief emergences into the real world for either training or a lesson, he had no age markers to measure by except by guesswork.

He might have been the equivalent of fourteen when he

figured out how to combine the two—flout and stealth. Flouting Detlev when he could be perceived by the Host or their minions had amused them, and each time he'd been caught he'd suffered the consequences philosophically. While Norsunder's lords, who rarely stirred from their timeless citadel, began to regard his errors as a typical for callow youth, he had learned from each.

The lesson he kept closest: the mind gained in strength along with the body only in the physical realm, where time resumed its natural progression, where there was sunlight and the fresh air that renews itself as it sweeps over pure water. But those excursions had to be brief, and always in obedience to someone else's plan.

When at last he dared venture on his own to explore the immeasurable realm between Norsunder's ageless, arid center and the world, he knew how to leave no physical trace or magical shadow. Detlev called that the hand through the water.

Finally, the most dangerous of all, he essayed single visits back in time, using the great window in the Garden of the Twelve at Norsunder's center. It was vital to be unperceived; an error meant far worse than the idle cruelties of those who found entertainment in such pursuits, it meant being forever lost in a fold of time.

And so, it transpired, learning to maneuver in Norsunder had prepared him for dealing with the anomaly the mages of Old Sartor had named the Moonfire.

He moved with practiced stealth, the stages of his plan ranked mentally in meticulous order, but found that this anomaly was far more slippery than Norsunder's magic-straitened boundaries. He had the *where*, but not the *when* . . .

One

Late summer, 4743 AF
Delfina Valley to the Border of Chwahirsland

MONDROS'S BEARD BRISTLED AS his eyes widened with horror.

"When I think," he said to Tsauderei, as thunder rumbled low in the distance, "how very close we came to knowing nothing whatsoever about this blood mage text, I'm afraid I am going to have nightmares for months. Years."

Tsauderei shook his head slowly. He, too, felt that unsettling roil in the gut that came with a sense that they had lost control of something important. "This is, in a way, worse than the time the youngsters took themselves off to Geth-deles without consulting any of us. What do you suggest we do?"

"What can we do?" Mondros asked, broad hands extended to either side on the word 'can'.

Tsauderei said, "Jilo, Senrid, the Mearsiean girls—it's their alliance again."

"Which was a benighted idea."

"But don't you see, I feel confident in stating that, except for Kessler Sonscarna, whose motivations are impossible to guess beyond an apparent animus against Norsunder, at every stage they thought they were doing their best. Jilo turns to Senrid of Marloven Hess, who turns to young Leander in Vasande Leror, who turns to his friends in Mearsies Heili, all using those young Colendi scribe students as a communications clearing house. The way they've been trained to serve."

"I see ignorant youths acting without due consideration, especially for their guardians." Mondros's deep voice rumbled low in his massive chest.

"Oh, and they're the first generation to do that," Tsauderei said sardonically.

"Granted." Mondros uttered an unwilling laugh. "My ire is entirely bound up in my sense of personal failure. I thought I'd established a good enough understanding with young Jilo to enable him to come to me. He faces a monumental task, one might as well say an impossible task. He cannot possibly succeed alone, and he seems to know it, yet there he is, laboring alone in that vile fortress where no one can get in to aid him in dismantling Wan-Edhe's architecture of evil."

"Mondros. Don't you see the problem?" Tsauderei said. "I do. At far too late an age."

"What problem?"

"The very reason we have mage schools, to provide a hierarchy as fallback. A trusted hierarchy. None of these young folk seem to have the luxury of trusted hierarchy, representing cumulative wisdom. Several survived by learning early they could not trust those in authority over them."

"So they trust each other instead. Yes, I see it." Mondros glared into space.

Tsauderei opened his hands. "When youth turns to youth for wisdom, it makes good sense to hare off the world to Geth-deles without telling anyone, and to translate and hide a blood mage text that Norsunder is seeking."

"But you had them living in your valley all last summer. You mean they don't trust you?"

"Atan does," Tsauderei said slowly. "Hibern as well, though I suspect she communicates with me on direct orders from Erai-Yanya. As yet, only a few of them know her well enough to trust her opinion. In any case, I think the problem runs back farther than last summer. It runs back before they were born, to when I turned down the offer to head the northern school because I was impatient of negotiation and compromise. My old friend Evend was more patient, but he's gone. I'm seen for what I am, standing outside the hierarchy, acting on my own, which suffices to justify Senrid and Jilo and the rest in acting on their own."

"So what do we do? Warn them?" Mondros asked.

"As if they don't know their dangers? I think they do, at least in part. The part that they don't understand is the perspective that comes with age, which leads me to suspect that they would take our cautions as more finger wagging. I think we need to convince them that they need us."

Tsauderei sighed heavily. "And the need is only going to get worse. We must establish good communication with all these youngsters as soon as possible, so that trust will come."

Mondros eyed him, hands on knees, elbows out. "Speaking of trouble, what do you make of these magical trespasses in Bereth Ferian? Local trouble brewing in the north?"

"Been pondering that." Tsauderei grunted. "Without further evidence, my instinct is to refrain from thinking politically. Chwahirsland, Bereth Ferian — my Delfina Valley. Look at the connections. Why would any mage venture past Oalthoreh's wards in Bereth Ferian, after all these centuries of relative quiet? Since nothing has gone missing, Oalthoreh's fear that the mage is after the Moonfire seems an unsettlingly good guess. At the very same time, why would Kessler Sonscarna dig out a blood mage text obviously secreted in Chwahir archives for at least as long?"

Mondros's heavy brows shot upward. "You think there might be some connection with the Venn?" His voice was a low rumble in his chest, unsettlingly echoed by the distant thunder; he heard it, and uttered an unwilling laugh. "Sinister, aren't I?"

"The Venn have always had that effect." Tsauderei stroked his mustache, which Mondros noted was beautifully groomed. "I would have said it's far more likely that the connection has to do with the Chwahir, and Wan-Edhe, except Bereth Ferian is way up north, one would think too far for anything of use to the Chwahir."

"But not far enough away for the Venn," Mondros said.

Tsauderei pursed his lips, and Mondros observed him as the elder mage stared upward in reverie. Rumor had it the old boy had been handsome and dashing in his day — popular with lovers, though he'd never settled with one. He still wore the long, closed robes of his young manhood, sporting that diamond in his ear and the long hair of those old fashions. Laughter flared in Mondros at the realization that we are never truly old inside our heads.

"So why now?" Tsauderei finally said, and Mondros's humor extinguished. "Let's assume the connection is the Venn. Norsunder has certainly wanted the Venn and their magic for centuries. Maybe it's become a primary goal now that they've been defeated again in trying to establish rifts big enough to bring their armies over from Norsunder-Beyond. But I don't believe the Venn have rift magic."

"We don't know that. We don't know what they've been up to inside their borders for the past six or seven centuries," Mondros said grimly, chill gripping the back of his neck. "You think it's a Venn renegade mage? Risking the treaty?"

They both knew that the ancient treaty stated that any Venn mage caught practicing magic outside their border could be executed on sight. That is, if that the Arrow wards didn't destroy them first.

"It's possible, after all these centuries. I think we need to find out."

"But no mage is permitted inside their border any more than their mages are allowed out in the world. Only traders can enter their harbors, and those apparently don't get into the Venn cities." Mondros swooped his hand, suggesting a dive into tunnels.

"*We* couldn't," Tsauderei said slowly, "but someone young might. Someone used to travel. Learns languages fast and gets along well. Skilled in the ways the Venn once admired, and probably still do . . ."

Mondros stared back uncomprehending, and then thrust his fingers through his beard. "You mean Rel? You want me to ask him, scarcely a month after he found out who I am? I feel guilty enough leaving him asleep to sneak away for this conversation!"

Tsauderei waved a hand to and fro, hiding how astonishing he'd found his old friend's confession that Rel was his son. As old as he was, he could still be caught by surprise. But now he comprehended Mondros's reluctance to talk about his past. "I understand. He's your boy. But Mondros, I did listen to the youngsters last summer, even if they didn't turn to me for advice. I believe he'd like to be asked."

"Humph."

Tsauderei said provocatively, "If I'd known who he was, I might have made an attempt to become better acquainted."

Mondros, stung, said, "I never told anyone but Raneseh. It seemed safer. You know how deadly Wan-Edhe is." He shook his head.

"This was not an accusation, merely a reminder of the effect of keeping secrets for what seem to be the best of reasons," Tsauderei said gently, and seeing that tough, wary, reclusive Mondros was genuinely upset, he went on. "So you didn't know where Rel was. Or that he was in the midst of the fighting, until after the fact. That was a necessary ill. You were vitally employed in making certain that Norsunder's war did not become a mage war. And rescuing Roderic Dei. Which no one else could have done."

Mondros's angry flush died away, leaving the downward gaze of remorse. "I could not find the queen. I still do not know if she lives."

"This is the price we mages pay," Tsauderei reminded him.

They both reflected on the fact that however much governments argued with one another, they were pretty much all agreed: mages must stay out of politics. It was an ancient prejudice, far too ingrained to overcome. Mondros's efforts on behalf of Everon would never be known by more than a few, and certainly never acknowledged.

"So you think I ought to ask Rel to go to the Land of the Venn?"

"I think he would be complimented by the trust implied, and I believe he would enjoy the challenge. He's an excellent observer, and travelers are often the best placed people to hear general talk of events inside a country. If there are great changes talked of by ordinary people inside the Venn kingdom, then that might warrant further exploration, including diplomatic pressure."

"True enough."

"Further, if he tells his allies that you are entrusting him with a crucially important task, perhaps they, in turn, might begin to extend their trust past him to you."

"All right, then," Mondros said. "I'm willing to try that, since I have so obviously failed with Jilo, struggling alone in that damned city. And Rel doesn't know any magic, so there's no residue around him." Mondros slapped his knees. "I'll put it to him when he wakes."

You would think that father and son reuniting would be an

occasion for joy.

In a sense it was, but Rel was aware that he should be happy, that one day he might feel happy. It would be a mistake to say that finding his father was a disappointment, because that was not at all true. It was more that "father" in Rel's mind took an amorphous, ideal form. Until he found him his father could have been anyone.

But now "father" had a face, a form, and his own goals. His own life. As the days went by, they worked together, and studied Ancient Sartoran together, both preferring quiet. On the surface they got along well, but then Rel got along well with most people, and Mondros strained every nerve to anticipate what Rel might want, from choice of food to subject of study.

There were times as the days turned into a week, then a month, that Rel would catch himself as he sat across from this strange man at his rough table, or watched him poring over his books, or listened to his deep breathing in the other bunk in the loft bedroom — his overwhelming emotion was a sense of unreality. And at times, awkwardness.

Mondros felt the awkwardness when he saw it in Rel, and each hesitation, each down-and-away glance, hurt him. But he strove to hide the hurt, grateful because he sensed no anger or resentment. Perhaps Rel, who might have lain awake thinking he could be anyone from anywhere, was having a rough time adjusting to the fact that he was not only half-Chwahir and a descendent from one of the most infamous families in that kingdom, but his other half a disinherited exile from a kingdom with a sinister reputation.

After the conversation with Tsauderei, Mondros intended to get right to the Venn problem, but he spent a couple of days trying to find a way to bring up the subject without it seeming as if he wanted to rediscover his son in time to use him.

Over breakfast one morning, after a disturbed night, he finally forced himself in what he considered an uncomfortably snaky way to mention Tsauderei wanting to find an experienced traveler for a scouting mission.

Rel's chin cut upward no more than the width of a grass blade, but the reaction caught Mondros by surprise.

Tsauderei was right, he thought grimly. He didn't know his own son at all. "I do not want you feeling any obligation," he said anyway, because that much he'd planned. "But if you want to hear it, I'll give you a report."

"Please," Rel said.

And Mondros did. Rel's obvious interest caused him to think that Rel was like him after all, liking a defined goal, and the prospect of action.

He was partly right. Rel gazed down at the breadcrumbs on his plate, almost giddy with relief. As soon as he recognized that inward release, he tightened up again with remorse. He shouldn't be so grateful for a natural exit, but he was.

Mentally he stuttered over the word 'father,' and the past night or so he'd been wondering how long he was supposed to stay. Winter would be arriving soon in these high mountains, making travel impossible. He didn't know if he was expected to call this cottage home, even though he didn't feel any more at home here than he did at Raneseh's holding.

Less.

Raneseh had trained him in etiquette, but there was no rule for this situation.

" . . . there are Destinations in the lands at either side of the Venn border, but I'm told the patrols are formidable, as are the penalties for being caught crossing. I know the Venn trade, but that is limited, and every scrap searched."

"It sounds interesting," Rel said. "I've never been up that far. Captain Heraford said once that there's plenty of ship trade. Captains who can deal with the constant storms, and pass Venn inspections, stand to make a lot bringing out those porcelain stoves they make, with the enameled knotwork decoration. And they take in grains and foods they can't grow underground. I can always get work on a ship, as I can hand, reef, and steer."

"Shall I send you by magic?"

Rel smiled into Mondros's dark eyes so much like his own, and guilt harrowed him again at the anxiousness he saw there, almost a plea.

"No need. If they are as wary as you say, I'll want to learn my way, and I'll do that better traveling as I usually do. Since there doesn't seem to be urgency."

Mondros agreed, understanding what was not said: Rel would be gone before he could be mired in the cottage over winter. "But I'll still give you a transfer token. For in case."

Rel thanked him.

Over the following night, Rel was subliminally aware of the whispering drone of Mondros's voice, rather than the deep breathing of sleep. When he woke, Mondros was still at it, his voice a low, hoarse rumble. As Rel washed up and packed his things, he reflected that if all that magic work was the spells for a transfer, no wonder those things were so costly.

Mondros set out fresh bread, shirred eggs, three kinds of fruit, and a stoneware jug of pear cider. As Rel loaded his plate, Mondros laid a Sartoran coin between them. "You can always trade that for the gold in it. Before you do, be aware that you have not only a transfer spell on it, it's warded in every way I could think of. That's the hard part, the protective wards. To complete the transfer, simply hold it and repeat Tsauderei's name twice. You don't even have to keep a Destination in mind — it will safely bring you back here."

Rel perceived in that tired gaze that any guilt he felt was a candle flame to the guilt of a father who had left his child, safety notwithstanding. Impulse prompted him to stretch his hands over the table and clasp Mondros's heavy shoulders. The muscles under his fingers were rock hard with tension.

They both stood, and Rel came around to pull Mondros in for a rib cracking hug. He heard in the slight catch of breath from Mondros that this was right, it was better than any words.

Before the sun had lifted a finger off the eastern horizon, he was on the road south.

Mondros watched him until his tiny figure vanished for the last time around a fold in the lower valleys, then trod heavily inside his cottage. He sat down, scowling at a piece of paper, considering. Finally he wrote:

> *Jilo, what have I done to cause you not to trust me? Why did you not bring the blood mage book to me?*

He sent that off, walked back out, and stood on the edge of the cliff, staring down at the empty road.

When Jilo found the note in his golden case, he scowled at it owlishly. He'd utterly forgotten about the blood mage texts, which he was sure Prince Kessler still had. That was probably how he'd broken that spell over CJ's arm.

Then he remembered that Leander Tlennen-Hess had been planning to translate the books. That meant he might have made a copy.

He brooded for a time, then wrote to Karhin in Colend for the sigil to Leander's golden notecase. Because he was a Chwahir, who knew little of the rest of the world's politesse, he wrote in careful Sartoran: *Leander, did you translate that text I brought? Jilo.*

At the other end, Leander took the note out. It was late at night, and he had been wavering between sleep and a little more study.

He considered how much to tell Jilo—and more importantly why.

He walked to his window and stared sightlessly out into the dark courtyard, as night birds swooped and drifted against the peaceful stars. With those few words he was thrown back to the horror he'd felt as he got further into the translation, and the conviction that had caused him to rise and chuck the entire thing into the fire.

He liked Senrid. He trusted Senrid—no, he wanted to trust Senrid, but he knew what a burden Marloven Hess's crown was. Even without the threats Detlev had made against Senrid.

Leander could too easily see Senrid, driven to desperation, wanting to use that blood magic for the best of reasons . . . and using it again. And again.

And so he'd stood over the fire until the last vestige of his painstakingly made copy had turned to ash, so that if the day came bringing Senrid to ask about the book, he could tell the truth: it was gone.

What should he say to Jilo? He glanced at Jilo's blunt note, deciding the simplest truth would do. He sat down and scrawled, *It was evil so I burned my half-finished translation.* And send the note off.

But there was no satisfaction in so doing, even if he'd kept the thing out of Senrid's hands. (And Senrid, so far, had never asked about it.)

Because the original book still existed out there somewhere.

Mondros stared in bemusement at the hunch-shouldered, awkward figure in rusty black who sat on the bench where Rel had eaten his last breakfast that morning, lank black hair hanging like claws in his eyes.

". . . and so he said he burned it. Wherever it is, I don't have it," Jilo was saying. "It wasn't a matter of trust, but habit."

""Habit," Mondros said gently, "develops out of trust. I'm not leveling any accusations at you, Jilo. I admire you for what you're doing, but at the same time I fear for you."

Jilo's head dropped, so all Mondros could see was the tops of his ears, and his thin, knobby hands as he worked them on his knees. He mumbled something that seemed to be some sort of apology.

Mondros did not let him tangle himself up further. "There is also the matter of Wan-Edhe's infamous enemies book, which I've learned third-hand actually exists. And in your possession."

Jilo's head came up. "Yes." He stiffened warily.

Mondros sighed. "I'm not going to attempt to take it. Can you tell me how it functions?"

"It tracks the magic transfers of enemies. It has limits," Jilo said. "One limit is, it only traces Destinations that Wan-Edhe was able to ward. I think there might be other ways around its spells. Because there are gaps. Like, it will say that Detlev is at Norsunder Base, and then again at Norsunder Base, and then a third time. Without any sign of where he went between those times."

"Maybe he goes to Norsunder-Beyond. I should think even Wan-Edhe was unsuccessful in laying wards *there*." Mondros thumped his fists on his knees once, twice. "May I put a request to you?"

Jilo's shoulders hunched a notch higher.

"If you see any patterns of movement in the world by Detlev or Siamis, will you let me or Tsauderei know?"

Jilo's expression cleared. "Yes," he said. "That's easy enough. Though Siamis hasn't shown up at all for a long time."

"I expect it's too much to hope he's dead," Mondros said on a sigh.

Dramatis Personae and Glossary for
RISE OF THE ALLIANCE

(These are individuals and concepts established in earlier books. **New characters are not listed here**.)

NORSUNDER (definition in glossary below)

Bostian: Ambitious Norsundrian military captain.

Dejain: Mage specializing in dark magic, one of a succession of Norsunder Base commanders, who tend to be summarily replaced by violence. She has no objections to others dying by violence, but she'd prefer to keep her hands clean.

Detlev: Chief visible mage and sometime military leader, answerable to Norsunder's Host of Lords. Born four thousand years ago, has lived in and outside time ever since. Like his nephew Siamis, has **Dena Yeresbeth**.

Henerek: Ambitious low-ranking young Norsunder military captain, originated in Everon.

Kessler Sonscarna: Renegade Chwahir prince with considerable military abilities, forced into Norsunder as a result of treachery by the mage **Dejain.** Currently used as an errand runner. (SEE **Chwahirsland** below)

Lesca: Apparently lazy steward in charge of Norsunder Base. Overlook her at your peril.

Siamis: Nephew to Detlev, recently emerged (it is believed for the first time) in four thousand years, as a young adult. Formidable mage, and like Detlev, has **Dena Yeresbeth.**

LIGHT MAGIC MAGES AIDING THE ALLIANCE

Tsauderei: Oldest of the senior mages, independent of the two leading mage schools, living in a historic mage retreat located in the mountains bordering Sarendan and Sartor in the Valley of Delfina.

Erai-Yanya: One of a long line of mages dwelling in the ruined city of Roth Drael. Trained partly by the northern Mage School at Bereth Ferian, and partly by Tsauderei, she works independently, her specialty magical wards. She has one son, '**Arthur**', who was adopted by Eveneth and became the titular Prince in Bereth Ferian. Erai-Yanya's student mage is the Marloven exile Hibern Askan.

Evend: Onetime colleague of Tsauderei, king of Bereth Ferian (a courtesy title only) and head of the mage school there, he surrendered his life to bind rift magic from being used in Sartorias-deles by Norsunder. His place as titular king was taken by **Arthur**.

Murial of Mearsies Heili: Recluse mage, living hidden in the western wilds of Mearsies Heili. Born a princess, she supported the transfer of the throne to her niece **Clair** on the death of her sister. Protecting the kingdom from a distance, she has seen to it that Clair gets magical training.

THE YOUNG ALLIES and OTHERS, Listed by Kingdom

BERETH FERIAN

Arthur: Named Yrtur, he adopted the name Arthur after his rescue by young world-gate crossing friends. Son of mage Erai-Yanya, he early showed great ability in learning and magic, but he was unhappy living in isolation. He was adopted as heir by **Evend**, the head mage of the Bereth Ferian Mage School, and presiding King of the loose federation headquartered at Bereth Ferian.

Evend: (see Light Mages)

Liere Fer Eider: Also known as the Girl Who Saved the World, she was the first of her generation to be born with **Dena Yeresbeth.** At ten years old she left her small town to escape being captured by Siamis, who had extended an enchantment over the world, which Liere later broke. The enchantment is generally known as The Lost Year, as most lived in a dream world while it lasted.

LAND OF THE CHWAHIR (aka CHWAHIRSLAND)

Jilo: Son of a lowly sergeant, heir to elderly **Prince Kwenz Sonscarna**, he finds himself acting king of Chwahirsland, after Norsunder's removal of the previous king, who had ruled for more than a century.

Prince Kessler Sonscarna: The single living descendant of the ruling Sonscarnas, who were systematically killed off by Wan-Edhe, blood relations notwithstanding. Prince Kessler escaped at a young age, made his way to a martial arts group, where he mastered military arts. He allied with a Norsundrian mage, Dejain, and began to assemble followers for his plan to remove all the hereditary rulers of the world, and replace them with his followers, chosen solely on merit. When defeated, he was forced into Norsunder by Dejain, who betrayed him.

Mondros (Rosey), Mage: His origins are a mystery, his intent to battle Wan-Edhe from a distance. He has looked out for some of the Young Allies Wan-Edhe has tried to suborn, and to kill. He lives in a cottage on the border of Chwahirsland.

Wan-Edhe, King of the Chwahir: Descendant of the ruling Sonscarna family, has ruled for close to a century. A powerful dark magic mage, he has managed to create a powerful citadel in the heart of his kingdom, where time itself is distorted.

COLEND

King Carlael Lirendi: Regarded generally as Mad King Carlael. He is as beautiful as he is strange. He seems to exist in a world of dreams, from which he emerges now and then, very alert and very aware. There is a loose council made up of the chief nobles who oversee the kingdom when he is unable to respond to the world around him.

Prince Shontande Lirendi: Son of Carlael, King of Colend, and crown prince.

Karhin Keperi: She is a teenage scribe student in a small town in the west of Colend, who volunteers to function as the center of the young allies' communication network. An indefatigable letter writer, she first met Puddlenose of the Mearsieans, and gradually got drawn into the Alliance.

Thad Keperi: Red-haired brother of Karhin, also a scribe student, but much less passionate about the scribe life. Very social, and friend to all the Alliance.

Little Bee and Lisbet Keperi: Younger sister and brother of Thad and Karhin. Little Bee is blind, has Dena Yeresbeth, though the family is not aware of it.

EVERON

King Berthold and Queen Mersedes Carinna Delieth: King and queen, survivors of rough earlier years. Mersedes, daughter of a con man, became one of the Knights of Dei, dedicated to protecting the kingdom.

Prince Glenn Delieth: Heir to the throne of Everon, and convinced that a strong army solves all questions, especially the threat of Norsunder attacking.

Princess Hatahra Delieth (Tahra): Younger sister of Glenn, passionate about numbers.

MARLOVEN HESS

Senrid Montredaun-An: Young king of Marloven Hess, a mage studying both dark and light magic. First friend to **Liere Fer Eider**, and second to make his unity in **Dena Yeresbeth**.

Retren Forthan: A young man from a farm background, Forthan is the best of the leaders to come out of the military academy. Senrid, the young king, hopes that Forthan will one day lead the Marloven army.

Commander Keriam: Career military man, now head of the Marloven military academy, also titular head of the Palace Guard. Acted as guardian and foster-father to Senrid, protecting him from the regent as much as possible.

Hibern Askan: Light magic student, tutored by Erai-Yanya of Roth Drael, who learned in the northern mage school. Hibern was exiled by her family.

MEARSIES HEILI

Clair of Mearsies Heili: Young queen of Mearsies Heili, a small agrarian polity on the northeast corner of the continent Toar. Niece of the hermit-mage **Murial**, and cousin to the wandering boy known only as **Puddlenose**, she has adopted a group of girls, most of them runaways. Her right-hand and designated 'heir' is **C.J.**

C.J. (Cherenneh Jenet): Found by Clair, who traveled through the World-gate, C.J. is from Earth, adopted into Clair's gang of runaways and rejects. She learns magic fitfully, and is generally regarded as the leader of Clair's gang of girls.

Murial: (see Light Mages)

Puddlenose of Mearsies Heili: Bereft of family at a very young age, and used by The King of the Chwahir in his complicated plots, he was rescued several times by Rosey (Mondros, see Mages). He wanders the world, determined to have fun. His chief companion is a world-gate wanderer from Earth named **Christoph**, but sometimes he's joined by **Rel**.

Rel: Known as Rel the shepherd's son, and more widely as Rel the Traveler, he was happily raised by a guardian in Tser Mearsies until wanderlust caused him to leave home. Met **Puddlenose** of the Mearsieans, and consequently became tangled in some of the Mearsieans' adventures. Friends with **Atan**, and one of the **Rescuers** (see **Sartor**) He was the only outsider ever invited to join the **Knights of Dei** in Everon.

SARENDAN

Peitar Selenna, King of Sarendan: Reluctant king who would rather study magic, he came to the throne after an especially vicious civil war. He, nephew to the former king, Darian Irad, was one of the leaders of the revolution, but advocated non-violent means. His accession was a compromise between the commoners, who adore him, and the nobles, who recognize that at least he is nominally one of their own.

Lilah Selenna, Princess of Sarendan: Younger Sister to Peitar. She, with friends **Bren** (artist), **Innon** (a noble-born accountant at heart) and **Deon** were deeply involved in the revolution.

Derek Diamagan: Charismatic leader of the revolution, a commoner who wished to overthrow all the nobles, and institute common rule. He was a far better speech maker than he was an organizer; his revolution was a disaster. Close friend of Peitar Selenna.

SARTOR

Queen Yustnesveas Landis V (Atan): New young queen of Sartor, after the oldest kingdom in the world was removed from time by nearly a century. She was found on the border by Tsauderei the mage, and raised by him before the enchantment was broken. She began her queenship as a mage student, with little training in statecraft, but well-read in history.

Mistress Veltos Jhaer: Head of the prestigious Sartoran mage guild, until the enchantment the foremost mage school in the world. Now a century behind. She is further burdened by guilt for having lost the kingdom to enchantment.

Hinder and Sinder: Morvende (cave dwellers), friends of Atan.

Rescuers: The name given to a band of children who had lived in a magic-protected forest during the enchantment. They sheltered Atan before the enchantment was broken. Ostensibly highly regarded as heroes by the Sartorans, there are the aristocratic Rescuers, and the non-aristocratic, Rel among them.

VASANDE LEROR

Leander Tlennen-Hess: Like Senrid, a young king, though of a tiny polity that historically belonged to the Marlovens, then broke away four centuries previous. Leander and Senrid have a lot in common, and would be friends, except for Leander's jealous step-sister:

Kyale Marlonen: Adoptive sister to Leander, relishes being a princess, and is jealous of Leander's attention.

Llhei: Sarendan-trained nanny (sister to Lizana, nurse to the royal children of **Sarendan**), governess to Kyale, remained after evil Queen Mara Jinia defeated.

Alaxandar: Captain of royal guard, quit under evil queen Mara Jinia, protected Leander.

GLOSSARY

ANGELS

The indigenous beings of the world, in their first attempts to communicate with the human beings who had appeared through the World Gate and were spreading so rapidly, assumed illusory human forms in order to facilitate communication.

The forms they took were intended to be the most appealing human forms; they did not at first comprehend myth or its power, and were perceived as angels. Subsequently beings have appeared in the world from elsewhere who are not easily categorized, and some of these, too, have passed into history as angelic visitors. Therefore this particular item from the humans' earth backgrounds persists in popular culture, though otherwise there is no organized religion that would be recognized as such.

That is not to say that the religious impulse is gone — far from it. But on a world where magic works, where souls (identities) are recognized as discrete, it has taken a different form. Some see a logical connection from there to creative forces behind the universe, and others don't; for those who do there is no call to propitiate such much less define them or it. There are also no concepts such as luck, or destiny in the sense of foreordained actions outside of choice; the word fate is interchangeable with consequence.

ANIMALS

Most were brought deliberately when humans came to the world, and a few (like rats and mice, along with their various parasites) came along secreted in various vessels; numerous birds were either brought or flew through on their own, and all proliferated on Sartorias-deles and two sister worlds. The indigenous life forms of this world first gave the early mages to understand the connections between disease and parasites, so when life forms recognized as parasites they were eradicated.

This is not the place to go into detail about the relations between humans and animals, as effected by the changes wrought by the early mages [see **BIRTH SPELL and MAGIC**]; suffice it for now to say that as humans gradually began to evolve both because of their contact with the indigenous races and the subsequent magic spells to improve life, so too did animals.

The immediate result was that humans abandoned the consumption of mammal flesh as well as the use of animals' fur and other parts. Hunting for sport evolved into wreathing, *i.e.,* riding close enough to the target animal to toss with one's own hands a wreath of ivy or flowers over the creature's head. (This sport has persisted for centuries, and animals were bred for speed and cleverness.) Animals that litter were limited through magical interference to one litter; animals that bear a single offspring were not interfered with. Blood hunts tend to be human against human.

BIRTH SPELL

Probably the strangest of the spells but the most far reaching in effect granted by indigenous beings to the early mages, who were women. (It was women who made first contact, and kept to themselves what they learned first as a defensive measure, subsequently as a rule that took a long time to rescind.)

When humans first arrived, they brought their appalling birth rates and reproductive habits, producing unwanted children that had to be dealt with one way or another, as the price of relations, which included forcing a woman or child, will. Only the Mage Council now knows just how close humans came to being perceived as vermin and eradicated from the world; the early mages strove desperately to rectify the ills they were aware of.

Magic therefore was used specifically to improve life [see **WASTE SPELL, WANDING**] and almost the first thing these mages achieved, with the willing cooperation of the indigenous beings (whose motives are nearly impossible to comprehend for certain but who were probably dismayed at the rapid proliferation of humans) was universal birth control. The egg dissolved as soon as it was released, unless the woman's blood chemistry was altered by her having partaken of root called gerda, gedi, gi, bitterroot, etc.

The effect on human culture was stunning. To keep this brief, one of the most obvious results was an unbalance in societal power, as females could totally control birth, especially as the women mages were also embarked on a desperate and at first secret quest to avoid eradication by the killing of all sexual predators. First those who preyed on children, then those who used sex as violence and domination without the consent of the partner, until the urge was nearly completely bred out of the human population.

But as female control increased, so did male reaction, especially when the next goal was the male drive to violence. A confrontation and then negotiation and cooperation between the rising schools of male mages and the old female Mage Council led to the joining of these organizations and the emendation, and finally the eradication of the selective genocide.

That part of history is no longer generally known and is seldom talked about except at the very highest mage circles.

The first cooperative effort was a second change to the Birth Spell, which enabled men, or anyone, actually, to give birth to a child by using a specific form of the Spell. Again, this was only achieved with the aid of the indigenous beings, and their contribution is still debated in contemporary times, for with their added magic anyone could have a child if they "heard" the Spell.

A healer or mage could only give them the beginning; the rest would come or not, and no one has ever successfully determined why the spell either completes or doesn't. (For the curious, the DNA derives from a single parent's past, or from a blending of both partners if two people handfast and complete the spell, but is only possible once the parent has been in the world more than sixteen years, which was the average age of the onset of reproductive possibility as observed by indigenous beings.)

The child appears at proper term, which argues for the magic including manipulation of time and space of which only the indigenous life forms have mastery; long debates have taken place about the origins of said children, if they are from a parallel timeline or world, etc.

The most obvious overall effects were to slow the population growth, and to alter the attitudes toward children since it now took specific efforts to produce them. These changes established the more firmly when the Mage Council subsequently managed the third emendation, which was magic that prevented pregnancy in anyone who could not deliver normally. Thus, a woman who has a preexisting condition that would preclude a safe birth could not get pregnant, even if she chewed or drank steeped gerda root.

Because the records from this time were mostly destroyed, no one really knows how long it all took, but the guesses are at least a thousand years. A less obvious effect would be the change rung on the matter of intimacy as it is regarded in cultures; trying here to be brief, there is no shame attached to it, and there is no value placed on virginity, but there is a deep sense of privacy, arising out of that early conditioning by ancestors to "hide" intimate congress from those all-seeing indigenous beings.

The unexplained workings of the Birth Spell serves as a reminder of those beings still there—somewhere—resulting in mating, whether for sport or for procreation, being universally preferred as a private act—even a group will generally want no windows and closed doors, even if they cannot define why. Another result is coverage, not just of privates, but of nipples—male or female—which are rather ambiguous symbolically. (And everyone likes the corresponding charge when the person chooses to unrobe.)

DENA YERESBETH

One of the skills thought lost forever when Old Sartor was nearly destroyed in the Norsunder War called The Fall, four thousand years ago. Dena Yeresbeth—"Unity of the Three," cohering body, mind, and spirit in ways impossible to humans after the Fall, as begun emerging again. It manifests in different ways; Liere Fer Eider, regarded as the first of her generation, heard others' thoughts.

MAGIC

The easiest definition is "energy." Many indigenous life forms of this world do not have a material presence, though in the early days they attempted various illusory forms in order to comprehend the humans who were first propelled through a universal gateway to their world. Humans were eventually taught to shape magic mentally (see **Dena Yeresbeth**), an ability they lost when they nearly destroyed themselves and the world what is generally regarded as four thousand years ago. (Time is not always reliable on this world, any more than is physical distance.)

Since then, humans have recovered, painfully reconstructing magical knowledge, with the idea of improving life and maintaining such improvements, among other motives. Mind-shaped magic was nearly eradicated, and mages required safe ways to access magic and use it. The worlds and gestures that are now regarded as "magical language" are remnants of the earliest form of Old Sartoran that is now all but lost, except to scholars. These words and gestures form units of finite utility, but most mages at lower levels of learning think them inherently magical in themselves.

HEALERS

A subset of mages trained mostly by the Mage Council, adept in doctoring skills as well as herbal knowledge and also what we would call psychology. They earn their pay by differing methods in most lands, but the Healer Oath established by the Mage Council requires them to never deny service. The Mage Council-trained healers are the highest in demand the world over.

As for their magic, there are no universal fix-it spells. Physical repair of any kind is extremely exacting, just as is surgery. However, the repair is mostly for damage — birth defects or incorrect birth-assigned gender being considered under this heading. Very early in the history of humans' discovery of magic, one of the first goals was the eradication of disease. Because microbes and harmful insects, etc., came over from earth and were not a part of the environment of this world, the eventual eradication of fleas, for example, did nothing to the biosphere, which was still adjusting to the influx of life forms through the universal gateway.

Specific diseases were isolated one by one and eradicated, thus there are, for example, no plagues, no STDs whatsoever on the world. People can and do get sick, though almost always through depressing their immune systems, a syndrome understood by healers, whose approach is holistic. Virus-transmitted disease hasn't been entirely eradicated, as viruses mutate too fast to be isolated, but their effect has been considerably reduced from the devastation of the early days.

MAGE COUNCIL

Its history is long and varied. Its earliest days belong exclusively to women, who were the first to recognize that the world humans had come to included other sentient life forms, and to discover access to magic. Some of the early Council's decisions are briefly touched on elsewhere, the most deeply guarded secret being the systematic purge of sexual predators, impelled not just by collective anger (though that played a significant role) but by the drive to keep humanity from being expunged altogether by said sentient beings, whose first introduction to the concept of evil came into the world with the humans.

By the time men joined the Council its main purpose was already the betterment of human life. After the Fall of Old Sartor, the Council was as dead as its members, but reformed again by surviving minor mages who embarked on the centuries-long quest to recover what had been lost.

For most of those early centuries just maintaining the basic Spells was about all that could be done. As the potential of magic slowly regenerated and old knowledge was painfully reconstructed, eventually magic could accomplish more. For the most part mages were regarded as builders and makers, and as such seldom came to the notice of kings outside of the need to provide for the hire of mages to maintain bridge, fire, road spells, etc.

This persisted until a few centuries after Inda's time, when the rapid proliferation of magical knowledge gave rise to the empires of the sorcerer kings. After those broke up, a mage school in the far north was established. It and the Sartoran mage guild are where most light mages are trained — but not all.

MORVENDE

Humans from Old Sartor who withdrew to caves beneath the mountains to escape the terrible war. (mor (removed, outcast) fen (group of people) de (plural). They did not emerge for centuries; they preserved the most of the old knowledge, strictly kept to themselves for the most part. Melanin is all but gone from their hair and skin due to the many centuries underground. Their fingers and toes were altered by magic early on to enable them to cope with underground life, thus they have talons instead of nails. They emerged into surface history for a relatively brief and disastrous time roughly around the first rise and spread of the Sartoran and Venn empires, after which the remainder withdrew for another long stretch of centuries.

NORSUNDER

From 'norss-en-dar', ('enemies, of the norss,' the latter being a group of mages from one of the other planets in their system) a creation by a specific set of extremely powerful mages as a retreat when their attempt to take control of the world failed in what was subsequently termed the Fall of Old Sartor. Removed in space and time from the world, its geography is created and destroyed at their whim, and one can withdraw into its central force while centuries pass on the world. More about the mages is dealt with elsewhere, but let it here be noted that they have all their old abilities, that they lie in wait for the world to recover and be worthy of a second effort.

Known as the Host of Lords, their chief maintains their powerbase by the consumption of the particular energies of identity and spirit, preferably against the wills of the victims, thus the term "souleater," one of the worst terms of invective in any language. People who choose Norsunder as an alternative to death are said to be damned; they may have plans for the accrual of power, but when they do make it to Norsunder they are left in no doubt whose will prevails.

SARTOR

Oldest political polity on the world, formed after human women made first contact with indigenous beings there. "Sar" connotes lordship or leadership (devolved to king and queen), "tor" people. Located at the opposite end of the continent from Iasca Leror, its influence on life in the southern hemisphere and the southern portions of the northern has been pervasive, despite its long, sometimes spectacularly broken history.

TIME

Sartorias-deles completes a revolution around its sun, commonly called Erhal, in 441 days; the largest satellite, called "the moon" by humans who were used to seeing moons, completes twelve cycles in that time. [there are actually several satellites, but only one large enough to be recognized in the early days as a moon; the smaller ones were regarded as stars]. The Sartoran Calendar, universally used in the south and in many places in the north, is divided into 73 seven-day weeks, as the concept of the seven day week was brought by humans to the world.

There are eight days comprising New Year's Week at the darkest time of the year in the south, and the longest day of the year is called Midsummer's Day and added to the calendar as a discrete day. The calendar otherwise is twelve months — the lunar cycle is just short of 37 days — of 36 days each. (Northern hemisphere lands that use the Sartoran calendar thus have a single New Year's Day, and eight days of Midsummer, or else mirror the count of days, which makes dating difficult if dealing with the south.)

Thus every year begins on Firstday. The day is divided by most people into six segments. These time units are broken into units of four in some places, making a 24 hour day. (the numbers three, four, and twelve carrying symbolic significance, some of which was brought to the world even if the originating reasons have long been forgotten.) Thus the Sartoran-influenced lands also use a base twelve counting system for magical purposes, though base ten (corresponding to the number of fingers) is common for trade and measure.

WANDING

Wands have spells on them to break down and transfer animal waste underground. (For the curious, the spell removes the waste as far as the noses and eyes of humans are able to detect, but leaves enough residue for dogs, cats, etc. to detect territorial markings, because the mages who cast the spells did not know the extent of the animal olfactory sense.) This Guild is universal, and is most often joined by young people who don't have any skills for other work, or who just don't want to do other work, whether for life or for a short time.

A Wander never goes hungry, has a place to sleep, and can wander about all day. Young people who cannot figure out a job, or itinerants, or those without any particular calling will often become wanders, as there is no real skill involved. In some cultures Wanders are drawn from those who've committed minor crimes, and are ordered to perform public service in this manner. In some areas, pigs are kept to eat scraps, and their leavings are used in truck gardens as fertilizer.

WASTE SPELL

The simple definition is that these few syllables, whispered when a human being lets go of waste, gets rid of it. Waste includes vomit, and with a syllable attached, menses.

The Waste Spell dates back to the earliest days after humans first found themselves on this world, and the indigenous beings, discovering that not only were humans fast befouling the environment, they were making themselves sick, communicated the connection to the early mages, who, when they comprehended the connection, not only arranged for this magic (for the curious, the waste is broken down chemically and transported underground), they arranged for spells that could be performed over specific items, such as buckets, that not just cleaned the water of bacteria, but cleaned items dipped into the buckets.

This concept was then extended to baths; the spell on the baths included the cleaning of teeth, so tooth cleaners were generally used on the road, unless one stuck one's entire head into a bespelled bucket. The spells also extend to industry, for example to catch wood chips from floating downstream from a carpenter's workplace, chaff from a miller, etc. Guild dues cover the maintenance of such spells in cities.

As magic returned to the world, eventually cleaning frames were developed, that wick away grime, filth, dead skin, etc from the person who steps through. If the person fell into mud, only the water remains.

About the Author

Sherwood Smith writes fantasy, science fiction, and historical fiction. Her full bibliography can be found on her website at https://www.sherwoodsmith.net.

About Book View Cafe

Book View Café is an author-owned cooperative of professional writers, publishing in a variety of genres including fantasy, science fiction, romance, mystery, and more.

Its authors include New York Times and USA Today best-sellers as well as winners and nominees of many prestigious awards such as the Agatha Award, Hugo Award, Lambda Literary Award, Locus Award, Nebula Award, RITA Award, Philip K. Dick Award, World Fantasy Award, and many others.

Since its debut in 2008, Book View Café has gained a reputation for producing high quality books in both print and electronic form. BVC's e-books are DRM-free and distributed around the world.

Book View Café's monthly newsletter includes new releases, specials, author news, and event announcements. To sign up, visit https://www.bookviewcafe.com/bookstore/newsletter/

Printed in Great Britain
by Amazon

52786377R00153